George and the Reich

George and the Reich

Stuart Nicholls

Set in Garamond, a serif typeface named for sixteenth-century
Parisian engraver Claude Garamond

*To my long-suffering wife Harriet
and daughters Maddie and Louisa,
and for Mum and Dad.*

❧ *The last morning* ❧

George woke up to the usual dawn chorus; not the birds outside cheerfully oblivious to the fact that there was a war on, but his mother frustratedly calling up the stairs, 'George! Are you up yet? Your breakfast is ready and if you don't get a spurt on you'll be late for school, let alone Granddad!'

Then he heard the clunk of the heavy front door being closed and the metallic clack of the latch dropping back into position.

George then counted, '1, 2, 3.' 'Morning darling,' he said in exact mimicry of the events being enacted downstairs, then he pursed his lips and let off an exaggerated kissing sound, 'Mmmwah!'

'All ok?' He continued to mimic the parental exchange. 'Yep, fine! Back in one piece!'

'Oh, thank God!'

'Is he up?'

'What do you think?' was the reply from George's mum which he lip-synced perfectly. He heard the tell-tale creak of the third stair as his Dad made his way up. George retrieved his special box from under the bed and unfolded his map of Europe, on which various points and cities were marked. Just then his bedroom door opened.

'Dad!' he shouted 'How did it go? Where were you? Did you shoot any down?' A volley of excited questions came seemingly without drawing breath.

'It all went fine and we all made it back, not sure if we hit target; heavy cloud cover.'

'What was the target?' George asked, his pen poised to record it on the map.

'Now you know I shouldn't say!'

'Oh pleeeeaaaase!' George pleaded.

'Alright,' his Dad said with a chuckle, 'the target was near Frankfurt.'

George quickly found and circled this on the map. 'Wow!' he said, 'New target.'

'Right! Flight Sergeant! Up, dressed, breakfast, Granddad, school,' his dad ordered.

'Yes sir!' George replied leaping out of bed.

Minutes later George flew down the stairs, two at a time, fully dressed and in one fluid motion sat down and began tucking into his breakfast. His Dad was already sitting at the heavy wooden kitchen table his hands clasped around a steaming mug of tea; a habit which dismayed most of his family. He always argued that he should be able to drink tea from an old boot, should he so wish and he did not like a bone china cup and saucer as he only got a mouthful from those; after all, beer and milk come in pints why shouldn't tea? Everyone, including Rachel, had given up that argument a long time ago.

'Anyshing ecschitin hacken lasht night?' George asked though a full mouth of porridge, showering soggy oats over his side of the table.

'George! Don't speak with your mouth full!' his Mum chastised. 'How many times, Urchin?' she asked rhetorically, utilising his nick-name within the family. A name which he'd rightfully earned over many years of grovelling around anywhere grotty and only washing under protest. This provided his Dad with much amusement and frustrated his Mum; she was convinced he should have grown out of this by now.

'He's his father's son, no doubting that,' she said turning around to face the table and giving John the 'It's all your fault' look. 'Right! Time you were off to school,' Rachel said pointing to

George and then the direction of the front door '…and time you were off to bed!' she said with equal authority to John gesticulating toward the stairs.

Still chewing his last gargantuan mouthful of porridge he hugged his Dad and kissed his mum goodbye. He ran to the front door picking up his school bag from the porch without limiting his stride and was about to exit the front door at high speed when his Mum shouted. 'Gas Mask!' one instruction he did obey. Then he galloped off in the direction of the village.

The Brigadier

George's trip to the village school took him along the main road which linked the two villages between which he lived. However, the road was little more than a farm track which in summer was dry and dusty, and in winter may only be described as soggy. The track meandered its way between orchards and hop fields before delivering its various travellers to the edge of the picturesque village. The village bore much evidence that it had remained relatively unchanged for hundreds of years. The houses were either thatched black and white Tudor wattle and daub or Georgian brick and slate, and had suffered few additions since.

Because of the increased traffic, much of which was still horse-drawn, George now took to the narrow pathway which ran each side of the ancient cobbled roads that twisted their way through the village. As he ran towards the village centre he passed many of the shops which catered for the villager's every need and shouting 'Good morning!' to the shopkeepers as he ran past their open doors, all of which responded with a cheerful 'Good morning George'. But at the speed he was running he was long gone by the time they replied.

The main village street culminated at the village pub and opened out into the village green. The pub was an ancient tavern and coaching inn, the cellar of which was rumoured to be Roman and haunted. The pub was simply called The Block, hailing back to the time when one of the main activities conducted in the village centre were the public executions. Indeed the village green was still colloquially known as the scaffold, which children had further shortened to the scaff. George rounded the corner at the block and then darted across the road which encircled the scaffold toward the house on the opposite side of the green.

This imposing double-fronted Georgian house, which lorded over all it surveyed, was the home of his grandfather, whom everyone in the village knew and addressed as the Brigadier. A veteran of the Sudanese campaign, the Boer War and First World War, he had been a lifelong career soldier who found civilian life a completely foreign concept and was thus viewed by all who came into contact with him, bar none, as rather eccentric. Although now retired from the army, old habits die hard. His life was still run with military precision, observing many of the ingrained protocols which had dominated his world. When he retired from the army the batman who had faithfully served him for the last twenty years, Ives as he was known to all, had also retired and come to live with the Brigadier, immediately resuming the vast majority of his previous duties.

George and most of his friends, for varying reasons, gathered each morning at the Brigadier's house just prior to school for the raising of the flag, a ceremony which was now a well-known village spectacle. At 8.30 sharp the Brigadier followed closely by Ives would march stiffly out the front door to the flag pole which stood centrally in the front garden. While Ives would attach the flag and make ready, the Brigadier would call the ranks of schoolboys to attention and continue with a brief inspection of those assembled. Once complete he would turn to Ives and order him to continue. At this point the whole thing took on a completely comedic air; however all laughs and sniggers were kept well-hidden as none relished the thought of being torn off a strip by the Brigadier. Because the Brigadier did not have the luxury of a squad of men with which to conduct the ceremony, Ives had to make do. At this point it has to be said, that at no stage during Ives's military career was he trained in the playing of any musical instrument. Therefore the 'tune' he played from the bugle held in his right hand, whilst hoisting the flag with his left, held no resemblance to any tune the army had ever used. Once raised all assembled, on the Brigadier's mark, saluted the flag and again held the salute for as long as the Brigadier. The ceremony complete the Brigadier dismissed the ranks who descended immediately back into a schoolboy rabble; pushing, shoving, running and jeering. George then shouted, 'Bye granddad! Bye Ives!' as he ran off with the rest of the pack.

Minutes later they arrived at the school playground, where the jostling jeering and noise of morning greetings amplified tenfold. The school had been built, according to the stone above the main entrance, in 1892 and was an austere-looking Victorian redbrick institutional building, which stuck out like a sore thumb in the village. It had been built to replace the old single room building which had had no need of demolition; it had obligingly fallen down of its own accord. The perimeter of the school yard was delineated by a low wall predominantly constructed from dark red brick but topped with sandstone. The wall for the most part was two feet tall from base to top with six-foot pillars of similar construction at each corner and spaced along each of the four sides. The pillars used to support metal railings which sat on the wall and filled the gaps between the pillars. These had disappeared shortly after the start of the war as the rush to produce munitions had gone into full swing and all available metal had been collected by the government.

George arrived at the playground and surveyed the scene exchanging morning greetings with many of those he passed. He noticed a huddle of several boys all seemingly tightly packed around one fascinating spectacle. The huddle broke out into violent shoving; the group simultaneously began chanting, 'Conshie! Conshie! Conshie!'.

Whoever was the centre of attention, and George now had a good idea who, was the one receiving the shoves. Without thinking further George waded into the group, pushing boys aside, who quickly closed behind him for a better view, until he reached the subject of the hustle. In the centre of the group was the small crouched snivelling form of Peter Dulac. Peter had consistently been the victim of the playground bullies since it had become common knowledge that his father had been interned as a conscientious objector.

Even before his Dad's apparent disgrace Peter had been easy pickings for the bullies. He was a small boy for his age who found it hard to make friends. He was as his name suggests of French descent; his father's parents had both been French. His name and ancestry had given rise to much spiteful name calling. As George got Peter to his feet from the gravel, he dusted him off brushing off the playground detritus from his grazed knees, clothing and face. The baying crowd, which had failed to disperse at the disruption of its fun, began chanting again, led by the king bully Gordon Savage, 'Coward Conshie! Coward! Conshie!...'

Gordon Savage was an evacuee from London who'd been sent to the country to stay with his aunt due to the bombing, or at least that was the story, other rumours had been rife around the village. Gordon's aunt was Mrs McWorthy the local policeman's wife who was known for not being able to hold her tongue. Gordon was as big for his age as Peter was small. Whilst he may have been at the front of the queue for physical stature he had definitely been at the back when the brains were distributed, in fact most suspected he'd taken that day off. He had also taken six of the best from the ugly stick. He was over five feet tall and growing; his girth was also reaching similar proportions. His nose was fairly flat resembling that of a boxer and his jaw had a very pronounced under bite which gave him the overall intimidating look of an aggressive warthog.

George first turned to Peter looking at his forlorn face with tear tracks running from both eyes and his runny nose. He gave him his hanky and said, 'Here, clean yourself up.'

'Th-a-ank y-ou' Peter said in mid-snivel.

Then George's face turned to thunder as his gaze ascended to meet Gordon's.

'And what'ya gonna do about it?' Gordon said looking at George and then round at his cronies laughing which was sycophantically copied.

'What has he ever done to you?' George replied rhetorically. 'Maybe his Dad is a conshie, it doesn't mean he is, so leave him alone!'

'Why don't you make me?' replied Gordon squaring up for a fight.

George looked straight at Gordon with an undisguised glint in his eye and devilish smile. 'OK!' he said 'why don't you tell us: What's your dad doing for the war effort, hmm?'

'You know! He's away in the Navy' replied Gordon with a nervous look on his face — even his limited intelligence had an idea of where this was going.

George's smile now broke into open laughter, a ploy designed to make Gordon lose his temper, and it was working. 'Which ship is he on then?' Not permitting Gordon time to reply, George answered his own question: 'HMS Wormwood Scrubs!'

The rest of the children in the playground, who had all now gathered around to observe events as they unfolded, in unison burst into laughter and pointed at Gordon.

'That should do it,' George thought.

And sure enough Gordon's right arm was swinging in George's direction with a clenched fist at the end of it. The playground audience began the requisite chant, 'Fight! Fight! Fight!' Gordon's arm looked like the boom of a sailing boat in mid gybe. George ducked the punch and just at the point when Gordon was most off balance, when his arm was at the end of its swing, George pushed as hard as he could on his right shoulder, causing him to irrecoverably topple and fall face-down. Gordon scrambled back to his feet, knees grazed, gravel and dust stuck to his face, his nose had begun to bleed and tears were streaming from his eyes. Not risking another punch Gordon ran to grab George but at the last possible second he crouched to the left, leaving his right leg extended which tripped Gordon who, once again came crashing to the ground face-down.

Just as Gordon was scrambling to his feet for another pass and roaring like an injured bear, the headmaster Mr Batt and a teacher, Mr Pritchard came purposefully across the school yard. Mr Pritchard was ringing the school bell which indicated to the children that they had to get in line ready to enter the school. Mr Batt grabbed both of the aggressors by the tuft of hair just above the ear and, with them both on tiptoe in an attempt to alleviate the pain, frog-marched them both to his office.

Whilst the school settled down to the usual morning ritual, the two boys stood in silence in front of Mr Batt with only his heavy mahogany desk between them. The headmaster sat gazing alternately at the boys with his piercing slate grey eyes, leaning forward, his elbows on the desk tapping his fingers together in a rhythmic sequence. George stood in front of the desk looking across at the man all the schools kids called 'vampire'; half on account of his surname and half because of his similarity with the cinema image of Dracula: pale, pasty complexion, deep set cold eyes and his dark, greying at the edges, hair scraped back flush with his scalp with liberal quantities of hair oil.

Mr Batt leaned back in his chair resting his hands momentarily on the leather arms. He then leant forward again reaching out with his left hand for the top drawer. George, being a veteran of the headmaster's office, knew exactly what this meant. Gordon however was blissfully ignorant of what was about to come. His face changed to one of fear, he gasped and began to snivel, as he saw the cane appear in Mr Batt's left hand. Gordon was a typical bully; he could give it but couldn't take it. For effect the headmaster leant back in his chair once again. Still holding the cane in his left hand he took hold of it with his right and slid his right hand along the length of the cane to the other end. With a wicked look of enjoyment he bent and straightened it several times. Then he began, with a quiet monotone delivery, 'Gordon Savage, you are new here and whilst you may be excused for being unsure of many things in your new environment I am sure, without doubt, this behaviour would be unacceptable at your school in London, hmm? Well boy! Am I right?' he finished by shouting the question.

'Ye-es s-s-sir, errr, No s-s-sir!' snivelled the confused and quivering Gordon Savage.

'George, you have no defence whatsoever, even if this was one of your crusades to protect the weak. I expect more from you at this crucial moment in our county's history, I would also expect more from a boy whose father is a commissioned officer of the RAF.'

'Sir!' was the bold one word reply which George offered. Thinking of the laughs he had had with his Dad at home, the subject of which had been Mr Batt, George looked at the ground after answering so that he could hide the huge smirk on his face and recompose before lifting his head again.

'...And you boy!' he turned once again to Gordon, 'I expect better behaviour from a boy whose uncle, with whom you are currently living, is an officer of the law!'

Mr Batt stood up, still flexing the cane in front of him, 'if I have either of you two in my office again this month you *will* feel my cane!' he bellowed, raising the cane high above his head and, on the last word, bringing it down hard on the desk with a thwack. George knew this tactic of fear and didn't flinch. Gordon on the other hand yelped and visibly jumped. That wasn't all; he then had to be excused to go home and change his shorts.

Home time

The rest of the day was the usual uneventful day at school, lessons, lunch, more lessons. Absolutely no sign there was a war on. The school bell rang promptly at quarter to four, cueing a repeat performance of the morning's mayhem. The school vomited yelling children from every doorway; the rivers of children gathered in a violent sea in the playground.

George didn't hang around to take part. As usual he pushed his way through the treacle-thick slick of turmoil to the relative tranquillity of the school gate and the road home. On breaking free of the bedlam he broke instantly into a sprint, which Jesse Owen would be proud of. George always ran home as quickly as he could so he could have a few minutes with his Dad before he went to the airfield.

He arrived home and stopped at the Garden gate to regain his breath and composure, then sauntered into the house. 'Mum! Dad! I'm home,' he yelled.

'We're out here, Urchin!' his Dad called from the garden. The garden fell gently away from the back of the house after the small walled patio down to the mini orchard at the bottom. It was almost completely lawn, apart from four large rose beds which bisected the lawn approximately half way down. They were sitting out at the table on the patio just behind the house drinking tea and enjoying the late afternoon sunshine.

'A little birdie tells me you've been fighting again!' His mum said scowling at him.

'A little bat more like!' George snapped.

'Well what have you got to say for yourself then?' she continued.

'That thick oaf, Gordon, was picking on Peter Dulac again… and stirring up a gang to chant at him. I told him to back off but he wanted to fight. But I didn't hit him at all… he kinda… fell over… twice!' George finished with a grin on the right side of his mouth.

'Good for you, Urchin, looking after the underdog… and no one likes a bully, well done!' George's Dad chuckled.

'John! Please don't encourage him!'

'He was sticking up for someone who couldn't stick up for himself. I don't see a problem,' he retorted. 'Anyway it's nearly time for me to make a delivery to Adolf.' He finished, standing up and stretching his arms and back with a big yawn.

'I wish you didn't have to, tonight'

'Only two more Rachel, then its R&R. Maybe we could go away for a couple of days, the three of us?'

'Oh that would be nice,' Rachel said with a dreamy tone and a contented smile, facing toward the warming sun with her eyes closed. 'It's such a shame we can't go to France anymore; I often wonder how the Beauchamps are doing!'

George had taken the opportunity, while the focus was no longer on him, to make himself scarce.

'I'm going to get changed,' John said 'Charlie will be here soon.'

'OK,' Rachel said not moving her sleepy stare from the warming afternoon sun.

Charlie's real name was John Chaplin. But on a crew of six, where three were called John, it was easier to have nick-names. John Chaplin got his for two reasons: one; after the silent movie star Charlie Chaplin and two; he was a rear-gunner; who in the air force was known as a 'tail-end Charlie', so he was stuck with the name Charlie. George's Dad, John Scott, imaginatively was known as Scotty.

John finished getting changed then as usual he sat at the kitchen table with a mug of tea to wait for Charlie to toot his horn. George sat down with him.

'Where are you going tonight, Dad?' he quizzed.

'George! How many times? You know I can't tell you. I shouldn't tell you when I get home. Anyway I won't find out until the briefing with the CO… So I'll tell you in the morning,' he replied ruffling up George's hair.

'But what if….?' George didn't finish the sentence.

'What if I don't come back?' His father finished the sentence for him 'I'll leave a clue in my locker. But what good it'll do you I have no idea!' he finished, and continued sipping his tea.

Very soon there was the sound of a car pulling up outside then a beep, b-beep beep.

'Right, that's me,' said John standing up kissing Rachel and ruffling George's hair again.

He grabbed his bag and walked towards the front door. George and Rachel followed. John threw his bag into the back of Charlie's small open-top sports car and then with a joyous wave he leapt into the passenger seat. With a few revs of the engine and some more beeping of the horn the small car disappeared in a cloud of dust.

'Right you! Dinner, bath and bed!'

'Awwh!' was the only reply he could muster in minimal defiance.

Planes

After his bath he watched all the planes fly low overhead from his darkened bedroom after they'd taken off from the nearby airfield counting them out as they passed. He lay awake listening to them fading into the distance. Long after the hum of the engines faded the silence was dramatically broken by the sobering wail of the air-raid siren. This gave way to the altogether more sinister drone of the approaching German bombers flying high above George's house. He sneaked a peak through his blackout curtain. He then checked the silhouette against the images in his plane recognition books 'Heinkels!' he whispered to himself. It was apparent from their direction and height that his little country village and indeed the airfield were safe, 'It's London they've got it in for. There are hundreds of 'em,' George said under his breath. 'Crikey! They're in for a pounding!'

Sure enough some time later — although how much later, George was not sure, he must have fallen asleep — there was a continuous deep resonant pounding. He peeped once again from his window to view a distant glow like the last remnants of sunset.

But at midnight it can only be one thing, it was London, the blitz. George's mind wandered to the London evacuees that were now staying in the village and attending his school. 'It must be really hard being away from your family for so long, especially if you don't know if they are safe,' he thought to himself.

Just then his thoughts were completely erased as he heard the anti-aircraft batteries closer to home start firing again — 'They must be on their way home'. Suddenly George's attention was transfixed immediately to the crackling sound of machine-gun fire. His eyes scanned the sky overhead frantically to spot the next burst and the tell-tale tracer fire. 'It must be a Beaufighter giving it to one of those Nazi gits!' he whispered excitedly to himself. There were another couple of bursts of tracer fire, now heading off to-wards the Channel. Then a small fire in the sky, and the sound of a distant engine gasping for breath, the flames took hold with furi-ous vigour. The sound being emitted changed to a higher pitch, as the wounded German aircraft plummeted toward the Kent coun-tryside, huge flames belching from one of the engines as it disap-peared out of sight behind a distant hill. There followed a split second of silence which seemed to last for hours, George's eyes fixed on the spot where he last saw the flames. The silence and darkness were simultaneously broken as a small piece of the Nazi

George and the Reich

war machine met its end in one last violent act of destruction. '*Yes, payback!*' the overexcited George shouted at the top of his voice.

'Get away from that window and *go to sleep!*' his Mum shouted with an extremely agitated tone from her room; evidently having been woken up by George's outburst and not the dog fight. George said nothing in reply. He had learnt that engaging in any exchange of words at this juncture would be futile and not of benefit to him whatsoever; instead he leapt back into bed and pulled the cover over his head in one fluid movement.

Dad shot down apparently

George woke up, rubbed the sleep out of his eyes and went across to the window, stubbing his toe on the cast iron train that was lying in the middle of the floor. 'Damn, blast, crap!' he shouted as he hopped around the room clutching his throbbing toes.

'Mind your language!' the matriarchal voice of authority shouted from downstairs.

'Sorry Mum!' George conceded.

'I've told you so many times; tidy your bedroom, it's like a pig sty, it's your own silly fault!'

'Yes Mum,' George said reluctantly, pulling a defiant face.

'…and take that look off your face!' she said intuitively.

'How does she know!?' he exclaimed, looking upwards for divine response his arms extended outwards.

George finally got to the window and looked out over what he could see of the Kent landscape in the late summer mist. He gazed across towards the general area of last night's drama but the mist was too thick and he could see no evidence. He conducted a scanning search of the panorama from his window moving his eyes closer to the house each time. Nothing, not a single trophy, not even a piece of shrapnel. He glanced down at the garden, 'That's strange, Dad's usually back by now.' He ran down stairs in a panic 'Mum! Mum! Dad's not back! What's happened? Where is he?' George shouted in a barrage of questions.

'Yes, he is a bit late, but it's happened before when they've been on a really long one, or that time when they couldn't get in at their airfield because of the fog and got diverted. That's most probably what's happened,' she reassured George 'Yes, that's what's happened,' she repeated to reassure herself. 'Now, breakfast…'

The continuing conversation was cut short by the sound of an approaching car. 'See there he is now' Rachel said instantly relaxing. They both ran out of the front door and into the garden. The euphoria was short lived as they were stopped in their tracks, their momentum having been stunted by what seemed like an invisible wall. Rachel dropped the frying pan she was still holding. Their eyes firmly fixed on the car as it came to a halt level with the garden gate. An airman jumped out of the driver's seat and trotted the two steps to the offside passenger door and the familiar figure of the airfield commander; Group Captain Victor Hawkshaw, emerged from the opened door. There was an unmistakeable solemn expression firmly fixed on his face. George's Mum succumbed to the stress of the moment and fainted.

Rachel awoke less than an hour later to find herself on the couch in the drawing room being viewed by the gathered faces of George, Victor, Doctor Pickle, the Brigadier and Ives. As she surveyed the faces, all but George with veneered smiles in a poor attempt to reduce the severity of the truth.

The doctor began with, 'Mrs Scott, I've administered a mild sedative and prescribed some more. I recommend complete rest for a few days and…' By now her semi-dazed gaze had moved from the doctor and fixed on Victor. 'He's been shot down, hasn't he?' she quizzed the Group Captain directly, her eyes fixed and narrowed in anticipation. 'Err, yes. We believe so.' Victor hesitated in his reply, 'He had made target and they were one hour into the home run when we believe they were hit by ack ack. Luckily, in some ways, it was such a calm clear night that Johnny, err, Flight Lieutenant Hayes, saw them go down, they all jumped clear and all six 'chutes opened.'

'So he's alive!' Rachel exclaimed tears of joy welling in her eyes. For the first time that morning she allowed herself to relax and a beaming smile emitted from her face. Ever cautious not to give false hope Victor said 'Well, it's a safe bet to say he was alive when he left the aircraft and therefore most probable that he made it down, no ground fire reported. After that we won't know until we hear who, if anyone, has picked him and his crew up.'

'When will we know? Who will tell us? How do we find out? What happens next?' A tirade of questions emitted from George's mouth before he had thought about speaking.

'George, Rachel,' Victor began, looking at each of them in turn, 'I'm sorry, we won't know anything for at least twenty-four hours maybe, and most probably, longer. If they go it alone it could be days, even weeks. If they are picked up by the Germans we should find out within forty-eight hours of their capture. If they make contact with the resistance we should hear something within twenty-four hours. I'm sorry I can't be more precise.'

'You said they went down one hour into the journey home?' George confirmed, 'So where were they at that point?'

'George, you know I can't tell you that,' Victor said in a half-sympathetic half-condescending tone.

'OK,' George replied reluctantly. Then with a rekindled enthusiasm he said, 'So what was the target then?'

'George, if I could tell you I would.'

'Well, did Uncle Johnny say whether it was raining? I'd hate to think of Dad having to lie low in the wet, he'll catch a chill!'

'It was fine and visibility was fair; they even had a slight tail wind to help them on their way,' Victor said, momentarily dropping his guard 'Now I have said more than I should have.'

'That's enough now George,' said Rachel, 'Victor has told us all he can.'

'I've taken the liberty of bringing all of John's things with me, so they are here when he gets back,' Victor stated optimistically. 'I'll have my driver bring them in.'

The airman brought the box of various items into the kitchen and set them down on the table.

'I'm sorry Rachel, I have to go now, war to fight and all that. Just as soon as I have any information I'll let you know.'

'Yes of course, thank you Victor.' Then looking over to the Brigadier, Rachel said, 'Dad will you see Victor to the door please?'

'Of course my dear, a pleasure,' the Brigadier replied, gesturing to the door with an upturned hand and making eye contact with Victor as if to say, 'after you.'

'Thank you very much Sir,' Victor said honouring the Brigadier as a senior officer. 'Goodbye Rachel... George,' he said as he left.

'I must be off too,' said the doctor, 'if there's anything I can do please let me know. Don't get up, I can see myself out.'

'Actually doctor,' Rachel said stopping the doctor in his tracks, 'there is one small thing you could do for me if you're going back into the village.'

'Of course, what is it?' enquired the doctor.

'Will you run George in; so he doesn't miss school please?'

'Yes, of course no problem... c'mon then George,' beckoned the doctor with a friendly smile.

'Oh Mum!' George protested. Rachel glared at him; even in her semi-sedated state George didn't dare object again.

'Don't worry George, Ives and I will stay with your mother for the day, we'll look after her,' the Brigadier called as George sulked and kicked his way out of the house and climbed into the doctor's car.

Box & Plan

On returning from school George ran into the house and dived straight onto the box that Victor had brought from the airfield that morning; he began to rummage manically through them. 'Hello George, how was school?' Rachel asked putting on a cheerful voice. On receiving no reply from the very focussed George she then replied to her own question with over-emphasised joviality, 'Hi Mum, oh it was fine thanks!' After a short pause with no response from George, Rachel continued, 'George, what *are* you doing?'

He was looking for the clue that his dad had agreed to leave him. George didn't reply, he just carried on completely focussed. He picked up various items, dismissing them all almost as quickly as he had picked them up. Then he noticed a small bottle of aftershave. 'I don't remember Dad ever using this type,' George said thoughtfully.

'What's that you've got there?' Rachel enquired. George held the bottle above his head not looking round or indeed turning towards his mum as he did so. 'Cologne!' she said, 'he doesn't use anything like that when he's flying. 'Cologne… cologne… cologne,' he repeated thoughtfully, several times and then paused. He slowly looked up. The expression of concentrated puzzlement turned to one of euphoric clarity. *'Cologne,'* George finally shouted 'Cologne was the target!' He leapt to his feet dancing around his Mum as if having some kind of eureka moment.

Still clutching the bottle, George ran out of the room at the same moment as the Brigadier was entering, nearly knocking him off his feet. George did not slow down and continued the sprint up to his room.

'What's got into him?' said the lordly voice of her father. Rachel replied with a bewildered shake of the head and shrug of the shoulders.

'Mm-hmm. That boy needs more discipline, mark my words, more discipline! Anyway; Tea?' he loudly half suggested and half demanded whilst surveying the room in his regal manner. Rachel looked up and nodded.

'Ives!' the single word order from the Brigadier seemed to be all that the batman needed to understand what was required of him. Immediately and obediently he jumped to attention: 'Yes sir, right away sir!' Some moments later a tray of tea, cakes and sandwiches was presented with military precision and speed.

'Thank you Ives, well done!' congratulated the Brigadier. 'Call the boy will you?' he further ordered. 'He must keep his strength up.'

Ives called up the stairs, 'Master George, sir.'

'Yes,' replied George.

'Tea, sir'.

'OK! Thanks Ives, I'll be right there,' George called down from his room behind a closed door.

Meanwhile up in his room George's mind was working over-time. He was hatching a plan; lying on his bed perusing his map of Europe, the one with all his father's previous missions on. George was busy working things out in his head and unconsciously whispering to himself, 'Since they were an hour away from Cologne on the route home and a Wellington Bomber flies at 230 MPH. allowing for the homeward course, speed and slight tail wind,' he said remembering the words of Victor, 'he must have travelled around 230 miles which is about 2 and 5/16ths of an inch on the map.'

George put the pin of his compass on Cologne and drew an arc with a radius indicating this measurement.

'They must have ditched in the region of Ghent in Belgium. I reckon that, no matter whose *care* he is in, he'll move from that area quickly. If the Germans have them they'll be moved to a local detention for initial questioning. If not, so as not to attract the attention of the already alerted security services of Derrrrr Führer,' George said to himself exaggerating the 'der'. This made him chuckle, so he said it again a bit louder and more exaggerated '*Derrrr* Führer!' creating a greater laugh from within. He refocused his mind to the matter at hand, 'So therefore Dad will move closer to the Belgium coast, lying low in the daytime,' he continued to whisper, 'but where will he go after that?' George continued to try to second guess the outcome of each possible scenario.

He sat studying the map and the various items he'd gathered on his floor: compass, pen knife, sheath knife, small first aid kit, torch and survival tin to name a few. His survival tin was something he'd put together himself using an old tobacco tin. Among other things it contained some waxed matches, so they didn't get damp, a small piece of candle, some fish hooks and line, a length of fuse wire, a pencil and some safety pins. He pondered for a while in deep thought. *Dylan*! he whispered to himself, 'I wonder?' His semi daydream state of contemplation was suddenly broken. 'George! Tea! Now!' came a shrill and definite voice which, by the tone and delivery it would be a grave mistake to defy or ignore. 'Coming, Mum,' George replied in his best obedient voice.

'Now George! Ives has made the most wonderful tea and the least you can do is acknowledge that by enjoying it.' By the time George's mum had finished the lecture George had whizzed past her, sat at the table and was already tucking into a sandwich whilst Ives was filling his tea cup.

'George! What do you say?'

'Fa-choo, Isches,' George said with a face full of ham sand-wich.

'George! Don't talk with your mouth full!' came the chastising voice of Mum as she sat down and joined everyone at the table.

George looked up at the stern, slightly drawn face of his mother then across to the knowing smile of his grandfather, who on making eye contact winked and gave off a little chuckle. George couldn't help but reciprocate with a smile which he immediately, knowing he was being watched, tried unsuccessfully to wipe off his face.

'Dad, don't encourage him!' Rachel scolded her father, who replied in a subservient tone, 'No, of course, quite right, sorry,' and then tucked into a large slice of fruit cake followed instantaneously with a large slurp of tea in a vain attempt at hiding his embarrass-ment.

George and the Reich

After everyone had eaten their fill, George fled immediately to his operations room, the name that he'd now given his bedroom in his head. Rachel and the Brigadier removed to the parlour, leaving Ives to clear away the crockery and remnants of the meal. Behind the closed door of his room George could hear the intermittent sound of industry and activity as Ives cleaned up and his Mum and grandfather chatted. He heard the sucking sound of remonstration as a cork was bullied into releasing its grip on a bottle of wine. He knew then that he would have at least an hour before anyone realised that he was awake and only then would he be ordered to bed.

Sometime later George heard a loud deep creak; a sound which emanated from the third stair from the bottom. This meant someone was on their way up; it could only be mum. He rapidly tidied away the map and other bits and pieces with which he had covered his floor into his rucksack and stuffed it under his bed just before his door opened. He looked round rubbing his eyes. 'It looks like someone's really tired; come on, teeth and bed now George please.'

'But…!'

Rachel verbally stopped him in his tracks, 'No buts George! You are shattered and it's time for bed!'

George got the look and the tone again and decided in a split second to concede. 'OK!' came the reluctant submission. He got ready for bed, said good night and settled down to sleep. He concentrated on the conversation which was emanating from downstairs; he could make out a few words but the conversation was inevitably about his Dad.

Later, came the nightly air-raid warning. Knowing that his Mum and grandfather were ensconced in deep conversation regarding the grave situation over a bottle of wine, George took his opportunity to run down the stairs. He ran past the kitchen where Ives was snatching forty winks on one of the kitchen chairs, his head resting on the huge thick rustic table which dominated the room. As George ran past, his slipstream briefly disturbed Ives's sleep, momentarily vocalising his dream of some long-passed campaign. 'Fuzzy-wuzzies Colonel, bloomin' loads of 'em… zzzzzzz,' snoring as he slipped back into a deep sleep. '*Mum!*' George shouted as he entered the sitting room, which woke Ives instantly from his dream, causing him to fall off the chair which he'd temporarily occupied, finally jumping to his feet and standing bolt upright to attention complete with salute.

'There's an air-raid… it's a big one, listen.' George continued unaware of the consternation he'd caused in the kitchen.

Rachel and the Brigadier, for a moment, did as they were told and listened.

'Yes it is an air-raid, but it's going to London!' she said rather crossly, 'and you are going back to bed immediately!'

'Muuuum, I'm hungry, can I get a piece of bread and butter and a glass of milk?'

'Oh… OK!, but straight back up to your room and into bed and no peeping through your blackout blind!'

At that command George ran to the kitchen doing a sling-shot corner around Ives and then cornering in the opposite direction at the end of the table to the larder.

To call this a larder was an understatement, it was more of a room in its own right. In less austere times George had seen this packed full to the gunwales with all kinds of food. The shelves reached all around him, no wall space was spared from the floor up. There were game hooks in the ceiling which he couldn't reach and if he stretched out his arms he couldn't touch any two of the chalky whitewashed walls at the same time. He momentarily perused the fare on offer. He then began grabbing and wrapping slices of bread in greaseproof paper, then chunks of ham, hardboiled eggs, chicken pieces, tomatoes (though he hated them), apples and just about anything he could lay his hands on, slipping it all into a thick muslin bag, grabbing some boxes of matches as he left clutching the bag which was now bursting at the seams.

'Cor, are we hungry sir?' said Ives in his usual jovial manner.

'Extremely Ives, I don't know what's come over me!' George replied as he left the kitchen and went back to his room. He listened intently to see if any intelligence had been imparted... all was quiet. He set his alarm and stuffed the clock under his pillow to be assured it woke him instantly and then settled down to sleep.

The Channel

George awoke suddenly to the rapid but softened vibration of his alarm clock under his pillow. This was a ploy he'd used many a time in the past to be able to get up early to go sailing or fishing at first light without waking anyone else in the house. However, this was new as it was only just getting dark; the alarm had woken him at 9.30 PM just over an hour since he'd gone to bed. Quite uncharacteristically George rapidly, but quietly, got up and got dressed while standing on his bed. He listened intently for any sound. He could just make out the sound of quiet muffled chatter downstairs.

He opened the window slowly so the old hinges didn't complain and give the game away before it had started. Putting on his warmest waterproof coat and hat, he grabbed his rucksack which he had packed full and the canvas bag bursting with food. He placed them both out on the roof of the porch. He packed his bed up to look like he was still in it, should anyone just glance from the door. Gingerly he then climbed out of the window, pausing only to gently close the window. Slinging the bags over alternate shoulders he began to climb down the giant ivy which clung to, or possibly supported, the old house; it was that robust he could not define which. On reaching the bottom he put out his left foot behind him to test terra firma and then jumped off with both feet; stopping still and silent in a statuesque semi-crouch for a moment to ensure he hadn't been rustled. George then put his rucksack on his back; he put the food bag into the basket on the back of his bike. Carefully he wheeled the bike round to the front of the house before mounting and setting off into the night in the direction of the bay.

When he arrived after the five-minute bike ride, he looked up at a slender figure, slightly silhouetted by the dull moonlight. George dropped the canvas bag and took the rucksack off his back. He bent over and placed his hands on his knees to get his breath back and then looked up again. 'Hello *Dylan*,' George greeted the silhouette, 'we've got a job to do, and it's not plain sailing!' George took the canvas cover off *Dylan* and stowed it carefully in the watertight locker situated in the bow, along with his rucksack and canvas bag. Then George rigged *Dylan*'s sails in preparation. He clipped the wheels on to *Dylan*'s stern, which his dad had fashioned from an old golf trolley to enable George to get the boat out of the water alone; then he lifted the bow and walked the small boat down to the water's edge.

Once afloat George climbed in and removed the wheels from the stern and replaced them with the rudder and tiller. He quickly hoisted the jib, which quickly filled in the night breeze. They were underway. Once clear of the bay and shallow water George dropped the centre board to help prevent them from drifting and hoisted the mainsail, the wind sharply took up the slack of the canvas which jolted the small dinghy and instantly quickened the pace. He was now sailing out into the English Channel, something he had not done since before the war. This was totally new territory. So far the war had gone on all around him but had only become reality that morning. Now he was after a piece of it, like a Rottweiler after a bone.

He took a last look behind him as the English coast disappeared to a faint outline. He gulped and said, 'OK, this is it!' He took out the compass and torch from his coat pocket, checked his heading using the compass and adjusted his course. 'OK! France here we come,' he stated taking a deep breath. He looked up at the sky, there was a heavy cloud cover, no chance of seeing the stars; he would have to navigate by compass alone. The moon was a dim glow behind the cloud providing a dark camouflage for him and *Dylan.* Although the wind was fairly strong in the direction of France it had no more than a slight effect on the sea with minimal swell and thus provided fairly smooth and fast conditions. 'Hopefully we should be there by daybreak if not before,' he reassured himself.

It was a mild night and so George took off his heavy coat, his sweater was warm enough. He then stuffed the compass and torch into his trousers and stowed his coat and the wheels into the locker, he'd always been taught to keep a tidy boat for safety and efficiency especially at night. He and *Dylan* were now out in open water. Suddenly George was overcome with a cold dose of reality which made him physically shiver: 'I have every chance of being discovered by British, or worse! A German patrol! Either way I'm in the toilet,' he said out loud. 'OK, then. Might as well be hung for a sheep as a lamb,' he finished. The wind was directly behind them. Given the conditions George had *Dylan* running as fast as the little boat could go.

The night, except for the sound of the water slapping against *Dylan*'s hull, was quiet. There were no aircraft overhead and no sign of any Channel traffic. He listened intently all around, staring into darkness in the direction that he listened… Nothing! He sat at the stern constantly alert for any new sound, light or silhouette. Occasionally he checked the sails and confirmed his heading against the compass. All was well. He checked all around one more time before heading forward to the locker and reaching in for the bulging food bag. He took out a piece of cheese and a chunk of bread then replacing the bag carefully re-sealed the locker. His concentration temporarily lapsed as he alternately bit chunks from the bread and cheese.

Suddenly he realised there was a new sound, faint at first but getting louder. George dropped what remained of the food. He looked all around trying to pierce the darkness with his eyes looking carefully in each direction not being able to tell from which direction the sound emanated. He searched meticulously like a bird of prey searching the undergrowth from the air for a rodent. Then he saw it. There was a dark, small, ghostly image moving at a rapid speed just in front of the horizon. George assumed the worst that it was a motor torpedo boat on patrol though he doubted at this distance that they would spot him. As a matter of caution he dropped the mainsail to reduce the size of his silhouette. He watched the apparition continue at speed then it seemed to change course, the sound of the engine becoming louder. Was it heading for him? Had they seen him? The questions rapidly ran through his mind as he attempted to make sense of the situation. 'Oh, cripes,' he said. He jumped to the front and released the jib then he flattened it on to *Dylan's* deck. He felt the pace slow to a gentle drift.

All of George's senses were firmly locked on the dark image, which he had confirmed in his mind was a motor launch, but whose was it? It moved rapidly in a wide arc. Suddenly, George was instantly disorientated, thrown into a panic and fell back landing on his bottom in the puddle of sea water that had gathered in the bottom of the boat. The still relatively small launch had disappeared behind a giant black silhouette which was directly in front of him which, until then, had remained completely unnoticed, an enormous black hulk rising from the Channel a matter of feet away. George, petrified, looked up at the huge dark edifice. George and *Dylan* were drifting slowly but uncontrollably toward the dead-looking apparition with no power to change course. He could hoist a sail to regain enough speed but that might give his position away to the approaching motor launch; or he could sit tight and take his chances with the unknown. At that time it was looking to George like he had a choice between the frying pan and the fire. He took another look up at the huge black monster framed by the moonlit clouds. The outline was unmistakable; it was that of a submarine's conning tower.

He could hear the volume of the approaching engines increasing. The launch was very close now as if it was heading directly for the submarine as well. Still drifting closer and closer finally *Dylan*'s bow touched the side of the metal hulk with a deep resonant clang. George audibly gulped and froze. 'Crickey! That's torn it!' he exclaimed out loud. His eyes were the only part of his body that retained full movement; they were vigorously scanning the decks and tower of this thing for any signs of life. 'Any minute now,' he thought, 'there'll be dozens of weapons all trained on me.' This thought made him visibly tremble. 'I just hope it's one of ours.' Just at that moment *Dylan's* bow touched the side again sounding out a second loud clang. This made George suspicious and thoughtful. 'That noise was loud enough to wake the deepest sleeper!' he pondered to himself.

George's fear subsided enough for his limbs to regain movement. He began to look all over the vessel for clues. He couldn't see any flag, there was no movement or sound emanating from inside; 'It's dead in the water,' he concluded, 'but it's not drifting.' This he could tell because even in this light sea *Dylan* was bumping along the hull of the hulk. 'It must be moored here, so what's it for?' he wondered. George took *Dylan's* bow rope and fastened it to the metal ladder which ran up the side so as to keep them shielded from open water. As *Dylan* swung round slowly to come alongside the hull of the larger vessel, George dropped some fenders over *Dylan's* starboard side to prevent further noise or worse damage to *Dylan's* hull. Once this manoeuvre was complete he looked up again and took a much closer look at the hulk, well, as much as the poor light would permit. 'What is this?' he questioned, 'it's too short to be a sub, but if that's true; what's the tower for?' he puzzled further.

His pondering was disturbed when he heard the now unmistakable engines of the motor launch reduce to a slow, loud, chug as it made its approach. The launch pulled up on the other side of the conning tower which was all that obscured their view of George and *Dylan*; out of sight but only a few feet away. George took a deep breath and, gulped. He heard feet on metal and then a metallic screech made his eye's instantly fix on the top of the tower. This was followed shortly by a loud clash of metal against metal resonating like the giant gong at the beginning of the Rank Films.

His worst fear was then instantly confirmed when heard the spine-chilling sound of a commanding guttural German voice shouting into the vessel. It was definitely German; 'Oh, cripes!' George whispered. He roughly understood that they were enquiring to see if anyone was inside. A second voice shouted a question which the first voice answered, '*Nein!*'

George then heard what sounded like an order barked at the crew. The man at the top of the tower replied, '*Jawohl!*'

There was an instantaneous scrambling of feet back toward the launch, the crew had evidently been ordered back on board. The engines roared and the launch sped away.

Very soon he could once again hear the sound of the sea lapping against the boat instead of that of the engines, and his heart pounding. His attention turned back to the huge floating thing; his curiosity was killing him; he had to see inside. He decided it was his duty to explore it. George grabbed his torch and pointed it carefully at the side. He was careful where he pointed it so that as little light as possible spilled past the object and unnecessarily alerted any unwanted attention from either side, or both. 'Cor that'd be a disaster!' he said to himself, 'I'd be grounded 'til I was 65,' he chuckled 'I'm probably going to be anyway!'

He lit up the side of the tower, painted on it was a huge red cross. This intrigued him even more; it couldn't be an ambulance — not out here and couldn't be a hospital. So what was it? He used his torch to look for the foot holdings so he could climb aboard.

He slowly pulled himself and *Dylan* back along the side of the hulk until they were directly beneath the tower and in line with the ladder welded to its side. George tied *Dylan* off there and gave the rope a good tug to ensure it was fast. George stuffed the torch into his pocket and clambered onto *Dylan*'s bows in preparation for boarding the strange floating object. He took a deep breath and blew it out in one single puff through tightened lips inflating his cheeks as if blowing out a large candle. Without further hesitation he grabbed one of the rungs and hauled himself across to the ladder bringing his other hand across and holding tightly whist feeling his way with his feet to ensure a safe foothold. He began the climb to the top of the tower. Half way up he paused, looked all around and listened; he was, thankfully, all alone, the coast or rather the Channel was clear. He carefully and quietly continued his climb to the top. The climb was completed in almost perfect silence. When he reached the top he questioned himself: 'Why do I have to be quite so quiet? There is no one around. For miles!' he added hopefully. Well he was certain there was no one around outside and pretty sure there was no one inside. 'Well, with all that noise, no one could have failed to have heard that, even if they were asleep,' George reassured himself. When he arrived at the top he checked around the hatch, there wasn't much to see, just a wheel lock to unfasten the hatch which he did. It took all his strength to throw back the hatch, and it made its full resonating signature noise. George looked wide-eyed into the black hole.

Removing his torch from his pocket he shone it into the tower. He could see a ladder leading down the inside of the tower to the bottom which seemed to open out into a larger room or rooms. The décor, from what he could see, had the usual military warmth and class that one would expect. He swung round on his stomach and lowered his legs into the tower, feeling for the ladder with his feet. Once he had located the ladder he moved his hands inside and climbed down into the belly of this floating mystery. On reaching the bottom he first firmly touched the floor with one foot, keeping firm hold of the ladder. When he was sure it was solid he let go, turned around and took his torch out from his pocket again. From what he saw, at first view, he'd descended into what looked like a single fairly large cabin.

George slowly turned completely round on the spot, scanning the room with his torch; taking in everything that the torch light fell on. It seemed to be of hexagonal construction with double bunk beds against two of the walls and a configuration of shelves and cupboards on a third wall. The walls between each of these items were bare, save for a small table on the wall between the two beds which also sported a picture of Adolf Hitler. He felt like Sherlock Holmes about to make an instant and conclusive deduction as to who dunnit; or in this case what was it? The first conclusion George arrived at was a fairly easy one. 'This is definitely one of theirs,' he said decisively; not a difficult conclusion due to the swastikas and picture of Hitler on the wall.

'I'd best not stay here too long,' he thought, 'just in case I'm rumbled.'

He quickly and systematically searched through the drawers and cupboards, making sure he didn't disturb the contents too much. Opening one of these drawers caused him to audibly gasp as the torch beam fell on the contents. 'Chocolate!' he exclaimed.

George couldn't resist; he stuffed two bars quickly into his pocket. He also pinched some first aid supplies and a bottle of fresh water. Then after one last quick scan, he climbed the ladder out and resealed the hatch after him.

George clambered back down the outside of the tower and into *Dylan* and very soon he was back underway in full sail, making good headway. He checked the heading on the compass and adjusted the tiller slightly. Settling back with the tiller under his arm he took a good long drink of the water he had pilfered from the Germans. He slapped his tongue against the roof of his mouth and smacked his lips together several times in the tasting routine. 'Our water's better than yours, Adolf!' he announced to the open sea at the top of his voice.

He heard a thud! 'What?' he said as he sat bolt upright. It was the bottle of water as it hit the deck. He must have dozed off, but for how long he was not sure. George rubbed his eyes and chuckled to himself. He again adjusted the heading after checking the compass, as *Dylan*'s bow returned to the correct heading; simultaneously he saw a light flicker, in what looked like the middle distance, and heard the engine noise again. He strained his eyes and saw the small silhouette of a motor launch. 'Crickey!' he exclaimed, 'they've come back around again!'

There's was nothing he could do, he couldn't outrun them and their fire power would blow him and little *Dylan* to smithereens. What could he do? They're getting closer now. He could see the silhouette was getting rapidly larger. They were headed directly for him! 'This is a time for action not dithering!' he said in a state of panic, although this time he was not frozen to the spot, 'come on make a decision. That's it! We'll capsize!' He could do it; he'd done it hundreds of times, when he was playing pirates with his friends. But this wasn't his friends; it was a crew of Nazi Germany's finest wrapped up in several tons of floating guns and ammunition. It was the only chance he had to make it look like his boat had come loose from its mooring and capsized. He dropped the sails, climbed *Dylan's* small mast, tied a rope to the mast and threw the sea anchor, at the other end, hard into the water. To speed up the process he leant his weight in the same direction; the boat began, slowly, to list over and then finally the mast hit the water. In what seemed like an age to George, as he watched fixated on the rapidly enlarging shape of the patrol boat, but really was a few seconds, the boat was fully inverted.

George took a deep breath and then swam under water and popped up under the upturned boat. He gasped in a huge breath of the trapped air, trying to fight against his body's natural reaction to cold and fear to breathe rapidly. He pulled down the centre board and disconnected the rudder and left it to float on its tether to make it look completely abandoned. He ensured all his equipment was still stowed safely. He stayed motionless, mainly because he was petrified and listening intently to the boat's engine as it slowed sharply. They'd spotted *Dylan's* upturned hull, at least if he got away with this they wouldn't turn back again. As the boat pulled alongside its engine slowed to a low drumming resonance. Search lights were now firmly fixed on *Dylan's* hull. George could see the beams of light refracting in water below. Poles or hooks were clawing at the underside which was now strangely and disconcertingly above Georges head. As he refocussed he could hear the guttural harsh discussion being conducted no more than a few feet from him, in German. His understanding of German was sketchy although he picked out one voice of authority suggesting that the boat is retrieved as a present for his little boy back in the fatherland. George gritted his teeth: 'Over my dead body' he quietly growled. The response came from another voice which was evidently superior, *'Nein.'* The first voice now rather subserviently said, *'Jawohl! Herr Kapitan!'* Suddenly there was an explosion nearby; orders were barked out and in a mix of excitement and panic. Faster than the boat had arrived, it was gone.

George took a deep breath, checked the coast was clear, righted the boat and carried on. Once he had *Dylan* back on the correct heading, he changed into some dry clothes from his bag in the locker. Some way behind him there were further explosions and gunfire being exchanged. George looked over his shoulder to see the accompanying bursts of yellow and white in the distance.

George reassured himself that since he had encountered a German patrol boat, which was now otherwise occupied, and a German a rescue buoy that he must be at least half way across, maybe more. He checked his watch '1.45 AM' he said 'We'll have to go some now to make the French coast and find the cave before day break, come on *Dylan* we need to really go now!'

Going in

George reached the French coast less than an hour before daybreak; it was still dark twilight. By his reckoning and navigation skills the peninsula and therefore the cave were near. Luckily it was a dark misty morning perfect cover to break up the silhouette of a small boat from watchful binoculared German eyes scanning the coastline. The cover, which was his saviour, also worked against him, visibility was low. If the tide was too low or he misjudged the location it would be disastrous; the jagged rocks could rip a hole in *Dylan*'s hull as easy as a hot knife in butter. George knew from the coast line that he wasn't far from the cave; it was only a short distance to the south-west. As he turned *Dylan*'s rudder to navigate the new course, he kept his eyes peeled for the landmark which would indicate the cave's location, whilst the entire time keeping one eye on the coast for any signs of the Germans.

Just then George spotted exactly what he'd been looking for, the unmistakable rock formation which marked the cave's location. He knew from the position of the rocks that he was too close to shore for comfort and immediately changed course to sail out a few hundred yards from the coast. He had to pass them and then turn directly inland between the two largest rocks; he knew from past experience that there was an almost straight channel of safe water leading to the cave entrance. This was experience he'd gathered the hard way one summer, by tearing the bottom out of a boat he'd sailed straight over the jagged rocks that lurk just below the surface on either side of the channel. The two rocks he was about to sail through looked as if at some time in prehistory they'd been the entrance to a much longer and wider cave. They seemed, for some reason to have been granted a reprieve by erosion while the rest had long since been taken by the sea.

George lined *Dylan* up for the last, and potentially most hazardous, leg of the journey. The wind wasn't ideal; it was blowing easterly across the shore which meant he would have to sail across it, in what sailors would call a broad reach. This meant that if he kept the sails tight to go fast the boat may be blown diagonally onto the rocks. He took a deep breath as he sailed *Dylan* into the channel through the prehistoric markers, keeping as close as he dared to the rock on the portside, to permit a little drifting.

The night was now fast releasing it grip, as early morning bullied its way in with a misty twilight; 'Not excellent visibility but good cover,' he thought. George sailed the little boat as fast as he dared. He needed to reduce the time that they might visible, to the guards on the cliffs above, to the absolute minimum. He checked forward to the cave mouth, which was now just about distinguishable, and then back to rocks. The wind was stronger than he first thought. 'Cripes! We've drifted!' He said correcting the course urgently to port to get them back into the channel. As *Dylan's* stern pivoted round there was a heart-stopping crunch, followed by deep grinding noise, accompanied simultaneously with a violent vibration in his right hand. 'Crikey! The rudder!' he exclaimed in a loud whisper. He looked behind to splinters of wood in *Dylan's* wake. He panicked. 'Oh no! We've lost the rudder!' He moved the tiller back and forth to see how much, if any, of the rudder was still there. He felt a slight resistance and the boat rocked and wiggled slightly. 'There's still enough there to steer with,' he said as he blew out a huge sigh of relief. 'We'll worry about that when we're safely in the cave, *Dylan,'* he said patting the side of the boat with his left hand.

As they approached the shore, to avoid the risk of further noise, George dropped the mainsail and lashed down the boom; he'll make it in on the jib alone. This strategy will be slower but quieter. It should provide him with more thinking and manoeuvring time, with the added benefit of reduced physical presence; at a key time when *Dylan's* outline may be definable, despite the poor visibility. He knew he was now in the danger area; this was not a natural danger, this danger was completely man-made, he was out of open sea but not home and dry. He was getting closer all the time. He knew from the height of the rocks that the tide was low and possibly coming in but he still couldn't define how low. In high tide he could sail straight into the cave easy as pie; at low tide he would have to drag *Dylan* across sand and pebbles. This would surely attract unwanted attention from Jerry. That's if they hadn't seen him already.

As George approached the mist was clearing and he could see the sheer face of the cliff in what was now almost daylight. His eyes traced the rock up and up; to his relief the top of the escarpment was visibly obscured by a capping of thick fog like an oversized meringue on top of a pie. It meant he couldn't see what was waiting up there but, by the same token, they couldn't see him. He heard a scrape, '*Blast!*' he said in a loud startled whisper. He leapt forward and released the centre board before it had a chance to drag on the bottom again or worse still, make a resonating thud into a submerged rock which could bring the boat to an abrupt halt preventing him from making it the last fifty yards or so and alerting every goon for miles around of his presence.

He knew now the tide was very low; because the centre board had touched the bottom he knew that there was no more than a foot of clearance between him and the beach. Ahead in the dark rocky outcrop he could see part of the cliff toward the bottom which was darker and roughly the shape of an archway like the entrance to a cathedral. This was it — the cave mouth. As he approached he still couldn't see if there was water in the entrance. In a split second he decided not to take any chances. He dropped the jib and jumped out of the boat, once again he was in the channel this time only up to his thighs. His plan was to lead the boat into the cave by hand ready to drag if need be; he looked up at the cliff top which was still obscured. He took a deep breath and began wading and pulling, maintaining vigilance all around and above. As he approached the entrance to the cave the water was becoming shallower and was now below his knees. The view of the cave mouth was much clearer, he could see there was water but it was not nearly deep enough. He stopped and clipped on the wheels. He returned to the front of the boat and continued pulling when suddenly he could hear voices, German ones, from the top of the cliff. From his knowledge of German he could make out that they were cursing about the fog, the lack of coffee and the useless sergeant amongst other things.

The water was now only just covering his ankles. The bow began to scrape the shingle in the shallow water, George lifted the front of the boat and at that moment he felt the wheels make contact with the bottom; he was nearly in the cave. He paused and gulped then he took a final glance upwards; the layer of mist still separated all view of him from the prying eyes above. With a deep breath he tugged with all his strength and dragged the boat across the short stretch of shingle. The short stabbing sound of crashing shingle broke the early morning tranquillity on the beach and lasted for a split second. He made it to the cave as fast as he possibly could and onto the rock floor and then stopped. He almost sprinted back the two or three paces to the cave entrance and listened intently to the banter between the German soldiers, his heart pounding in his chest and ears making it hard to hear the faint conversation so many feet above his head.

One of the voices had shushed the rest and said he'd heard something. The others were teasing him saying, 'They'd better inform the Führer that the invasion had started.' Another voice said, 'Well I'm not repelling any invasion until after breakfast, even if it is Churchill himself.' Another German said, 'If it is Churchill, we'll have time for lunch as well! He'll never climb that cliff. We should have afternoon tea ready for him… He'll need it by then!' and what sounded like the whole garrison broke into the most raucous laughter. George breathed a huge sigh of relief. The only soldier to hear anything had been ridiculed by his peers. He knew for the moment at least he was safe. His heart had slowed and he began to feel a cocky confidence and satisfaction at his achievements. Then

George remembered why he was here. He couldn't let this minor success make him arrogant and careless. After all, if he was going to make it, he still had to get across France, on his own, through some of Germany's finest, to a yet uncertain destination. If that wasn't enough, provided he made it that far he'd have to make it back again! 'Oh my God, what have I done,' George thought, the magnitude of the situation hitting him like a freight train for the first time.

'I'd best get *Dylan* hidden, then try to get some rest until the evening,' George thought to himself. He turned around sharply from the cave entrance to make his way back into the cave. With his first step a crippling sharp pain shot up his leg from deep within his left ankle. He dropped to the cave floor like a sack of potatoes, his ankle seemingly unable to take his weight all of a sudden. He rubbed the offending area to sooth the pain that was making him wince. He had to consciously suppress the natural urge to yelp like dog whose tail had been trodden on; in the certain knowledge that if he didn't the full complement of soldiers, whom he'd heard laughing some moments ago, would land on him like a ton of bricks.

He got back to his feet standing on his right foot gaining additional support from holding on to the cave wall. Slowly, and quite gingerly, he put his left foot on to the ground. With a gradual transfer of weight the sharp pain returned each time he put pressure on the foot; each time transferring his weight back to the right foot. He was able to get enough weight onto the left foot to limp the rest of the way back to *Dylan*. He sat on the edge of the boat and getting his leg into the most comfortable position, removed his back pack from the stowage compartment. He took out the first aid kit. He was pretty sure that he had done no lasting damage like a break, but was certain that he had unwittingly sprained it, ironically when he was giving himself the mental lecture about arrogance and carelessness. He strapped the ankle up using a bandage and safety pin.

The early morning mist was burning off and light was now beginning to flood the cave. A gentle breeze was blowing into the cave from the sea and already he could feel the air was warmer. He changed from the clothes that he had worn that night, which were now also fairly damp, into a fresh set from his bag. George stumbled up and down the cave floor a few times, all the time increasing his tolerance of the pain. He had to get *Dylan* hidden before it was too late. He dropped the mast and lashed it down ensuring all the sails and equipment not necessary for his further journey were stowed away properly, as he limped his way round the little boat.

Cautiously, he pulled *Dylan* around the corner of the cave out of direct view from the cave mouth. From the tide line on the cave floor he knew that the sea didn't rise this far in. George climbed back into the boat and finished checking through all his things that he'd packed back in his bedroom at home. His mind wandered to the safety of his bedroom and the warmth of his bed; what he wouldn't give for an hour's sleep in that bed, right now? It suddenly dawned on him his Mum would soon find out he had gone; he sniffed back a tear. In order to distract his mind from the upsetting realisation he completed his preparations and the battening down of *Dylan*. He unpacked *Dylan*'s tarpaulin and covered the boat, all that is except for the bit he was sitting on.

George could still hear the faint goings on and the odd excerpts of conversation and barking of orders. He concentrated intently on all the external noises trying to filter out the natural ones leaving all that is man-made. From the locker he took out the blanket he'd pinched from the rescue buoy and some of the food he had snaffled from the larder and tucked into bread, cheese and an apple, washing it all down with a good gulp of finest Kentish water. The hours of exertion, concentration, stress, cold and lack of sleep had now all taken its toll on George. He finished his cloth-bound banquet and wrapped himself in the blanket using his coat to rest his head. The warm morning breeze gently ambled into the cave and politely caressed George's already rosy cheeks like a silent lullaby. His concentration wandered from the faint chatter and clatter of the cliff top garrison to the rolling hypnotic sound of the waves breaking on the rocks outside like a metronome setting a largo beat. He struggled to fight his heavy eyes; he was so exhausted that he couldn't lift one eyelid, even if he could use his hands. George finally gave in the struggle with his fatigue and slipped into a deep sleep.

Meanwhile back in England…

The phone was ringing in the Police house with a strange sense of urgency. 'I wonder who that can be at this ungodly hour?' said Mrs Macworthy, who was fond of her sleep: it was well noted throughout the village. 'It's six o'clock in the morning! Are you going to answer that?' she exclaimed nudging her snoring husband in the ribs with her elbow.

'Who, what, follow that cab… Arrest him!' were the first utterings of the morning from a disorientated Sergeant Macworthy as he rubbed his eyes trying to make them focus.

'Are you going to answer that?' Mrs Macworthy barked again like an irate Jack Russell.

'Yes I am! It could be a serious crime at this time in the morning!' Sergeant Macworthy enthused, as he stumbled bleary-eyed in the general direction of the impatient phone.

'Serious crime!' Mrs Macworthy sniggered 'The last serious crime we had around here was two weeks ago. I bet little Mark

Smyth'll get life for scrumping those apples.' She chuckled to herself as she snuffled like a sow and settled back down back to sleep.

'Good Morning Police ho…' He didn't get to finish the greeting before the plaintive voice at the other end went into full flow like a sobbing machine gun. 'OK Mrs Scott… OK!… Now…. please calm down. Right then; George! What's happened to George?' Sergeant Macworthy said in an attempt to calm Mrs Scott down so as to get at the facts. 'Yes, Mrs Scott I'll come right away, just stay there and don't do anything. Make yourself a cup of tea and I will be there soon.'

The rather stout Sergeant Macworthy now moved faster than he had in years. He ran up the stairs; the last time he'd done that was the day of the Wall Street crash eleven years ago. He paused at the top to get his breath. After getting fully dressed in his uniform he ran back down the stairs, missing some steps and slipping down the rest landing in a heap at the bottom. He picked himself up rubbing his head, and bottom, both of which had taken the brunt of the fall. He put his helmet on after finding it under the kitchen table. Once he'd found his shoes, he put them on one at time hopping across the kitchen; on one foot then the other as he fastened them, bumping into several pieces of furniture and the door frame as he went. 'Will you stop making that racket, some of us are

trying to sleep!' shouted the voice of Mrs Macworthy from up-
stairs.

As he left the house putting on his bicycle clips, he mumbled,
'Proper police wives would have got up and ensured their hus-
bands at least had a cup of tea and a piece of toast inside them
while serving the public!' He made sure this protest was not quite
loud enough for his wife to hear. The Sergeant then mounted his
bicycle and wobbled off in the direction of the Scott house.

Sergeant Macworthy arrived at the Scott house twenty
minutes later; after riding a distance most people walk in half the
time. He propped his bike against the fence which, when he let go
and walked to the gate, promptly fell over with a tuneful metallic
clatter. He let go of the open gate, turned around and bent down
to pick up the offending bike. Just as he had a hold of the seat and
handle-bars the gate swung back and hit the policeman squarely in
the seat of his pants; the impact caused the already off-balance and
rather portly peeler to join his bike on the road. By now the noise,
in an otherwise tranquil and bright morning, emitting from the
tangled mess of bike and bobby had attracted an audience: Rachel,
the Brigadier and Ives. They observed the slapstick fiasco as it unfolded with an incredulous chuckle from the doorway. It was welcome light relief; however spectacles of this nature were not un-
common where the Sergeant was concerned.

George and the Reich

He finally scrambled to his feet; propped his bike up, securely this time, against the fence and attempted to smarten himself up again, whilst walking through gate. He tucked his shirt back into his trousers, whilst pulling them back into position, straightened his helmet and then unsuccessfully attempted to brush the dust, picked up from the road, off his uniform. He approached, his audience, not realising that the left side of his face was pebble dashed with dust and gravel.

The Brigadier, handing Sergeant Macworthy a handkerchief, said, 'You might want to.' He gesticulated the rest of the sentence by waving his index figure at the offending debris, accompanied with a delicate clearing of his throat.

The Sergeant felt his face, blushed and accepted the handkerchief. He cleared what he could with the hanky, which couldn't touch the more stubborn imbedded stones. These had to be painstaking removed one by one, as he followed Rachel; a hand gesture from the Brigadier indicated he should do so.

They walked round the outside of the house to the garden. They knew from experience to keep the clumsy policeman where he could do the least damage. As the entourage took their seats at the table just to the rear of the house on the terrace, Ives appeared from the French doors with the tea tray. Sergeant Macworthy scanned the tray as Ives positioned it on the table and smiled when he spied the large rack of toast and pot of jam. Ives poured and distributed the tea and plates of toast with unobtrusive military proficiency and silently disappeared when his task was complete.

'Now then Sergeant. Down to business,' commanded the Brigadier.

'Oh!… err…yes of course,' replied the Sergeant as he fumbled through his pockets attempting to retrieve his note pad; which, along with the pencil, was on the table at home in the police house.

'I… err… wonder if you have a…' He didn't finish the question; Ives had already mysteriously reappeared and thrust two sharpened pencils and a wad of paper into his pudgy hand.

'Right… oh… yes… thanks!' he spluttered in response.

'After yesterday's traumatic news, Ives and I stayed here; moral support and all that,' the Brigadier dictated in his regal booming voice. 'George went off to bed at around 8 PM; can't be sure exactly, you know. The last any of us saw of him was shortly after when he came back down stairs for a little snack.'

'Actually sir,' Ives piped up 'master George's snack wasn't that little, it took both arms to carry it.'

'Well, why didn't you say so before, Ives?'

'Well, begging your pardon sir, I've only just recalled it.'

'Hmm, we shall have words later,' warned the Brigadier.

'Oh, Dad, do leave him alone,' Rachel said sympathetically.

'So he came downstairs for a snack?' asked the Sergeant.

'Well, yes Sergeant but it was a bag full.'

'What would he do with all that food at that time of night?' Sergeant Macworthy pondered, seriously.

'I think it's now clear that his lordship had some kind of plan. This wasn't spur of the moment,' the Brigadier hypothesised.

'He's probably just run off after the news of his Dad. He'll be back soon. You'll see,' said the Sergeant trying to offer comfort whilst eyeing up the toast and jam.

'*No!*' Rachel snapped 'This has got one of George's plans written all over it. All we have to do now is work out what he's up to.'

'Well. What's missing? What does it look like he's taken with him? Where could he go: friends, relations and how's he going to get there?' Sergeant Macworthy said, finally asking some thought provoking questions.

'OK,' said Rachel. 'Ives, you check the shed to see if his bike's there. Dad, you get on the telephone and call: Daphne in Staplehurst, John's Sister Margaret in Canterbury and Auntie Rosemary…'

'But she doesn't have a telephone,' the Brigadier puzzled.

'No, you'll have to call the post office next door; I have the number for emergencies. They'll run around and get her; the number's in the book next to the phone.' Rachel replied, '…and I'll check his room for what's missing, although how I'm going to know in that mess is anyone's guess.'

Ives was the first back to the garden table. The Sergeant, still sitting there, looked up. His hamster-like cheeks were full to bursting with toast, Ives quickly deduced from the empty plate and smudges of jam round his face.

'As far as I can see the bike's gone.'

'B.i.k.e g.o.n.e,' the Sergeant said as he wrote a note.

'Nope, can't really see if much has gone,' Rachel said as she walked out onto the terrace 'All I *can* see is that his backpack has gone. And that could be filled with anything,' she despaired. 'Although apart from his desk the room is unusually tidy.'

'Well, no one from the family has seen him, that's for sure,' said the Brigadier resuming his seat. 'I took the liberty of informing Victor whilst I was making calls; he will keep an eye out in case George turns up there.'

'Where can he be?' Rachel said with tears welling in her eyes.

'Listen!' commanded the Brigadier, 'He is made of stern stuff, that boy. He knows his way around and can take care of himself. We'll find him soon, don't worry; will we not Sergeant?'

'Yes sir! Of course we will,' replied the Sergeant with a splutter of tea from his fourth cupful. 'Right! I'll get going and start the investigation.' The Sergeant continued getting to his feet.

'I will see you out Sergeant,' volunteered Ives.

First Foot in France

George heard German voices shouting, close by. He couldn't quite make out what they were saying. He knew it wasn't friendly. There was a sound like hundreds of jack boots on gravel. He sat up looking directly into the eyes of a German soldier who was shouting incomprehensibly, like a distressed seagull.

George sat up with fright. Sweat was dripping from his brow, his hair was damp. For a few seconds he was completely disorientated. He looked round. No Germans! It was a bad dream. He could hear gulls in the mouth of the cave shrieking and fighting on the gravel. George blew the stress out with a huge sigh. 'My Germans were seagulls!' he sniggered.

He looked at his watch, it was 4 PM. This was it; it was the right time to make a move on the next leg of his, thus far, completely un-planned and probably doomed quest. He knew that his next place of safety should be the hotel of Madame and Monsieur Beauchamp: L'Hôtel de la Manche. This was the preferred place to holiday for the Scotts prior to the war. Over the years the two families had become friends and George was praying this was still going to be the case. Although the war was still fairly young and France had only recently been occupied, he'd heard rumours of French collaboration. This would be a leap of faith, a chance he had to take. He'd come this far and was not going to turn back now. Suddenly George was distracted by a different sound in the gravel at the mouth of the cave, this time it *was* feet, human feet. From the voices he knew instantly they were German feet. George froze — all his senses were focussed on the mouth of the cave. He couldn't see the cave entrance from the dark recess where he had stowed *Dylan* and himself. Although, he could hear from the tone and echo of the footsteps and voices that they had entered the front of the cave. George's heart was audibly pounding. Sweat was running off his forehead and his hands. Then he heard one of them say, in German of course, 'See I told you it was just seagulls, come on it's time for a drink.'

George then took a deep breath of relief. 'Why am I putting myself through all this?' he muttered quietly. 'Dad!' was the single word answer he gave himself. This seemed to be the internal order to move. He swung his legs out of the boat and jumped off in a single movement. As he landed on the rock floor an excruciating pain shot up his leg from his ankle. George just managed to prevent this reaching his mouth and manifesting itself in a scream. Even in the dimly lit cave he could see the ankle was swollen. He scrambled to his feet and limped back over to *Dylan*. Each step sent a pain up the centre of his leg, like an upward thrust of a dagger causing him to wince. The effort and concentration necessary to suppress the natural reaction to scream caused his face to contort and sent floods of tears rolling down his cheeks.

He removed his pack from the boat and tied down the tarpaulin. Slinging the pack over his left shoulder he patted *Dylan* with his right hand and said '*Au revoir, Dylan!*' He slowly, tentatively made his way to the rear of the main cave where he paused. Sitting on one of the higher rocks he removed his shoe and began to lash a bandage, which he'd taken from his pack, as tightly round his ankle as he dared without cutting off the blood supply. After admiring his handiwork he carefully put the shoe back and cautiously stood up taking most of his weight on his good leg and arms as he hopped round to face the rock and pushed with his arms to gain an upright posture. As he transferred more weight to the bad ankle he could feel the extra support the bandage was providing. With a slow uneven gait he moved further to the rear of the cave and the narrow passage which would lead him out into France and behind the enemy lines. As he walked up the ever steeper rocks he tried with each step to find the least painful way of setting his foot down. The last few feet he had to climb on all fours to the ledge and entrance to the passage. He removed his pack and pushed it into the passage ahead of him and crawled slowly in. He found the exercise of crawling distinctly less painful than walking. Luckily it seemed not to have rained for several days and the passage was quite dry.

He remembered one holiday when he'd crawled through this tunnel in the middle of a heavy downpour which had made the passage like an underground stream. He'd arrived back at the hotel soaked and covered from head to foot in mud. He had been immediately ordered to take all the dirty clothes off in the yard and was hosed down before being allowed in the hotel to take a bath. George chuckled to himself when he remembered the ticking off he'd had from his Mum during which his father had been making faces behind her, making him laugh and getting him into more trouble.

He reached the end of the short passage pushing his pack out before him and emerging into the relative cover of the small wood. The thick knitting of undergrowth, as ever, camouflaged the tunnel entrance and George's emergence. Although small it was a fairly dense wood and afforded him a hidden vantage point to survey the coastal track which would lead him to the Beauchamp's hotel. The scene had changed little apart from the abundance of loud Teutonic banter clad in grey-blue uniforms; it was still an un-made dirt track although at present thanks to the warm weather it was very dusty.

Between the road and the wood there was a narrow shoulder of rough grass about five yards across. Crossing this strip of grass was potentially very dicey, mainly from the point of being spotted by the soldiers than the possible further damage he could do to his ankle. He reviewed the panorama. Apart from the abundance of German soldiers there were very few locals going about their business. This was the best possible scenario as too many strange looks from the locals may be enough to alert the suspicions of the occupying force that he may not be what he seemed and, ultimately, cook his goose.

A small convoy of various military vehicles drove past where George was peeping out of the wood stirring up the dust to an audible chorus of coughs, splutters and curses from the soldiers working nearby. He took a deep breath and gulped. 'This is it!' he whispered to himself. Then he strode forward again forgetting about his ankle and instantly ending up in a heap on the woodland floor. George got back to his feet taking hold of a sturdy looking stick to lean on. He limped out of the woods and on to the coastal path. He knew that the hotel was usually about a fifteen-minute walk but in the state he was in it could take more than half an hour.

With the exception of the odd one giving him the briefest of glances, the German soldiers carried on with their duties, oblivious to the slow, listing, passing presence of this boy. This gave George some confidence that his attire and indeed demeanour were appropriate. All along the path the soldiers were digging holes, filling sandbags and setting up machine guns. Along the way he had to step off the path at various times because of vehicles, at one point to avoid being run down by a convoy of trucks all towing various things some of which were large field guns.

He was now about halfway to the hotel. The late afternoon was warm, and a fresh sea breeze blew inland as he approached a group of stationary vehicles and trailers on the left. They were parked in a regimented courtyard formation with one large armoured-looking trailer in the middle. All of them had been drably painted in field camouflage utilising various shades of grey-blue. He could see from two hundred yards or so away that as one motorbike sped away from this conglomeration another one halted and its uniformed rider ran in.

He slowly approached, with his pronounced lopsided gait, what he now assumed to be a command post. His throbbing ankle was metering a regular beat. The flag pole at one end of the central trailer was sporting the unmistakable red, white and black emblem of European domination. Defiantly it flicked from side to side in the Channel breeze, occasionally lashing out aggressively with a loud crack, whilst the Anglo-Saxon wind maintained its defiant irritation on the swastika.

On the other side of the track directly opposite the trailers, a group of soldiers were enjoying a welcome break from their labour. Some were sitting, evidently on whatever could be found that would serve as a chair, others simply lay in the drying grass one hand lazily draped across their face to shield their eyes from the afternoon sun. All had removed their tunics and casually rolled up their sleeves. They were drinking from steaming mess tins; George believed this to be coffee. He had heard stories that the Germans were drinking coffee made from acorns. George made the *'yuk'* sound in his head. Coffee was a drink he had not learnt to enjoy and the thought of it being made from acorns: 'Why would you bother?' he thought.

Now passing between the soldiers and the trailers George glanced with what he hoped seemed to be a slow careless look in either direction. He heard a loud voice in a semi-shout say, *'Heil Hitler!'* He looked over in that general direction to see a soldier dropping the extended arm Nazi salute and then run from the central trailer, start his motorbike and ride off back along the cliff road, along which George had walked. He could see through the windows in the various trailers that there were several personnel in each, with what seemed to be a meeting of officers in the central one, all facing each other wearing their peaked caps with the high points at the front. George glanced back across at the relaxing soldiers, several of which had by now, with nothing else to engage their attention, taken the most superficial of interests in this limping boy passing them by. This somewhat unnerved George and sent a shiver of paranoia coursing through his body. This caused thoughts of utter fear to circulate round his head: They were watching him. What were they thinking? Had they rumbled him? He tried to regain composure and looked away, first up the road in the direction he was travelling and then towards the trailers. This made things worse; the officers were now standing outside the main trailer smoking, as if taking a break from running this section of the sprawling third Reich and they were also all looking directly at him.

George could feel the panic building inside him. The pain in his ankle was reducing; probably due to the abundance of adrenalin sprinting through his veins. Sweat was gathering in large droplets on his forehead. Oh! And now he needed to pee! He looked back up at the soldiers, then at the officers and then back to the soldiers, all their eyes were still fixed on him. Just then while not watching his footing he kicked a large rock with his bad foot. He felt a razor-sharp pain shoot up his leg; George yelped in agony and dropped to the ground in a heap of tears, his face contorted by the pain.

L'Hôtel

George began to open his eyes. He could hear a lady's voice softly saying, 'George… George are you awake?'

'Yes Mum I'm awake; it can't be time to get up is it?' George said dreamily still not being able to quite focus although he could just make out a figure in front of him. 'It must have all been a dream,' he said rubbing his eyes. Then he heard footsteps and the lady simply and quietly said, 'Shhhh, you must pretend to still be asleep.'

'But why?' George questioned still rubbing his eyes.

'Because you are in France and that is a German medical officer coming to check on you!'

'What?' George exclaimed in a loud whisper whilst simultaneously sitting bolt upright.

'He brought you in yesterday afternoon,' whispered Claudine Beauchamp. 'Now lie down, quickly!'

George closed his eyes and laid back down feigning deep sleep, something which he was well practised at doing, whenever he heard the stairs creak at home. Just as he did so the door opened and in stepped the German doctor.

In perfect French he formally greeted Madame Beauchamp and enquired how the patient was.

Claudine replied, 'He seemed to sleep soundly for most of the night; there was one point where he called out as if in some horrific nightmare calling after his parents.'

'Did you find anything in his things to identify him or help track his parents?'

'No, nothing, sir,' she said.

'Poor lad, it would seem he may be a victim of this damn war, there'll be many more before it's over, I'm sorry to say. You'd have thought we'd have all learnt our lesson twenty years ago, wouldn't you?' the doctor said rhetorically. 'But I haven't said any of that, understood?' he confirmed quietly.

'Of course, sir,' replied Claudine.

'And stop damn well calling me sir, Claudine, please call me Reinhard,' the doctor appealed.

'Yes Reinhard,' Claudine said with an embarrassed grin.

'I'll check on him this evening, he should be awake then; I should be able to examine that ankle properly then. In the meantime don't let him out of bed and make sure he eats something and most importantly get some fluids into him. And if he is composed enough, see if you find anything out about him,' the doctor instructed.

'Yes Reinhard, absolutely,' Claudine said.

Then the doctor left the room. George sat up immediately and was about to speak when Claudine put a finger on her lips and shushed him.

Very quietly she said, 'Wait for the front door to shut.'

A few moments later the front door, which was big heavy oak affair, shut with a thud that sent a shock wave through the room. Then the light sound of a single pair of feet on the gravel, a car door opened and shut, the engine started and the car drove away fading into the rest of the day's background noise.

Once the car had gone, Madame Beauchamp looked him straight in the eye and said in English, 'You have some explaining to do. What are you doing here for pity's sake; it couldn't be more dangerous here for an English boy right now!'

George then explained the whole thing so far; about his dad getting shot down and what followed including how he got there.

'*Mon Dieu!*' she exclaimed in mild Gallic blasphemy. 'You are lucky you have made it this far with just a sprained ankle.'

'We have to work out how we are going to get you home, but first we have to get your story worked out,' Madame Beauchamp dictated.

'Story? What story?' George exclaimed.

'The story which is going to keep you, and ourselves, out of the hands of the Gestapo,' Claudine retorted brutally.

'Oh crikey! I hadn't given it any thought at all,' George worried.

'And we have to work out how to let your Maman know where you are.'

'Where is Monsieur Beauchamp?' George enquired.

'Luckily today is the day he goes to the market for vegetables. He can make contact with the resistance to see about getting you home. But you cannot leave until your ankle is better so we have to get your story right.'

'OK,' he replied.

Over the course of that afternoon they worked out George's story and went over and over and over it to ensure it was watertight and that George knew it inside out. The doctor had given them the perfect alibi, almost like he knew George needed a story. He was to be an orphaned boy, the victim of vicious fighting in which his house was destroyed and parents killed by a stray shell just before the Dunkirk evacuation. He ran away from the fighting then, and had been running ever since, sheltering where he could, scrounging and working for food and money. All his identification had been destroyed with his home, all he had was what he stood up in and what he carried. With the new story came a new name; while he was in France he would be known as Luc Loiseau.

Once they had completed the task of providing George, now Luc, with his new identity, Claudine brought Luc a tray of food.

'I could have come to the kitchen for that,' he said.

'No you couldn't!' barked Claudine. 'Didn't you hear what the doctor said? You must stay in bed, eat and drink plenty of fluid.'

'Cor! French onion soup and a huge cheesy *croûton*, oh how I've missed this,' George attempted to say although it is not easy to talk with a mouth full of very runny soup, which ran down his chin and on to the bedclothes resulting in a half-hearted scowl from Claudine.

'Madame Beauchamp,' George led into a question, 'how do you know that German medical officer so well?'

'He is billeted here,' she replied 'Our hotel has been commandeered by the Germans for their officers. But we are lucky because we are so far out of town; the younger ones didn't want to stay here, so we get all those like Reinhard who want a quieter life and aren't really that keen on Hitler. Thank heaven we have no SS,' she exclaimed.

'Crikey!' was the only response that George could initially muster. 'So I am here, an English lad right under the nose of the German high command,' George proudly mused to himself with his hand nonchalantly behind his head.

'No, not the German high command, remember we only have seven rooms, just seven. OK Luc!' Claudine said sternly, 'You need to *be* your story, so no more talking in English — while you are in France you will speak French from now on so that if you talk in your sleep it is in French.'

'*Mais oui, bien sûr,*' George said using his French for the first time which means: but yes, of course.

'*Très bien!*' Claudine cheered. 'Now finish your soup…,' she continued in French, '…and then get some more rest, I'll wake you before he is likely to return so you get no surprises.'

'*Merci, merci beaucoup,*' George replied. He finished the food; Claudine removed the tray and left the room.

George snuggled down in his bed and listened to the sounds outside his window. The birds were merrily chirping unaware of the potential catastrophe which was unfolding around them. Trees rustled in the wind, the odd engine chugged past in the distance. Although he had received some painkillers his ankle throbbed lightly. As George lay there snug and warm he couldn't help but wonder what drama was unfolding at home. Where was his Dad? And how was he going to find him? The warm late summer sun glistened, its soporific hand seeping through the window closing George's eyes and stroking his brow, ensuring he slipped away into the most restful sleep.

When George awoke again it was dusk and his stomach was rumbling. The last red and orange glimmers of the sunset were dying away as the day gave in to the onset of night and the first stars appeared. He settled on his side with the bedclothes up high and tight around his ears to watch this magical transition. George wanted to see if he could tell at what point day stopped and night started. Just then he heard footsteps walking along the corridor and getting louder. The footsteps, he could tell from the irregularity of the rhythm and the different tones, belonged to more than one person. This assumption was confirmed by the murmuring of voices obviously kept deliberately low for his benefit. He could make out the voice of Madame Beauchamp but was unsure of the second one. It was definitely male but not harsh enough to be German, not even the doctor's when speaking French.

The door opened slowly, Claudine Beauchamp entered followed closely by a figure that George initially couldn't make out in the dimly lit room. Then the man stepped out from behind Madame Beauchamp. George could see it was Monsieur Beauchamp with a fairly excited look on his face. George sat up excitedly. 'Monsieur Beauchamp!' he exclaimed quite loudly forgetting his French accent.

'Sshh!' Claudine gestured for quiet with her index finger over her lips. She glanced outside the room, up and down the short corridor. With a nod, she signalled to her husband that the coast was clear.

Jacques Beauchamp moved closer to George. He spoke quietly in French. 'I have left a message in town for a contact with the resistance. They should be in touch soon.'

'Will they be able to find out where my father is?' George asked.

'It is possible,' Jacques replied 'but it is more important we find a way to get you back across the Channel to safety.'

'I don't want to go back until I've found my Dad!' He said looking Jacques squarely in the eye.

'Well, we will know nothing until they make contact. Anyhow *you* can do nothing until your ankle is better,' Jacques concluded.

To this at least George was in full agreement.

George opened his mouth to speak when the evening tranquillity was broken by the sound of a car approaching on the gravel drive. It halted in the front court yard with a crunch. There followed a dull thud as the car door was slammed shut, then loud footsteps stabbed at the gravel as they approach the door.

'It is the doctor!' Claudine exclaimed. 'He will be coming in to see you, now. So pretend to be half asleep.' Claudine ushered Jacques out of George's bedroom and into the kitchen to start preparing the evening meal.

'When the doctor has finished with you, I'll get you some food,' Claudine said as footsteps were heard on the stone steps leading down to this corridor.

Claudine whispered, 'He is coming, now remember your story!'

Just then the door whined open and in walked the doctor. 'How is the patient?' he enquired in perfect French almost concealing his German accent.

'He has slept all afternoon, and ate all his lunch,' she recounted.

'So, what do we know about our young mystery guest?' asked Reinhard.

Claudine answered, 'His name is Luc Loiseau, and it would seem you were correct in your earlier assumption.'

'Thank you Claudine.' The doctor now approached the bed and briefly glanced at George's face before focussing at the base of the bed. 'Now then young Luc, let's have a look at that ankle,' the doctor said pulling away the bedclothes at the end of the bed. 'Tell me how you did it and how you came to be lost with no papers, hmm?'

The doctor felt the ankle all around with a firm but gentle pressure which made George wince each time. 'Come now Luc, you can tell me.' He glanced up at George, with a gentle smile, then back at the ankle comparing it to the good one. 'Don't let this uniform deceive you, in reality I am a just a family doctor and a grandfather as well. Look! These are my grandchildren,' the doctor said showing George the pictures in his wallet.

George smiled at the doctor feeling somehow strangely reassured by this. He cleared his throat and in his best French he recounted the rehearsed story as if it had really happened. During this time the doctor checked his general health and spoke only to get him to breathe deeply while he listened to his chest. The doctor seemed to finish the examination simultaneously with the end of George's story. Claudine beamed with pride as she silently sighed deeply with relief. It was then that she realised she hadn't breathed at all during George's account to the doctor.

Reinhard turned around and addressed Claudine. 'The ankle should mend fully in a week; it's not broken although it is a nasty sprain. I recommend bed rest for the next twenty-four hours then some very light exercise to start with. Otherwise he is in excellent general physical health.'

'This is excellent news, is it not?' Claudine asked optimistically.

The doctor was displaying a furrowed brow of worry. 'His physical health is of no concern to me, it is his mental health which is worrying me, no child should have to endure what he's been through.'

'Indeed not,' Claudine agreed.

'Our new friend Luc here, is obviously severely traumatised, did you notice Claudine there was little emotion in his recount of events?' he said almost rhetorically. 'Eventually he will have to be placed in an orphanage but I think it will do his psychological and physical health some good to stay here for a while, so he will be in your charge if that will be OK with you?'

'Oh, but of course!' Claudine replied unable to prevent her face from smiling.

'Don't be completely soft on the boy, when he's recovered he can earn his keep with a few chores, after all work makes you free you know,' he said with a wry grin. 'In the meantime I'll arrange for replacement papers for him, they should come through in a few days.' With that the doctor left the room with a wave to George.

Claudine and George waited for the sound of the doctor's footsteps to disappear up the stone steps; they looked at each other and burst into fits of laughter simultaneously. This had seemed to go better than planned.

The door to the bedroom swung open again; Claudine and George instantly froze glaring wide-eyed at the now wide-open door and in walked, Monsieur Beauchamp carrying a tray of food.

'Oh! You silly fool!' she chastised him, 'we both nearly died of fright!'

'Well who else would it be?' He asked 'And I've brought George…'

'Non, non!' Claudine interrupted, 'I think you mean Luc, don't you?'

'Ah, yes, Luc,' Jacques agreed 'Well, Luc I have brought you some supper, one of your favourites, if my memory serves me right.'

'Oh yes!' George exclaimed as he was presented with a mixed plate of French cheeses, cured meats and salad accompanied by a generous hunk of French bread and a large tumbler of watered wine. The feast was soon scoffed. Claudine closed the shutters, collected the tray and said goodnight to Luc.

Resistance visit

The next morning, shortly after the officers had departed the hotel to their various posts, there was the indication of a presence at the back door; the door to the kitchen. There wasn't a knock, more a sound of light activity outside. The kitchen door opened out onto a small cobbled yard, two sides of which were walled in by the L-shape of the hotel and a third, directly opposite the kitchen door, led to the old stable. It had been a long time since the stable had been used for keeping horses. Part of it was used as a garage and workshop and the rest, much to Claudine's annoyance, was full of junk.

Claudine opened the door to find Monsieur Bisset taking off his bicycle clips and untying a basket of vegetables from the back of his trike. He turned round rather quickly, almost knocking Claudine over with the basket. 'Bonjour Monsieur, but what are you doing here?' Claudine greeted and questioned in one breath. 'Jacques has already picked up our vegetable order.'

'I know but…err we didn't have his full order ready so this is the rest of it, is Jacques here?'

'I am not sure what you are talking about, I'll get Jacques,' she replied and then yelled at the top of her voice, '*Jacques!*'

There was an obedient reply from behind the doors of the stable: 'Coming my love!' Then Jacques appeared on the opposite side of the court yard covered in dust and oil, wiping his hands on an old rag. Walking toward the kitchen door, Jacques greeted Monsieur Bisset, who had yet to be invited in.

Then before anyone else had a chance to utter a word Claudine said with a domineering excitement 'I've told Monsieur Bisset that we have our complete vegetable order and besides, we have no need or use for any more, he said you did not get the full order, well I know you did because I checked it all and put it away.' Once Claudine's rant was over she stood red-faced, breathing like a long distance runner and looking alternately at each man for agreement or explanation.

'Let us all go inside where we are less likely to be heard,' said Jacques. Monsieur Bisset nodded in agreement and walked past Claudine, into the kitchen. Claudine quietly obeyed with a puzzled look on her face. They all sat at the kitchen table and Claudine politely poured Monsieur Bisset some coffee, then Jacques and finally herself.

'So what is going on?' she demanded.

'Well,' Jacques began, 'I have asked Monsieur Bisset to come along to verify George for the purposes of reconfirming this to the British authorities, so when he is better he can be repatriated.'

'Oh, I see!' said Claudine, 'Huuuh!' She took a sharp intake of breath, as the realisation hit her 'You are with the resistance?'

'Shhhh… Claudine!' Jacques said, 'Not so loud!' as Monsieur Bisset went ashen and broke into a cold sweat. Trembling he removed a handkerchief from his pocket and mopped his own forehead and the back of his neck.

'It is OK,' she said, 'all the Germans have gone for the day, only George is here,' she assured them.

'Nevertheless, Claudine we cannot be too careful,' Jacques replied.

'Anyway,' Monsieur Bisset piped up, 'yes, I am with the resistance and we can get a message to the British. But they will want to confirm he is who he says he is before risking an extraction. So I will need to meet with the boy.'

'OK, I think he is awake now,' Claudine replied, 'we can go to see him, if you wish?'

'Yes, please'.

Claudine led the way from the kitchen along the ground-floor corridors to George's room.

Claudine opened the door slightly and peered around it. 'Luc!' she said using his assumed French name, 'there is someone here to see you.'

'Really,' he replied excitedly, 'who is it?'

'It is Monsieur Bisset; he needs to talk to you, OK?'

'Okay, but who is he? And why would he want to talk to me?' he puzzled.

'It is fine, but I shall let him explain.' Claudine finished speaking as she walked in the room followed by Monsieur Bisset in a worn light-brown jacket and dark-blue beret.

He approached the bed and looked at George. 'How on earth did you make it across the Channel?' Monsieur Bisset asked without preamble.

'*Dylan*!' George replied. 'Are you in the resistance?'

'Yes I am,' he said seemingly tired of this question already. 'But what is *Dylan*?'

'*Dylan* is my boat,' George said proudly.

'How did you avoid the Channel patrols?' Monsieur Bisset probed almost in disbelief.

'I didn't, I ran into two; well to be entirely accurate I ran into the same one twice, but that's a long story,' George said nonchalantly.

Monsieur Bisset shook his head in a mixture of a shudder and disbelief.

'Anyway, down to business. I need to know some details to pass on to the British to verify who you are and let your family know; I need some information from you that would prove you are you.'

'Are you going to radio it to SOE?' George said with wide eyes.

'Unfortunately, I can't tell *you* anything further,' Monsieur Bisset said rather abruptly. 'Now you must tell me some facts about you and why you made this very dangerous trip,' Monsieur Bisset demanded.

George recounted the story about how, and why, he had risked life and limb crossing the Channel.

'OK, now I need a word or phrase which will prove your identity; something that only your closest family will know.'

George didn't need any time to think. 'Urchin,' he replied immediately.

'Urchin?' Monsieur Bisset exclaimed and simultaneously questioned.

'Yes. Urchin,' George confirmed. 'You need a word to identify me to my family; Urchin will do it.'

Once he had all the information he needed Monsieur Bisset said, 'I'll pass this on to London. In the meantime you concentrate on getting that ankle better then we should have you back home very quickly.' George didn't protest again. But he had come this far to help his dad and he wasn't going back without him.

Monsieur Bisset wished George well and went to leave the room.

'Can you find out where my father is, please?' George pleaded.

'I'm not sure that will be possible,' Monsieur Bisset replied.

'Please!' George said again with tears running down his cheeks.

Monsieur Bisset looked first at Jacques and then at Claudine both displaying a pleading expectant expression, then he turned back to George, 'I'll see what I can do... but, I can't promise.'

'Thank you, so much.'

Monsieur Bisset simply smiled and nodded. Jacques and Claudine followed Monsieur Bisset to the kitchen to see him out. As he was leaving he turned and said, 'We should have an answer in a week or so.'

'That's perfect,' said Jacques, 'his ankle should be better by then.'

Back in Blighty

Group Captain Victor Hawkshaw emerged from the dense smoky atmosphere of the meeting room, a meeting to which he'd been urgently summoned in Dover in the early hours of the morning, in one of many underground rooms linked together by a complex web of tunnels. He made his way along the dimly lit and drably painted corridor, his footsteps echoing loudly as he ascended the steep staircase leading to ground level. At the top the two guards saluted as one opened the heavy blast-proof door, its hinges complaining at the effort. Victor tiredly returned the salute and continued up the last few steps outside which were flanked on each side by a thick wall of sandbags.

As he reached the top he checked his watch; it was just on 6 AM which meant he had been in there over four and a half hours. A chilly morning breeze was blowing straight up from the Channel. He rubbed his arid eyes and breathed in deep lungsful of the fresh, clean sea air in a vain attempt at relief from the hours of concentration, and attack by the clouds of cigarette smoke. In a rather cramped room of ten officers he had been the only nonsmoker; it was a pastime in which he never seen any benefit. He looked around in the first light of the morning, stretching out the inactivity and tiredness of the last few hours. Victor shook his head as he recalled the subject matter of the meeting with complete dismay.

He walked towards his staff car; through the wisps of mist he could see his driver in the front seat, and he couldn't fail to hear the very loud snoring coming from the same direction. 'You lucky blighter,' he thought. He knocked on the driver's window, the airman jolted awake, rubbing his eyes he looked round and saw his CO standing there.

'Oh my word!' he exclaimed, 'I'm so sorry sir! It won't happen again, I must've just nodded off.' In the time it had taken him to utter those words, he had jumped out of the car and was holding open one of the rear doors.

'Don't worry Smithy, at least one of us got some sleep,' Victor said as he got in and slumped back as far into the seat as he could go.

Smithy shut the door, jumped back into the driver seat and started the engine.

'Tough night sir?' Smithy enquired.

'No, that was the easy bit.'

'Back home, is it sir?'

'No, take me to Scotty's, please,' Victor sighed, 'now for the hard bit.'

'Pardon sir?' Smithy said from the front, the car already revving into action.

'Oh… nothing,' said the Group Captain nonchalantly, 'give me a nudge when we get there if I've dozed, please.'

'Absolutely sir.'

Approximately half an hour later the car ground to a halt at the Scott residence. Smithy jumped out of the car and opened the rear door.

'We're here sir,' he said in loud whisper.

Victor squinted, unable to fully open his still very raw eyes in the morning light. 'Thank you, Smithy,' he said taking a moment to wake up. Then, still bleary eyed, he stumbled out of the car. 'Wait here, will you please Smithy,' he said.

'Certainly sir,' Smithy replied.

As Victor opened the garden gate he recalled having to break the awful news about Scotty only days ago. He took a deep breath, composed himself and now reinflated, he walked briskly to the front door. As he went to knock, the door opened.

'Good Morning, Group Captain, please come in,' said Ives. The Brigadier had remained at the house since they received the news that his son-in-law had been shot down. Naturally wherever the Brigadier was so was his long-suffering, but cheerful, batman.

'Morning Victor,' came the authoritarian voice of the Brigadier from the far side of the room. 'Do you have any news?' he enquired.

'Well actually…,' Victor began.

'Is it John, George? Please tell me they're OK,' Rachel pleaded as she ran from the kitchen.

'Well… err… I wonder if Ives would take Smithy a cup of tea,' Victor enquired quietly with a gesture of one finger on his lips on view only to Rachel and the Brigadier.

'Ah… yes… of course,' said the Brigadier. 'Ives, would you take some tea to the Group Captain's driver, please?' he relayed.

'Yes sir! no problem, sir,' said Ives scuttling off to the kitchen, returning minutes later with a steaming mug and proceeding outside with it.

Victor turned to Rachel saying, 'Rachel, maybe you should sit down first.'

'Oh *no!*' exclaimed Rachel. 'They're dead! They're both dead!' she continued hysterically.

'No, on the contrary' Victor attempted a comforting tone. 'Unfortunately we have no news of Scotty yet. But George has, we believe, been found and he is absolutely fine.'

At this news Rachel began to sob uncontrollable tears of joy.

'Well, where is he then!' the Brigadier demanded.

'Ah, yes well, that's the thing. He seems to have managed, somehow, to make his way to France.'

'That's… not possible… how… or… could he…? Victor, what makes you think this? How can you be sure?' Rachel asked.

'We've had a vague, slightly odd, coded message from the resistance. We believe it is George,' Victor replied 'Now, so we can confirm it is him, does the word "Urchin" mean anything to you?'

'Yes! My goodness — that's his nickname in the family.'

'Excellent!' said Victor beaming, his bloodshot eyes smiling along. 'What we know is: as of yesterday evening George has made it to northern France and is in a safe house on the coast, although at present we don't know exactly where; we were hoping you might know something that may assist? You see the resistance are very cautious about transmitting locations in case Jerry has obtained the codes.'

'Yes, I think I might,' Rachel replied jumping out of her seat, 'Follow me!' she instructed, in a teacher like voice.

Victor and the Brigadier obediently followed up the stairs and into George's room.

'After he'd disappeared I spent some time in here trying to make sense of the whole situation, then I noticed something strange. This room is usually a wall to wall mess; complete pigsty. You'll notice the floor is completely clear but look over there; on George's desk there are lots of things which initially looked a mess but have in fact been neatly laid out on a carefully placed map of Europe. George never places anything neatly: this was done on purpose.'

The three of them gathered closer around the desk, studying the strange array of artefacts.

'Well beats me! Can't see any rhyme or reason to that lot,' barked the Brigadier.

'Nor I, unfortunately,' added Victor.

'Look closer,' said Rachel, whose instruction focussed them back on the arrangement. 'Look. There's a sea-urchin shell placed on a picture… of the hotel…' She stopped speaking, halted by the realisation of what she had deciphered from George's code. 'Oh thank God, he's with the Beauchamps,' Rachel sighed with utter relief. 'We know them; it's where we used to go on holiday before the war,' she explained.

'OK, that's good he's found himself a friendly pocket. However…' Victor's expression and voice tone changed to a greater intensity and he leaned in closer to Rachel and the Brigadier. 'I've just come from a high-level emergency meeting. It was convened to discuss one subject: George, and how to get him home. SOE are, as I speak, liaising with the resistance to ensure the proposed strategy is doable from their side. We should have an answer within forty-eight hours. At this stage that's all I am permitted to tell you. Apart from the fact that the resistance want him off their turf as quickly as possible; if he is discovered the consequences are potentially very grave indeed for all those sheltering him, and security will be tightened to an extent that the resistance and intelligence operations will be inhibited.'

'But if he's discovered what will happen to him?' Rachel cried.

'I put the same question to SOE: at best if he's discovered as British it may mean a Nazi orphanage or repatriation. At worst… well let's not go there.'

As they walked back downstairs and resumed their seats, Victor continued, 'There is one thing none of us could work out though: how did he get there in the first place?'

Rachel, with a very puzzled expression drew her gaze from eye contact with Victor to the floor then slowly to the ceiling for inspiration. Then her gaze fell on a framed picture of George taken with his boat. In a flash of clarity she turned her head sharply to look at her father, the shock and realization petrified momentarily on her face. Then turning back to Victor she exclaimed, '*Dylan*!'

'*Dylan*! Who's *Dylan*?' Victor questioned now looking completely puzzled.

'*Dylan* isn't a *who,* he's a *what,*' the Brigadier began to explain, 'a completely silly name for a sailing dinghy, I always thought!'

'So you're saying that he's made it across the Channel. Single-handed! In a sailing dinghy. At night?' Victor slumped back in his seat with incredulity at the situation.

'He is a very skilled sailor for his age and he's an excellent navigator, John taught him everything he knows,' Rachel assured Victor and herself at the same time.

'My word,' Victor exclaimed, 'so what we are saying is that George has made it across the Channel undetected at night, a feat which is difficult enough under normal circumstances and nigh on impossible in wartime.'

'Well it seems the only *plausible* explanation,' Rachel confirmed.

'Right, well, we need to check that *Dylan* has definitely gone and then I'll have to work out a way to credibly deliver this hypothesis to SOE and the general staff. Would you show me where *Dylan* is kept please?'

'Of course Victor,' Rachel replied, and then turning to the Brigadier said, 'Dad would you take Victor to the cove to show him where *Dylan* is usually moored, please?'

'Of course my dear, a pleasure'.

'We can use my car Brigadier,' Victor proffered.

As they made their way to the front door, Victor stopped in his tracks and rubbed his chin as if pondering some difficult puzzle. Turning round he cautioned, 'We best keep this among ourselves; does anyone else know?'

'Well, yesterday I panicked and called Sergeant McWorthy out.' Rachel replied biting her lip with regret.

'Blast! You can bet that the whole village knows now!'

Just then the phone rang. Rachel answered it, 'Hello.' Visibly she shuddered as if her blood had instantly turned to ice. It was the hideously smarmy voice of school headmaster Mr Batt.

'Ah Mrs Scott!' he began, 'I understand that George has disappeared and was wondering if there's anything I or the school could do to assist?'

Rachel knew he had no intention of providing assistance, nor did she want any from him, but the real purpose of the call was to glean any information that he could.

'Actually, Mr Batt, I'm glad you called,' Rachel responded lying through her gritted teeth, 'George came home not twenty minutes ago bringing with him a high temperature, sore throat, runny nose and chesty cough; so I've packed him off to bed. I was just about to call the sergeant to call off his investigation.' Although she guessed, knowing Sergeant McWorthy, that no investigation had started.

'So hopefully we will see him back at school soon, thank you Mrs Scott and goodbye.' Rachel sighed with relief as her conversation with falsely sycophantic Mr Batt ended.

'Well that should do it,' Victor smiled, 'well done. Let's hope we get him back before that cold wears off.' With that the two men left the house, some moments later the car started and the sound slowly faded.

Settling in

The week that followed Monsieur Bisset's visit was fairly uneventful. George's papers arrived via the doctor. He was able to
slowly put pressure on the ankle and he began doing chores
around the hotel. Towards the end of that week he had been ven-
turing into the village, at first with Monsieur Beauchamp in his van
and then on his own by bicycle. It was as if he had been born and
bred in the area; the general populace didn't give him a second
look and shop keepers and market stall holders greeted him warm-
ly with his assumed name, Luc, to which he was beginning to answer naturally. He soon realised that this gave him the ability to
move freely within the area, just like the locals; after all he had
genuine papers. He had become such a familiar sight to the garrison of German soldiers posted on the roads that he was rarely
asked to show his papers. In fact it was frequently the case that the
sentries would wave him on without the need to even slow the
pace of his bicycle yelling a friendly greeting as he passed.

He used this freedom to compile an almanac of the fixed and
mobile positions of all the German men and equipment; where the

men were billeted, where they were posted and their numbers. He also kept a detailed list of the equipment and its deployment. As he became bolder he spoke to the soldiers, learning more German and questioning them about the work they were doing. This helped him build a picture of the intended fortifications and supporting infrastructure. As he compiled this information he kept it hidden under a loose floorboard under his bed. He knew if he made it back to Britain this would be valuable information.

He had been back along the coast road several times on his bike. Now, he would wave to the officers in the command post, who would nonchalantly wave back. This was a purposeful exercise so he could become invisible. He had to go back to the cave to retrieve more of the equipment he would need to journey further south in search of his father. He had to be ready to go at a moment's notice before he was forced back across the Channel.

This day he rode back along the coastal track, he seemed invisible to all that he passed blending in as part of the daily sights and sounds. He approached the woods with a casual caution ensuring the speed of his bicycle was maintained whilst as subtly as possible carrying out a full 360° survey of his surroundings. No one was paying any attention. He rode into the wood, as far as he could. He pushed the bike in further laying it down in some thick undergrowth. He stood up behind a tree and peered round the trunk, checking out the road from left to right. No one seemed to have even taken the slightest interest. 'Goons!' George whispered quietly.

He then scampered further into the wood to the cave entrance, glancing up and briefly looking round like a meerkat before it disappears into its burrow. George entered the hole feet first and crawled down until the hole opened out into the cave. He paused again for a moment, listening for any alarming sounds. Then he climbed down to the cave floor. It had been two weeks since he had left *Dylan* down here. He pulled back *Dylan's* cover and took out all the equipment from the locker; he selected what he needed and packed this into the empty knapsack he was carrying and replaced the rest back into the locker. George replaced the cover over *Dylan* and without wasting any time climbed up the back of the cave to the tunnel.

As he crawled up the short tunnel he heard voices. 'Germans,' he whispered to himself. He got to the end of the tunnel keeping his head just below the entrance. He listened intently. The voices were too close to be on the track which meant they were in the wood. George had to think quickly; he didn't want to be seen in the wood at all. On the other hand, it is what boys from all nations do, play in the woods. There was one thing for certain: he didn't want them finding the entrance to his cave and discovering *Dylan* because that would cook his goose for definite. He listened carefully, still just below ground level. There were two, maybe three of them and they were just talking normally, so there was no emergency on. George slowly looked over the top of the tunnel entrance in the general direction of the voices. He could just see through the thick undergrowth that the soldiers were on the edge of the wood. He studied closely for a while longer. He could see they were very slowly walking into the woods. He had to make a move at the risk of being spotted. If he stayed put he would be discovered and so would the tunnel.

George quietly crawled out of the tunnel dragging his now fairly heavy back pack. He crawled toward where he had left his bike. Using a tree for cover, he looked up to see two soldiers walking into the woods rifles at the ready as if hunting. One of the soldiers suddenly took aim and fired almost instantaneously. George heard and felt the bullet whistle past his ear. He instinctively stood up with his arms raised and in his newly acquired best German shouted, 'Don't shoot! I surrender!' After the initial surprise the two soldiers lowered their weapons and now laughing said, in German, 'Ah! hello Luc so you want to surrender? Without a fight? Name, Rank and Number,' they shouted believing immediately that George was playing in the woods. He hadn't quite known what he was doing when he stood up or what reaction it would receive. After all, it was born from the fear of nearly having his ear pierced with red hot speeding metal. However it was as a good a reaction as any so he went along with the game.

He kept his hands in the air and said, 'Loiseau, Luc, lieutenant 646593. I have no choice but to surrender, you have me surrounded.'

'Yes,' said the German soldier giggling, 'The two of us have you and this entire wood surrounded. Now, you had better get out of the woods — no one is allowed in here any more it is *verboten*!'

'But why?' Luc asked.

'Because it is too easy for the resistance or escaping aircrew to hide in, so now it is out of bounds and we know anyone found here is a fugitive.' The German soldier replied.'

'How will you keep people out?' Luc asked.

'It is going to be fenced and trip-wired.'

George picked up his bag and nonchalantly swung it over his shoulder.

'What have you got in that bag Luc?' one of the soldiers asked.

'Grenades, two pistols and a howitzer,' he replied smartly, with his tongue stuck firmly in his cheek and trying not to look flustered. He could feel his cheeks beginning to redden and the sweat beginning to gather on the back of his neck and forehead.

The soldiers laughed loudly. 'Go on, get off home before we get into trouble for not giving you a harder time.'

He picked his bike up pushed it out of the wood and jumped on it as soon as he could.

On returning to the hotel he quietly put his bike away and entered via the kitchen door, briefly stopping to listen for the sound of movement. He carefully looked out from the kitchen into the passage. After checking both ways he sneaked quietly to his room ensuring he made as little noise as possible, peering round each corner first. He wanted the Beauchamps to know nothing of the contents of his back pack, so as not to give away his plan.

When he got to his room, he closed the door behind him quietly and stood with his back against the door listening once again for any sounds. Silence. He pushed a chair against the wardrobe and with a great deal of effort, given the weight of it, hid his backpack behind some pillows and blankets which were piled on top. The task successfully complete, George went back to the kitchen in search of a snack.

Repatriation?

George returned from running an errand for the Beauchamps; a routine trip to the butcher. Well, routine for anyone but George. These seemingly innocuous excursions had assisted George to construct a picture of the local garrison of such detail that if the Germans found his notes he would, he had only recently realised, certainly be shot as a spy. On the other hand some part of this information may be invaluable to British intelligence, if he ever managed to get it home, that is.

He parked the bike against the wall next to the kitchen door. He ensured his note book was firmly tucked into his jacket pocket, before lifting the basket off the front of the bike containing the real purpose of the trip. Before entering the kitchen, he paused briefly to look at the trike and trailer which stood in the yard; a large basket of fresh vegetables were fastened to the trailer. He did not pause for long; he knew this was the transportation of Monsieur Bisset the greengrocer who was also Monsieur Bisset member of the resistance. 'He may be bringing news,' George thought. He began to feel quite nervous and slightly nauseous. He took a deep breath and opened the kitchen door. As he expected Monsieur Bisset, Claudine and Jacques were all around the kitchen table drinking coffee. They all greeted him fondly as he entered. George put the basket of meat on the drainer near the sink and washed his hands. As he turned round, drying his hands, Claudine asked, 'What took you so long? You only had to go to the butcher.' George didn't acknowledge the question, instead he looked directly at Monsieur Bisset, 'Have you any news of my father?' he blurted the question out.

'I have news for you Luc,' Monsieur Bisset replied, 'firstly, we have intelligence that your father has been captured and is being held by the *Luftwaffe* in a transit camp; that is like a holding station, in the Alsace region of France. He is apparently due to be transported to a permanent POW camp in a week or so. I have no more information than that. Secondly, we have received a message from London, via the BBC. When we receive the second part of the message this will tell us that the operation is on that evening for definite.'

'Operation! What operation?' George exclaimed.

'Why, the operation to get you back to England, my boy.'

George tried hard not to display the inferno of raging defiance amassing within him. He bit his lip, 'Yes, over my dead body,' he mumbled through an intensely gripped jaw.

'Pardon?' said Monsieur Bisset, as if having missed something he should have been listening to.

'So what's the plan then?' George enquired, interested only so he could think of a way to avoid it.

'You will know what you need to know, when you need to know it,' Monsieur Bisset replied bluntly. 'It is sufficient to say that it will be any night soon, even tonight, we won't know until we receive the message from London. When we do, it will mean that the boat will arrive at 2 AM that night, I will collect you at 8 PM that evening. It must be 8 PM so we have enough time to move during the curfew and get to the beach, long before the Navy arrive. So you must be ready to go at 8 PM each evening until we go. OK?'

'OK,' George replied.

Briefing

In a small Navy briefing room, in Dover at around 19:00hrs, the Navy and commando officers, who were to lead and conduct that night's operation, were being given the final objectives and running through the mission in fine detail, once again. They were continually pouring over aerial photograph, charts of the Channel and maps of the French coastline whist reciting verbatim the planned sequence of events.

'…and remember!' Rear-Admiral Barton raised his voice to emphasise his point 'the objective is to extract that boy. Any diversionary explosions are just that, *diversionary*. And engagement with the enemy will be minimal and only defensive. The enemy need to think it is no more than a nuisance raid with zero strategic purpose, understood?'

'Sir!' replied Lieutenant Commander Thompson and Major Oliver in unison.

'Excellent!' said the Admiral, 'Well, I'll leave you chaps to brief your men and get some rest. We will de-brief here tomorrow on your return. Good luck!'

After shaking hands with the two officers the Admiral left the room.

As his footsteps in the corridor on the other side of the door began to fade, the two officers looked at each other with a mutual, unspoken, disbelief of that night's task. Lieutenant Commander Thompson threw his peaked cap at a chair and leant over the table littered with the maps, charts and photographs over which they had pondered for so long. 'Can you believe that?' he directed a rhetorical question of incredulity at Major Oliver, 'We have to execute a seaborne extraction on heavily defended enemy territory which is…'

'Dicey at best!' Major Oliver interjected.

'…absolutely!' Thompson agreed 'all for a kid who decided to go sightseeing on the wrong side of the Channel in the middle of a war,' he continued shaking his head in disbelief.

'At least we know he's got some nerve,' Oliver added.

'We'll all need nerves of steel if this all lights up,' Thompson retorted 'Well, we best brief our chaps as to what they're in for… and when the barrage of ridicule has died down we can turn in for a couple of hours.'

'I don't know about your mob, but mine are itching to do something for real,' said Major Oliver.

'Oh absolutely!' replied Thompson, 'If I tell my lot to clean or paint another thing they'll mutiny,' they both chuckled.

'Thompson, what did he mean about only defensive engagement?' Oliver questioned with a look and tone of false puzzlement.

'Haven't a clue, old chap,' Thompson grinned in reply.

'Oh well, I'm sure we'll work it out,' Oliver said rubbing his chin.

'Right, see you on board, with your chaps, fifteen minutes before zero hour,' Thompson said picking up the charts and the rest of his things. After which he promptly left the room, his heels beating a definite quick march stride which echoed from the corridor and quickly faded.

Major Oliver gathered his things together and exited the room shortly after.

His was an altogether slower and more thoughtful gait, more of a stroll, as if delaying the inevitable as long as possible. Something was playing on his mind. As he walked towards the exit he tried to put his finger on exactly what it was. He was so preoccupied that he neglected to return several salutes. As he walked along the corridor his behaviour became distinctly odd, looking as if he was conducting a conversation in whispers, including gesticulation, with an imaginary friend. Each hypothesis he suggested he dismissed as quickly as he'd thought of it. 'I know it's telling the men the objective, that's the problem, yes that's it!' he exclaimed. Then he realised that he'd said this revelation rather loudly as he looked up and around him several personnel of mixed rank were all looking at him.

'Are you all right old chap?' one of them asked.

'Oh yes, Colonel, thank you… sir,' he replied, noticing the pips on the officer's shoulder, 'just a bit preoccupied, got a bad feeling about this one,' he continued. He realised at that moment it wasn't the prospect of briefing his men that was playing on his mind at all. After all he'd done that plenty of times and had been ridiculed each and every time; that's what they did and it had never worried him. No, he had a bad feeling on this one. That's one thing he would never impart to the troops, they were superstitious enough as it was.

He took a deep breath, stepped off with his left foot and broke into a definite quick march stride, a gait which he maintained until he reached his car. Major Oliver continually went through the timescales in his head: it was now 19:30hrs, 'Half an hour to get back to base,' he thought. 'The briefing should take no longer than thirty minutes, so that's 20:30hrs we'll have to leave at 23:00hrs to be at the boat in plenty of time, so that's two and a half hours with my eyes shut.'

Ici Londres, ici Londres

It's 8 PM; there is a light knock at the kitchen door. Jacques opened the door. Monsieur Bisset is standing there, looking nervous and sweating.

'Come in René,' Jacques beckoned Monsieur Bisset into the kitchen.

As Monsieur Bisset brushed passed him Jacques looked out and scanned the moonlit yard. As he completed his scan, Jacques noticed two human silhouettes standing in the shadow; only given away by the tiny red glow of a cigarette. Jacques closed the door, gesticulating with his thumb over his shoulder he said, 'Will those two come in?'

'No. They will stay there until we leave,' René replied.

'Cognac?' Jacques offered.

'Please,' René replied, 'it will ah… take the edge off!'

Jacques poured them both a large drink and handing one to René, they both raised their glasses and simultaneously said, '*Santé! Vive la France!*'

René put his glass down heavily on the kitchen table. 'Now. Where is the boy?' he enquired, with a tone of we shouldn't be here any longer.

'I'm here,' exclaimed a voice from the hall door.

'Ah! Here you are Luc,' said Jacques.

'We have had the second part of the message Luc, we leave now,' said Renee.

Claudine came to the kitchen. She kissed George on each cheek: 'Good Luck, George!' she said with a tear in her eye, 'Give our love to your Maman, I know your Dad will get home. We'll see them, and you, after the war.' With that Claudine left the room.

'C'mon, we must go. Now!' exclaimed René as he beckoned with his hand and moved toward the door.

Jacques moved toward the door, his right hand resting on George's right shoulder and carrying George's bag in his left.

Jacques and George stopped at the now open kitchen door. Jacques handed George his bag, gave the boy a hug and speaking barely above a whisper said, 'Good luck, George!' With that, he closed the door and George was left outside in the dank, saline mist that seemed to have engulfed the hotel and all around. George noticed that he and René had been joined by two other men, who had been waiting under the eaves for them to emerge from the hotel. René crouched down and holding George by both shoulders looked him in the eye. Even in this darkness George could see this.

'You *must* follow our instructions to the letter. We all are in great danger, and will be long after you are safely in the hands of the Royal Navy. These men...,' René jerked his head upward, '...are not only risking their lives but those of their family, remember that. You only have to go down to the beach, we have to return home afterward, when it is most dangerous.'

'Yes, Monsieur Bisset, I understand, thank you,' George replied with a gulp.

The four of them set off towards the beach, stopping regularly to listen for any noise that might signify the approach of German units, or anyone for that matter. One of the two nameless resistance workers led the way, the other followed cautiously up the rear. George could see in the slight moonlight that both were carrying small machine guns nonchalantly slung over their shoulders. 'Probably Sten guns,' George thought, knowing these stripped-back machine guns were the weapon of choice in resistance groups. René Bisset stayed by George's side the whole time, constantly alert in a state of semi-panic, jolting his head to the left and right and continually mopping his brow and neck with his handkerchief.

'Why are we going this way?' George whispered to Monsieur Bisset.

'We have to go this way so we avoid the Nazi coastal patrols and we keep plenty of cover around us. Now shh! You must keep silent!' René whispered.

They continued walking for around an hour taking a very long route in a large arc. George knew, from his own reconnaissance, that this route avoided all open spaces and potentially dangerous areas. They stopped and crouched in a small thicket of trees. George knew that they were near the coast; apart from his local knowledge, he could smell the sea and although not a rough night he could hear the waves crashing on the rocks. The night was dark and damp; there was no moonlight and very few stars due to thick cloud cover, with a moderate wind blowing towards the sea. The conditions were perfect; if it was too light and calm the Germans would hear the Navy approach long before they were in sight.

'Now George,' René whispered, 'this is the most dangerous part coming up. We have to make our way to the beach between the coastal patrols and for the last fifty yards to the cliff we have no cover. If we get caught, it is everyone for themselves. We cannot be caught together; that would mean certain interrogation by the Gestapo. Once on the beach we have to hide out there until the boat comes.'

George could feel the adrenaline coursing through his body. He was wide-eyed and alert and very scared. He knew there was no way out of this now; he had to go with the Navy. He wanted to run from his escort so he could complete his personal mission, but he knew it was too dangerous.

One of the two resistance workers, who had been to reconnoitre their route to the beach, returned to the wood. 'René,' he said, 'there is a small German patrol slowly making their way along the coast road from the west. They have a search light and are scanning land and sea alike. Once they are well past we should be good to go. There was no sign of any other activity.'

'OK, Jean thank you.' René then turned to George, 'So we'll just lie low here till the German patrol has passed. We'll move back into the trees a little way and wait for twenty minutes.'

'OK,' George nodded.

He and René moved further into the woods for more cover. The other two stayed near the edge of the thicket laying down flat in the undergrowth, shielded by a fallen tree.

The twenty minutes dragged slowly. George could hear the patrol approaching at a leisurely pace. As it drew closer he was petrified by the search light. Each time it flashed its sinister beam on the trees directly above him it seemed to whisper, 'I know you're there! I will find you!' He began to sweat, shake and feel nauseous with an ominous fear. He'd been in much closer shaves with the Germans on his way across the Channel; at no time did he feel like this. 'It must be because this seems more real, it's not a game any more,' he reasoned in his mind, 'and I have to rely on others and not just myself. Yes, that must be it.' And he allowed himself a contented smile. But the feeling was still there. Something was wrong. 'What could it be?' Then it dawned on him, 'It's because I've failed to bring Dad home.' His chin and bottom lip began to quiver uncontrollably, his eyes filled, giving what light and images he could see a watery haze. A single tear ran down his left cheek before he attempted to wipe away all signs of emotion. He took a deep breath and recomposed himself.

The German patrol was now directly between them and the cliff edge. The four of them pressed themselves as far into the undergrowth as they could. George could see the heavily-manned truck followed by an armoured car. All the time the light was scanning the entire panorama. René whispered to George, 'As well as looking, they are listening.'

'Listening?' he replied.

'Yes. They have a direction finding aerial, they are looking for illegal broadcasts by spies and the resistance.'

'Oh I see,' George said, keeping any dialogue as short as possible and still with a troubling feeling in the pit of his stomach.

'Pssst! Pssst.'

George jolted his head in the direction of the noise. Jean was signalling to him and René that it was time to move. This was it. They would be on the beach shortly.

The four of them crept in single file to the very edge of the thicket. Jean, who lead the way, tentatively peered left and right rapidly several times and then again, this time slower and more deliberate, taking in more detail. He turned back and said, 'It looks like the coast is clear — we'll cross to the other side one at a time and take cover. Once we're all across we'll descend to the beach together. I'll go first.' With that he turned away again, he checked in both directions again, and then made the fifty-yard dash to the cliff. He ducked down and then peered up over the edge towards where the other three were still in the thick cover. René nudged George: 'Right, you next — check both ways, if it is clear run for it but keep as low as you can. Good luck.'

George took a deep breath. He peeped out from the cover of the trees. The road looked clear as far as he could see in both directions. Before he realised it, he was doing a crouched sprint towards the cliff where he could see Jean's head, just looking over the parapet. The track was a soft dusty texture which muffled the sound of his steps to a light thud. The weather had deteriorated to a heavy drizzle which the wind was driving on to his back. When he got to Jean's position he went to jump down to his side, but instead he half rolled and half fell in a clump. The other two followed shortly after crossing the open ground without a hitch.

After a moment to observe that they hadn't been followed or spotted, they proceeded with their trek down the short but steep cliff path to the beach. They set off in the same formation as before with Jean leading the way. There was a well-trodden path down the cliff which had a surface of rock, sand and dust, which had now turned to mud. The cliff was all knitted together by a tough weather-beaten grass which flourished everywhere but the track. The mud created by the evening's rain was making the venture very slippery, particularly for René who was not the most athletic of men. René found himself unsteadily sliding most of the way, more than once ending up on his *derrière*.

Once they reached the bottom they skulked their way carefully round to the west side of the beach. The wind was still blowing freshly seaward and the sea had an ample swell which sent white horses galloping across the rocky outcrops at each side of the large cove. Despite the sound cover provided by the crashing waves they could take no chances; each of them watched their footing, taking care not to make too much noise in the heavy pebbles. They stayed close to the cliff bottom, all the time making full use of the natural cover provided by the cliff and its dark shadows. On the west side of the beach, the conglomerate slope of rock and mud knitted together with grass gave way to a higher sheer bare rock face, with many overhangs. It was within the dark recesses of this cliff that they were to hole up until the Navy arrived at around 2 AM. There were several hours' silent seclusion to endure before then. George settled down into a deep recess and pulled his coat around him tightly, flicking the hood over his head. He leaned back into the corner of the recess and laid his head against his bag which he had wedged into the rocks as a make-shift pillow. He listened to the dramatic but rhythmical crashing of the sea. Being this close he could feel its regular crescendo though the rock, which had afforded him temporary shelter.

Home James

George had no idea how long he'd been asleep; however he woke up to look straight into the eyes of Monsieur Bisset, who'd been nudging him. 'You need to be awake and alert now! The Navy should be here in thirty minutes. Are you all set?' René said.

Rubbing his grainy eyes and still very sleepy George replied curtly, 'Yes!'

'You have been asleep for over an hour, I bet you could sleep on a battlefield,' said René, permitting himself a brief chuckle. 'Right,' he continued, 'this is what happens now. We will all leave the beach, one at a time, at ten-minute intervals which will assist us to avoid arrest for breaking curfew. If the Navy are on time the last one of us will be leaving the beach just before they arrive, OK?'

'Yes, all understood,' George replied in a softer tone.

'The Navy will signal to the beach with a light with four short flashes two long followed by three short, it is…'

'…Morse code,' George interrupted, 'that means HMS,' he said quite smugly.

'Very good,' said René. 'Here is a torch. You must reply with a 'G' which is…'

'Dash, Dash, Dot,' George finished René's sentence.

'Good. Right,' René said standing up, 'I must go now. *Bonne chance,*' he said extending his hand to shake George's.

'Thank you, Monsieur!' George said reciprocating the hand shake. Then René turned and scuttled off round the headland and disappeared into the night.

George now kept his gaze firmly fixed in the direction of the sea which was thick black in the distance with the occasional slate-grey fluffy image of a large passing cloud. Closer into shore, it was punctuated with the white lines of waves breaking on to the beach. His eyes and ears began playing tricks on him. Several times he thought he saw the defined outline of boat heading towards them and the sound of an engine, each time turning out to be a phantom.

The resistance worker, who had remained nameless, now stood up and quietly wished George *'Bonne chance,'* with a passing wave of his hand as disappeared into the night. George's gaze remained fixed, scanning the middle distance with total concentration. His concentration faltered when he heard the last of his escort, Jean, whom he had totally forgotten about in his single-minded state, start moving. He moved across to George in a crouched walk and looking all around patted George on the shoulder and said, '*Bonne chance!*'

'You too!' George replied '...and thank you very much.'

And Jean too was gone. So, there he was, an English boy on his own in the middle of the night, on a beach in occupied France. 'Unbelievable!' he thought.

Suddenly, there was a noise. It was faint but he was sure it was an engine. He listened for it intently; it was no good it had gone. 'Another phantom,' he thought with a deep sigh. He listened to the regular pounding of the breakers on the beach. Each crash was interspersed by a lighter sound of receding water. As he listened to this regular rhythm he became aware of another sound, audible in between the crashing of the breakers. He tuned his ears to extrapolate the sound; it grew stronger with each passing second. Now he could clearly make out the motorised sound approaching from the sea. It had to be the Navy. He scanned the sea for any moving shapes. The noise lowered in tone. George instinctively knew that the engines on whatever vessel that was, were slowing. It must be the Navy he thought, they're slowing as they approach to reduce the audible noise. Then the engines seemed to fall silent. He could make out the very faint silhouette of a launch sitting fairly low in the water.

He found himself staring so hard into the darkness that he forgot to blink. His eyes felt a little raw and began to water. Then he froze and shuddered. His fixed stare of concentration was broken by a small light flashing. He counted the flashes: four short, two long, three short. He gulped. His whole body was shaking with the instant rush of adrenalin. He picked up the torch and pointed it in the general direction of the silhouette. 'Oh crikey!' he exclaimed out loud in a blind panic, 'What's my reply supposed to be?' His mind was blank as he tried to recall René's instructions. He started reciting the alphabet, and dismissing each one in turn, in vain attempt at recollection.

'A, no that wasn't it. B, no not B, C no, D no…'

In the meantime the message was being repeated. He knew if he couldn't remember the reply the Navy would abort the mission.

'E, no don't be silly, F was it F…oh damn and blast what was it?'

The Navy repeated the HMS message for a third time.

George looked to the sky for inspiration. 'Come on George, think!' he said with his arms outstretched. 'G! G! it's flippin' G!' he said, as his hands fumbled with the torch in the darkness. He found the switch and immediately started sending two long flashes and one short.

The Navy stopped signalling, but George continued until he heard another motor. This one was high pitched compared with the first, like the drone of a bumble bee in flight. He stared at the sea looking for whatever was the cause of the new noise. Then he saw a small low image darting towards him, as if skimming on the water like a flat stone. As the craft came into the shallows he saw there were actually three of them. He continued to stare totally captivated by the scene emerging from the darkness. The craft slowed and then turned off the engines. He could see several figures jump out of the boats and drag them just out of the water. The first of these figures crouched just ahead of where the boats had been hauled. Others fanned out across the beach in his direction. Every so often one man would break from the formation and crouch on one knee. As they came closer he could see the crouched men near him were constantly on the alert for attack from the cliff. Their gaze permanently fixed high and their weapons at the ready. The crouched men formed a sort of avenue back down the beach to where the boats were waiting. The last few men landed at the recess in the rock where George had viewed the spectacle unfold. Several of the men crouched around the rocks facing outwards, in a similarly poised position to the rest. The last of the men approached George and introduced himself, in his best public-school accent: 'You must be George? I'm Oliver, Major James Oliver.'

'Pleased to meet you, Major.'

'Now George, not a good time for building sandcastles! What d'you say we get you back to Blighty before Jerry decides he wants to use us for target practice, huh?'

'OK!' George chuckled, nervously.

'Right George, this is the plan: When I say "go" you and I will make a run for it between the lines of men back to that middle boat. *If* it all lights up we will keep running, those chaps are armed with machine guns and light mortars, they will cover us, OK?' Oliver finished his speech with a thumbs-up, to which George reciprocated.

Then Major Oliver grabbed George's hand and looked at him 'Ready?'

'Yes' George said after taking a deep breath.

'*Go!*' Major Oliver Ordered.

George and the Major left the cover of the rocky recess at a fast pace. George ran as fast as he ever had. He got the impression that this was a light jog for the Major. As they ran between the line of men George could see their faces of composed concentration, all with various weapons at the ready. Most of the men were armed with Sten sub-machine guns, intermittently some were armed with the heavier Bren gun and along the line several light mortars had been set up.

George could feel the wet sand give beneath his feet with each step, making running all the more tiring with the sheer exertion and effort needed to maintain the pace set by the Major. He was constantly on alert all around. The fear and adrenalin rush gave him a heightened sense of awareness. He noticed that the men, who marked out the avenue of beach down which he and the Major were running, were moving into a closer formation once he and the Major were well past their position. Despite their apparent cold attention to duty and the silent sleekness to the movements he got the impression that the sooner they got off the beach the better.

Now halfway between the cliff face and the boats, George could feel the fresh briny sea breeze, salty on his face. He breathed the air deeply as he was beginning to tire. George continued to look all around him, watching the commando's scurrying around them like highly trained mice. Just then something caught his eye at the top of the cliff. 'Major!' he snapped.

'Can't stop now George, nearly there.' The Major replied to what he thought would be a request for a rest or at least a slowing of the pace.

'Top of the cliff just over my right shoulder, I saw something move!'

George and the Major both looked back at that spot; there was nothing.

'I swear Major! I saw movement,' George exclaimed.

'It's OK George,' the Major reassured him, 'stress and darkness can play awful tricks on the mind.'

Just as they were nearing the boats it was as if there was a sudden dull sunrise. The whole beach was lit up.

'What the…!' The startled Major began looking sharply up to the sky. 'We've got company,' he said to his men, not breaking his stride toward the boat. A short sentence of which the latter half was drowned out by noise, as hell was unleashed in their direction, the parachute flairs ensuring any night cover they had was now non-existent. Plumes of sand were being thrown up all around them as a blizzard of bullets hit the beach. Major Oliver's men instinctively began to return fire with machine guns and mortars whilst retreating to the boats. However they were at a complete disadvantage firing into the dark not knowing exactly where the barrage was coming from.

The Germans were peppering the beach with heavy machine-gun fire, mortars and grenades. With explosions and gun fire all around him, George dropped to the ground and froze solid. He could hear bullets whizzing past him on either side. Suddenly, the explosions intensified. He saw a large plume of mud and rock shoot up in the air like a giant rapidly growing shrub, and then there was another and another. A shower of mud, rock and sand joined the rain of bullets falling upon anything that was on the beach. As they ran past the last of the men remaining steadfastly in their positions, Major Oliver ordered, 'Smoke! Smoke!' This single order caused the men to reach for grenade-like canisters from which they pulled a pin and threw like a grenade. Clouds of smoke belched out of the twenty or so canisters which hit the beach simultaneously about fifteen yards from the lines of men towards the foot of the cliff. This cleverly obscured them from the German sights, although it didn't prevent the barrage.

'The smoke's drifting on the wind; it should provide us with some cover to get the boats off the beach. Now get in the boat!' Major Oliver shouted pushing George over the sponson of the large dinghy. 'The Navy are going to continue with the covering fire, here's our chance to get out of this bedlam,' Major Oliver shouted while signalling to the man at the helm to get them out of there. Two other men pushed the boat back into the water fully and turned it round. Bullets were still whizzing past the boat. George stayed as low as he could. All around were the flat staccato notes of hundreds of bullets quenching in the water. George looked up to see one of the men who'd pushed them back clambering into the boat being assisted by the Major. George looked around for the other soldier, thinking he was already in the boat, but he had disappeared. George tried not to think about this, the reality was obvious.

While the helmsman guided the boat out of the relatively small surf George maintained a low profile. Although the waves were not huge, as a first-time passenger in one of these boats George felt like he was going up a hill then being dropped down the other side, each time landing on the boat's floor with a thud. George kept low until he thought they were clear. He looked up at the Major who looked down and smiled at him 'Well, that was unexpected,' he yelled over the sound of the engine and gunfire 'You OK?' he asked.

'Yes, fine. I think,' George replied shakily.

'We're clear of the beach now, you should be able to sit up if you want,' said the Major.

George looked back in the direction they had come from. Following them were the other boats in a spread-out formation. Looking up, he could see the dull glow of the parachute flairs through the smoke haze.

The sea next to the boat suddenly exploded, as if Poseidon himself had arrived to show his displeasure. The shockwave jolted the dinghy violently and threw up so much sea water that everyone was drenched 'They've got some hardware on that cliff now sir,' the helmsman commented. 'So I assumed Corporal!' Oliver shouted intolerantly over the racket, 'Just get us back to the launch. Quickly!'

'Yes sir,' the corporal replied.

'Crikey!' George shouted at the top of his voice 'Major, would you take this?' George said handing him his notepad.

'What is it?' Major Oliver enquired.

'My note pad,' George replied at the top of his voice. 'In it you'll find full details of the German occupation: numbers of men, location of armaments, fortifications, mines and so on.

'My word George you have been busy, I'm sure that will be of interest to the intelligence chaps. Well done! Really, well done!'

George looked back towards the beach both horrified and completely entranced by the lethal barrage. So far he'd only felt like a spectator in the war, admittedly it had affected him in the most traumatic way but now for the first time he actually felt like a participant. Suddenly from the cliff top he saw a single flash of fire, followed by a blast loud enough to be heard over the commotion. Without further warning the boat following on their port side exploded in a mass of fragments and water. George sat there petrified, his mouth frozen in mid gasp. The magnitude of the danger he was now in, hitting him like a cricket bat squarely in the face. He looked back at the cliff; it was *déjà vu*, another flash, a loud bang.

George felt like he was flying. Then his nose painfully filled with sea water as he was plunged deep. Disorientated he panicked. He couldn't shout for help. He tried to scramble to the surface. Which way was up he didn't know. It seemed like he'd been under for ages. George convinced himself to calm down. His logic taught him that it would conserve his oxygen while he took stock of the situation.

'OK, which way is up?' he thought. He looked all around. He could see that one direction looked slightly lighter than all other directions. Because he had calmed his panic, his mad scrambling had stopped. In his motionless state he could feel himself moving.

He was rising! He could see the waning light cast by the flares dancing on the surface above him. The cracks and bangs of the mêlée on the surface were softened by the water. It was like he had his head between two thick down pillows as he had often done when there were dog fights at night over his village.

George broke the surface. 'At last!' he thought with a huge gasp as he spluttered for breath. He looked round but he couldn't see anyone else who had been in his boat. The Navy launch was still returning fire. He looked all around; the last boat was still intact and had slowed right down. It seemed to be searching for survivors. George waved his arm in the air shouting, 'Over here, over here!'

It was useless no one would hear him in that hullabaloo. Then he heard a voice, a loud authoritative English voice using a loud hailer: 'Return to the launch! I repeat return to the launch immediately!'

The last dinghy immediately made for the launch. George knew this was the Navy preparing to leave and that he couldn't swim there before the boat left. He could hear the sound of the engine revving in preparation for departure. His only chance was to swim for the rocky headland and his cave. He still had some clothes stashed in *Dylan* if he could get there. At least if he was caught then he may be able to bluff why he was out after curfew.

He knew with wet clothes from the sea that his goose would be cooked.

George didn't wait to watch the launch disappear on its voyage back to England. He began to swim as hard as he could toward *his* cave while the German's attention was still on the skirmish which was now completely at sea. Behind him he heard the launch's engines engage full ahead and power off into the distance. He didn't look round. George was waging his own private war against the sea. As he came closer to the headland the still powerful waves began crashing over his head in an effort to dash him against the rocks. He swam hard now using the force of the surf to power him diagonally toward the gap in the rocks and the shingle path to the cave entrance.

Cold and tired, he was now close and feeling for the sea bed with his feet. In the dip between the waves he felt the sea bed for the first time. This gave him heart for a final push to the cave. He began to swim harder his eyes fixed, in the dim light, on the gap in the rocks. Just then a large wave picked him up and carried him toward the large outcrop. He used the last of his energy to avoid the certain serious injury that would result from being dropped on to the rocks with such force. He glanced off the last protruding rock, grazing his left side in the process and was then deposited on the shingle wash outside the cave entrance.

Although exhausted he quickly got to his feet, the sea water burrowing into his grazed flesh. He remained in crouched position as he checked all around. The sky had now returned to night; the flares having since extinguished themselves. The barrage from the cliff had stopped. He listened closely. There was nothing he could see or hear close to him. He looked cautiously up to the cliff top, nothing. George knew he had to move, now. The Germans would shortly send detachments down to the beach to confirm it was clear and security along the coast would be tighter than ever as the security forces looked for anyone who might have been involved.

The tide was high and the cave entrance was flooded. George waded as quietly as possible calf-deep into the cave. He stopped just inside and pressed his back again the wall. He was listening to see if there was any sign he'd been spotted. In the distance, above the sound of the sea, he could faintly hear that the Germans were on the beach. Not that he could hear any excited chatter or shouting; it was the barking of dogs that gave it away. He was instantly thankful for the high tide, which should hide his scent from the keenest nose he thought. 'Best move quickly just in case,' he said to himself 'there's nowhere to run or hide in here.' Given the lack of light, as quickly as he could he went to the back of the cave, feeling his way with his hands and feet until he reached the hidden *Dylan*. He reached into *Dylan*'s locker and pulled out his spare

George and the Reich

clothes. After changing he lost no time. He bundled the wet clothes into a waxed canvas bag and set off up the tunnel to the wood. Cautiously George felt his way from the back of the cave to the small tunnel entrance, his hands caressing the rocks forming the pictures in his mind and guiding his feet to provide the purchase to effect movement.

The cool dank air of the night greeted his face as he crawled up the narrow tunnel. As he reached the level of the wood he could hear the continuing commotion along the cliff road. Gingerly, he peered slowly out of the tunnel entrance. His eyes could provide him with no more information than his ears already had. The thick wood made the darkness of the night absolute. He lifted his head higher straining his eyes to see over the undergrowth. Through the thick wood he could see shadows, human and vehicular, moving rapidly backward and forward.

George swung his bag over his shoulder. At a slow, crouched, semi-crawl he made his way to the perimeter fence which now surrounded the wood. Using the undergrowth for cover he surveyed the area through the fence. Vehicles, motorbikes and men were rushing back and forth in a scene of mayhem. George soon realised all the attention was focussed on the beach. This was his chance. As long as he kept off the road and made his way through the scrub, he knew he could make it back to the hotel. But, he had to go now, before the mêlée died down.

He looked to the top of the fence; even in this light, with the chaos going on it was too risky to climb that high. There would be a good chance of being used for target practice and this he was keen to avoid. As far as he could see in either direction there were no gaps in the fence. 'Under!' he thought. George put his hands at the bottom to his surprise the bottom of the fence moved; the Germans hadn't bothered to bury the bottom of the fence. He lifted the fence enough to push his bag through and then lifted it some more and rolled under. He stayed down and looked round, he hadn't been noticed. He checked the fence. As far as he could see in this light it was no worse than if a dog or fox had pushed their way under.

Once he'd left his cover, he had a short sprint of a few yards to get to the scrub. It should be safe enough under the cover of night. However, if it had been daylight it would almost certainly have been suicide. The scrub followed the line of the cliff, parallel with the coast road. It consisted of small grassy dunes, gorse bushes and the odd clump of a few weather-beaten trees. The scrub would provide adequate cover all the way to the hotel as long as the Germans weren't searching it. He got to his feet remaining in a low crouch almost as a runner on his starting blocks. He checked again. The coast was clear. He hesitated no more. He was off. He made it to the scrub in seconds although it had felt like minutes. He peered out from behind the cover, no one had seen him; they were too busy looking in the other direction. He used the cover of the scrub and worked his way closer and closer to the hotel. Occasionally he stopped and listened for unfriendly company and peered over the dune or round the bush.

Twenty minutes later, which was good going considering he had to skulk all the way, he'd made it back to the hotel, while the fracas continued. Unusually for this hour all the hotel lights were on. He peered round the last bush before the hotel. He could see Claudine and Jacques outside on the gravel drive evidently wanting to know more but not daring to venture away. He scanned the rest of the scene; all the officers billeted there were evidently closer to the drama. He took no chances. He crept back behind the bush and using the shadows dashed across the track into the side courtyard. It was in total darkness. He crossed the yard and pressed his back against the stone wall of the house. Slowly he edged his way toward the front of the house. He peeped round the corner, Claudine and Jacques were still there, now he was behind them.

He tried to attract their attention over the continuing noise "Pssst!" he spat. It was not loud enough, he tried again, but louder, '*Psssst!*'

Claudine looked round in the dim light; he could see her face was contorted with worry. It dawned on him that he was the source of her panic given the location of the disturbance. The look on her face relaxed then turned to elation when a little light, spilling from a downstairs window of the hotel, fell on his face as he emerged from the shadow. Sobbing with joy she ran to him and hugged him tightly.

As Claudine hugged George within an inch of his life, a new sound emerged from the background din. The sound of multiple engines could be heard above the noise.

'We should get inside and get George cleaned up right now!' Jacques said walking closer to them whilst looking over his shoulder. 'I think we may very soon have visitors. They will be extending the search back inland now!'

They all looked in the direction of the engine sounds; there was now the glow of headlights to accompany them.

'Quick inside,' yelled Claudine. They all ran in to the hotel.

'George, get cleaned up and into bed right now!' Claudine ordered.

'I have this bag of wet dirty clothes. What shall I do with them?' he panicked.

'Just give them to me and I will put them in the stove!' she barked.

George handed Claudine the bag and began undressing.

'You mean burn them?' he exclaimed.

'But of course!' she snapped 'The mood they'll be in... How do you think we'll explain the fact we have wet dirty clothes that just happen to fit you?'

George didn't answer, it seemed blatantly rhetorical. As he finished undressing, Jacques handed him his pyjamas and he went to clean up as best he could.

The sound of trucks cars and motorbike were now distinguishable.

'Quick George they will be here in seconds,' Jacques pleaded.

'Where are all the officers that are billeted here?' George asked as he leapt into bed.

'They are all out at their posts. They went as soon as the firing started,' Claudine said tucking him in and turning the light off.

Jacques ran to the stove and crammed the clothes in as fast as he could.

Claudine joined Jacque in the kitchen and they simultaneously gave out a huge sigh of relief. Their moment of tranquil eye contact was destroyed, as several vehicles ground sharply to a halt in the very spot they had all hugged some moments ago.

SS

The front doors of the hotel were violently flung open, followed by a rapid influx of German soldiers that seemed to disperse in different directions like streams of army ants. Claudine and Jacques stood in the hallway of the hotel observing the scene with horror, the swarm of soldiers noticing them only to navigate round them.

They were both filled instantly with abject fear at the realisation that these soldiers were all members of the SS; usually made up of fanatical card-carrying Nazis. The fear was compounded as the shadowy figure of the leader of the security service for the area stood in the doorway. Sturmbannführer Gerhard Stein surveyed the scene in a slow panoramic scan. His frosty black eyes, which matched the death's-head emblem on his cap, coldly took in every detail of the hotel's foyer: A medium-sized rectangular room with high yellowing ceilings, decorated predominantly in the dark orange of a warm summer sunset. It was commanded, at the far end, by the heavy dark mahogany reception desk. The walls were further intermittently adorned with works by the late nineteenth and early twentieth-century impressionists. The solid stone floor was softened only by the addition of a slightly worn, faded lime green rug.

Finally, his sinister eyes fell in an intimidating glare, on the two cowering figures in front of him. The icy dead-pan expression on his face cracked to an ominous smirk as he sauntered menacingly toward them. He knew full well the fear he instilled in the indigenous population, which he took pleasure in exploiting to the full; not only in the execution of his office but also for his own gain. Jacques was aware that Claudine was petrified; she was shaking, he'd heard her sharp intake of breath as Stein had appeared in the doorway. Jacques took Claudine's hand and gave it a reassuring squeeze. Neither of them dared to make eye contact with each other or indeed with Stein.

Stein took a few minutes to walk the short distance to the reception desk, by which the Beauchamps both stood, hardly breathing. As he approached, his eyes continued to survey the environment he had entered. Disdainfully, he glanced one by one at the paintings on each side of the room. He menacingly ran a black leather gloved finger along the heavy sideboard as he passed it, after which he briefly looked at his finger and then rubbed his thumb across it several times as if clearing it of dust and simultaneously tutting and shaking his head. Arriving in front of Jacques and Claudine he looked first at Claudine and then at Jacques.

'Your taste in art, if you can call it that, is disappointing. These are no more art than a child's kindergarten painting,' Stein said, partially turning to gesticulate towards the pictures with his right arm. His knowledge of art extended no further than that which the party dictated was 'good taste'. 'You may have heard a little commotion this evening,' he continued, 'We have to conduct some routine checks around all the coastal dwellings. There was a small landing of British commandos on the beach, about a mile away; there is nothing to worry about they didn't make it past the shoreline. Do you know anything of this?' he questioned, his eyes looking straight into Jacques' and then Claudine's' with an intensity which burned right through to the back of the skull.

'No! We heard a lot of firing but we know no more than that, Herr Sturmbannführer,' Jacques replied for both of them.

'I thought not,' Stein smiled, almost genuinely for the first time whilst removing his cap. 'But, there are some amongst us who do! The British were liaising with the resistance, we know that much. I need to see a full list of all those staying here, now,' he ordered.

Claudine immediately retrieved the guest book from behind the desk and passed it over. Stein snatched it and began to review the list.

'Would you care for some refreshment, on this unpleasant evening Herr Sturmbannführer?' Jacques offered in pretence of grovelling.

'A large cognac would be most pleasant,' he replied, not lifting his eyes from the book. Claudine took the opportunity to leave the room and compose herself while retrieving the Sturmbannführer's drink.

'I see all of your guests are some of our more mature officers,' he chuckled.

'Yes, Herr Sturmbannführer. I believe they enjoy this normally tranquil location.'

'Indeed,' he replied, 'Apart from you and your wife, is this a complete list of occupants?' he questioned.

Jacques knew he had to be truthful and mention Luc, something which he had hoped to avoid. 'There is one additional resident,' Jacques said trying to keep the resentment from his voice.

'Ah! And who is this?' he questioned as Claudine handed him his drink.

'His name is Luc… he is a homeless orphan… an unfortunate victim of this war. We are hoping to adopt him.' Claudine stepped in with refreshed confidence. 'We have no children of our own, and we have grown to love the boy.'

'That… may not be possible. I will have to see the boy. Now,' he ordered. 'He may be a prime candidate for the *Lebensborn* programme. If he is he will be sent to Germany to be brought up in the modern German culture. Where is the boy?' he further abruptly demanded.

'He is in his room, in bed Herr Sturmbannführer,' replied Jacques.

'You will take me to him, now!' he demanded.

'Of course, Herr Sturmbannführer, and right away.' Jacques politely gesticulated for Stein to go first with a subservient tilt of the head.

'Please, you lead the way,' Stein replied.

When they arrived at George's room, Jacques raised his hand to knock on the door. But before he had a chance to, Stein opened the door barging past Jacques and Claudine. George, who had been anticipating such an intrusion, sat bolt upright in bed rubbing his eyes and feigning a rude awakening.

'What is going on?' he asked in his best French accent.

'Ah ha, so you are the famous Luc?' Stein asked rhetorically. 'Where are the boy's paper's?' Stein asked without taking his eyes off George, holding out his right hand expectantly.

'They are in the bureau' Claudine answered, 'I'll just get them,' she said leaving the room rapidly.

'Get out of bed boy, and stand up straight facing the door,' Stein ordered.

'Why?' George asked with a bravado of nonchalance.

Jacques instantly winced and covered his eyes when he heard George utter the question.

'Do not question me! Do as I say now!' Stein shouted, red in the face and the veins popping out of his neck.

George leapt out of bed and stood to attention, knowing that he'd overstepped the mark.

Stein walked around him as if conducting a military inspection 'The boy has very good Germanic features and a healthy physique, he would be ideal to be brought up in the fatherland. I will arrange it immediately.' With that Stein left the room and then the hotel the way he'd come in. All the SS troops followed him out like rats following the pied piper of Hamelin.

This was the worst thing the Beauchamp's could have heard. What was worse, was that they were powerless to do anything about it.

In floods of tears Claudine gently put her hands on George's cheeks. 'Oh you silly boy you should have stayed in England, what will become of you now?' she sobbed.

By this time Jacques had also lost his masculine composure and tears were running down his face.

'Don't worry,' George said speaking plain English for the first time in weeks 'This is exactly what I need. It's a free bona fide pass to travel. With my travel papers stamped by the SS I am unlikely to be questioned by anyone,' he said smugly, lying back on his bed with his hand clasped behind his head.

'But they are going to take you to Germany and have you brought up in an SS orphanage or by a Nazi family,' Jacques exclaimed.

'Oh, don't worry I have the beginning of a plan… I won't reach Germany; well not on their terms anyway!' he replied confidently.

Empty-handed

In the early morning twilight, the dishevelled remnants of the thwarted British raiding party returned to the harbour that, bright eyed and bushy tailed, they'd left a matter of hours ago.

The shrapnel-damaged launch tied up at the quay and the depleted complement of commandos began to disembark. Cups of cocoa were offered to each man as he shuffled along the quay wall. Some wounded had to be helped by their comrades; this support was soon taken over by the awaiting medics and ambulance drivers, already assembled and ready for the worst. Finally, those who couldn't walk and the unconscious were carried off the launch on stretchers.

Standing on the front decking of the launch, Major Oliver and Lieutenant Commander Thompson exchanged glances and permitted themselves a mutual sigh of relief as they simultaneously looked back at the harbour wall. Instantaneously, the expression of relief drained from their faces and they both stood straight. The cause: Rear-Admiral Barton, red faced and puffing, was stomping towards them.

'He's not waiting for the de-briefing, he's coming now!' exclaimed Oliver.

'Need to brace ourselves for some rough weather, old chap!' agreed Thompson, as the Admiral was making his way down the short ladder onto the deck.

'Get your damn hands off me!' the Admiral bellowed at a sailor who'd offered a helping hand.

The shell-shocked sailor instantly jumped back a yard into a rigid saluted attention. His eyes fixed on his prey, the Admiral didn't return the salute, instead he marched towards Major Oliver and Lieutenant Commander Thompson.

Still puffing the Admiral barked at the two officers, 'Well! What the hell went wrong?'

'Poor show, bloody shambles!' Major Oliver replied.

'It was as if they'd been expecting us, sir,' added Lieutenant Commander Thompson.

Having now calmed down a little, the Admiral continued, 'Well, did you get the boy?'

'Er, no sir!' gulped Oliver, expecting a tirade of abuse. 'We had him, but when the shell fire turned the boat over... he was gone. He either made it to shore or joined Davy Jones, sir.'

'Blast!' shouted the Admiral. 'Well, I'll need a full report on my desk this afternoon, from both of you. Understood?'

'Sir!' replied Oliver and Thompson simultaneously.

'But what's really puzzling me...' the Admiral continued in a thoughtful half whisper, 'is how Jerry knew we were coming? The French chaps are all tried and tested.'

'Well sir, either it's a leak in the resistance or they had the hardware nearby quite by chance,' Thompson said, almost stating the obvious.

With a shrug, Oliver put his hands in his trouser pockets and felt the notebook that George had handed him some hours before, during the hullabaloo. 'Hang on, I wonder if this can shed any light on it?' he said taking the notebook from his pocket.

'What's that?' the Admiral barked.

'It's something George handed to me last night; he said it contained information that we'd find useful,' replied Oliver.

'Useful? A boy's notebook, *bah*!' scoffed the Admiral heading back towards the ladder. 'Reports! This afternoon!' he shouted back.

Oliver was already thumbing through the pages in complete disbelief. 'My word! He must have been invisible to them,' he exclaimed. '*Sir!* Admiral,' he shouted running after the admiral who was already pacing back along the harbour wall to his car. The admiral stopped and turned round to see Major Oliver running towards him.

'What is it man?' he growled.

'Sir, it's this book. It has more information in it about the German occupation in that area than we've ever had: Troop numbers and regiments, armaments and defences — even where the officers are billeted.'

'What!' yelled the Admiral snatching the book 'Well, I never did!' he exclaimed. 'How's he managed that, I wonder?'

'Well, I would imagine that being a young boy, he's inconspicuous, even invisible,' replied Oliver rubbing his chin.

'Well that explains it then, they've got some heavy stuff dotted along the coast. Maybe it wasn't all in vain after all. This is good quality; I'll get this to the intelligence boffins immediately. That boy's a natural,' declared the admiral. 'For everyone's sake, I hope he's made it.' With that he saluted Major Oliver and turned and made for his awaiting car.

To the Fatherland?

The next day George left the hotel with the SS officer who was to escort him all the way to Berlin. The train they were to travel on that morning was for German military personnel only going home on leave; it would take them directly to Germany. They walked together to a waiting car. The car was black and of German manufacture, evidently not usually used for anyone not of superior rank.

As they approached, the driver opened the door to the rear for them to get in, closing it behind them. The car started and almost simultaneously, very loudly, pulled away at high revs. The Beauchamps stood on the step of the hotel almost numb with the helplessness of the situation, not knowing what, if they ever saw them again, they would say to George's parents.

Jacques, had done all he could; he'd alerted the resistance who'd be aware of the situation throughout their various organisations and would also alert London, somehow. After the car had sped off into the distance they both turned and silently re-entered the hotel. As the tears welled in Claudine's eyes Jacques put his arm around her, in a forlorn hope to comfort them both. As they walked back into the hotel, quite dazed, Claudine opened a piece of crumpled paper she had, until then, had tucked firmly into her fist.

'What is this?' Jacques enquired.

'George put it in my hand, just as he was leaving.'

'What does it say?'

'Pass to resistance, for London: Urchin — eagle — pawn,' Claudine read 'But, what does this mean?'

'It is some kind of code, it is best we know no more. But it would seem that George was a little more prepared than anyone gave him credit,' Jacques commented.

'*Bonne chance Luc, bonne chance*,' said Claudine looking wistfully behind her.

The car arrived at the station early; the train wasn't due for another twenty minutes. George surveyed the scene. It was a typical continental station in that, unlike Britain, the platforms were low, meaning that you climbed up into the carriage, rather than merely stepping in. It was a station with which he was familiar from previous trips to Paris, although it was much busier than ever he'd seen it before. The station was amassed with all manner of

German military personnel and there was an atmosphere of jovial relief and spirits were high; they were going home.

The young officer's mind was not on his charge for the journey. No, this was a huge inconvenience. His mind was on the free schnapps to which he, as an officer, was entitled throughout the journey. This demeanour had not gone unnoticed by George.

Just as George was assessing the situation for himself, the station's public address system crackled out the tinny announcement of the imminent arrival of the Paris train.

'You vait here, I go to ze toilet,' the officer spoke harshly to George in his best attempt at French.

'Sir!' George said with a hesitant intonation to his voice 'Would you leave me your cap to prove that I should be here and won't be ejected from the station while you are away, please?' George pleaded pointing to his head and then the cap.

Without further words the officer disdainfully threw his cap at George.

A moment or two later a slowing train chugged into the station. George watched the Paris train slow and grind to a halt in a loud tumultuous belch of steam and smoke finishing with a screech of wheels and brakes. Since the time the officer had left him, George had nonchalantly sauntered and kicked his way along the platform, moving ever closer to the edge. He was now positioned by the first carriage of the Paris train. Glancing around he could see that he had the perfect smokescreen to hide his actions. He made his move. He jumped gracefully on to the carriage and made for the onboard toilet, where he stayed until the train was well underway again.

Still clutching the SS cap he wandered into the first class section of the train. He found an empty compartment and as he sat down, he contemptuously slung the cap onto the seat opposite. A few passengers who were still looking for seats half-entered the compartment and then retreated again on catching sight of the SS officer's cap. George had banked on this reaction to avoid any awkward conversations. He leaned back in his seat, quite pleased with himself that all had gone to plan. Quite what he'd do when he arrived in Paris he had no idea.

Just then he heard the conductor calling for all tickets to be shown as he walked down the corridor. George heard the compartment doors being opened and slid shut again with a loud clunk, each one louder than the last as the conductor progressed along the carriage. The conductor finally arrived at the door to George's compartment. He called for tickets before the door was fully open or he had even raised his eyes from the collection of tickets he was arranging in his hand. He slowly glanced into the compartment his eyes rapidly moving from George to the officer's cap on the opposite seat. After taking in this sight he seemed less at ease than before. He glanced back to George and simply said, 'Tickets please!'

'My SS escort has my ticket, sir,' George replied pointing to the unoccupied cap, 'I'm sure he won't be long.'

'That won't be necessary,' the conductor said 'I'm sure it is all in order, thank you.'

'One question if I may?' George said stopping the man in his tracks, as he'd already turned to leave.

'Of course.'

'How long is it to Paris, please?'

'All being well if there are no hold ups, around two hours,' the conductor replied through the closing door and then he was gone.

George spent the whole journey viewing the passing scenery. He was paying attention to none of it, as he wracked his brains for a plan of action when he hit Paris. The rural green countryside the train had ploughed its way through had almost instantly been replaced by the red and grey of buildings of the metropolis. He realised the train was close to stopping in central Paris and still he had no plan. It was no good, he'd have to wing it. He could hear the noise of the engine slowing, he felt the train braking. Quickly he checked the inside of the SS cap. Good, there was no name tag. He felt around the inside of the rim, his hand passed over something which felt like paper and crinkled. He tugged at the paper which came away easily. He unfolded it to find four ten-franc notes. 'Crickey! I'm rich,' he quietly exclaimed.

The train stopped and George quickly shoved the cap under the seat and stuffed two notes down each sock. He looked up and gulped; the station was mobbed. It was busier than he remembered. He knew he couldn't stay on the train; by now they'd be looking for him and one of the obvious places was the train that had left whilst his escort was in the toilet. He stood up, and had to push past the crush of people already boarding the train, which he did to an indignant tirade of Gallic abuse. He finally pushed his way off the train and on to the platform. Now it was his turn to get pushed and shoved from one direction to the next.

À Paris

George was being violently tossed around in a sea of people and was in a dreadful panic. All he could see was people. He was totally disorientated. Which way was out? He didn't know. Whilst the brutal jostling had subsided, he felt himself being carried along by the human current in one direction. A river of people, the banks of which were the train on one side, and a six- or seven-foot high wrought iron railing on the other. He had no choice; he had to go with the flow. The station was brightly lit and warm both of which were probably due to the glass roof and the bright day out-side. The surge of people was slowing and converging tightly to-gether. George could see he was approaching the ticket barrier. He had no ticket! This would attract the authorities unless he thought quickly. He looked down and saw many discarded tickets on the station floor. If he bent over to pick one up, he risked being top-pled and crushed; if he didn't he risked arrest and possible discov-ery. He quickly bent down and scooped up three from the floor. Holding them to his side he looked round, everyone had their tick-ets ready for inspection, they all had red tickets. He looked at the

George and the Reich

three in his hand; he dropped the yellow and purple and kept the red.

As the crowd converged on the ticket collector at the barrier, the official was methodically scanning the huge number of coloured rectangles presented to his eye-line and nonchalantly waving everyone through the gate. George could see the crowd the other side of the barrier was made up not only of civilians but a large proportion of German soldiers as well. As George's turn approached he kept looking around for a means of escape, if he needed one. He glanced back at the po-faced ticket collector, then again at the people around him; they all still clutched red tickets and were looking over him like he wasn't there. His heart was pounding. Sweat was gathering on his forehead, the back of his neck and the palms of his hands. He began to tremble. He had to pull himself together! Only the night before he'd been shot at and shell fire had tipped him into the sea and he was still here to tell the tale! He took a deep breath and composed himself. The trembling stopped. It was his turn. He looked squarely at the ticket collector as he showed his ticket and was waved through like the rest. He was out of the crush, the people dispersed, it was still busy but there was now room to move.

He noticed that he was briefly observed by two suited men in long coats speaking German and giving him a piercing glare and then looked behind him. George set away at a normal, casual pace, the panic was over. He allowed himself a huge sigh of relief. Then he heard, 'Hey boy,' in French of course, 'your ticket is invalid. You have to pay!' He didn't look round he just ran. He could hear the voice, which he presumed was the ticket collector shouting, 'Stop! Stop that boy!' He didn't look round in case he could be identified. He just kept running, he didn't run in a straight line, he tried all sorts of diversionary tactics. He ran around small crowds of people and behind crates stacked on the platforms and doubled back and then back again.

By now he was at the other end of the station and was aware that no one was chasing or calling after him. He'd given them the slip. He paused to regain his breath and composure. He permitted himself a brief gaze up at the ornate architecture of the station that had so captured his imagination as a young boy. He'd believed back then that the train had stopped inside a palace.

Slowly, he sauntered toward the nearest exit, looking around all the time. The bright midday sunshine was streaming in; the light was so bright that outside was a complete blur. He looked back into the now contrastingly fairly dark station. Still no-one had picked up his scent, or more likely didn't care.

George turned back in to the midday light. His pace quickened in an effort to further distance himself rapidly from the ticket collector and unwanted attention, looking behind him all the way. He was looking behind so carefully that he stumbled down the three steps out of the station. George landed in a heap on a very shiny pair of black riding style boots. He slowly looked up to see, a face of stone staring incredulously back at him. The SS Standartenführer, whose boot had been soiled, raised his ceremonial riding crop and issued a tirade of guttural Teutonic abuse at the terrified George. The entourage, who had moments ago been sycophantically laughing at the Standartenführer's jokes, gathered around the spectacle expecting some sport at the boy's expense.

As the now petrified George looked up into the soulless eyes of this SS officer, he could only manage a terrified, trembling apology in French.

His German was good enough to understand the Standartenführer's response between sadistic gritted teeth. 'Oh, you will be sorry alright you little French guttersnipe.' The only thought that went through George's mind at this moment was, 'Well, at least he doesn't know I'm English,' and at this thought he was helpless to prevent a slight smirk which only served to infuriate the officer further.

George was about to receive the thrashing of his life at the hands of the SS when there was the plaintive voice of a French boy. On first inspection George could see that he was of a similar age and was quite dishevelled in appearance. The boy shouted at George in French, 'Ah Pierre there you are!' George looked round to see who the boy was addressing; it must be someone very close but there was no one. The boy grabbed George by the face: 'Pierre! I've been looking everywhere for you, where have you been? How have you got in such trouble?' The boy then, in an obviously well-practised manner, subserviently pleaded to the officer to let 'Pierre' go, gesturing with his right index finger in a circular motion around his temple that George, or Pierre, was a few centimes short of a franc. The officer told the boy that his friend must be careful who he ran into in future; he may not run into someone as lenient as him. Then he indicated to them to get lost before he changed his mind. They both ran as fast as they could to get away. The officer was so amused at the fear he had instilled that he broke into a rapturous laughter which was echoed by the gathering around him.

George ran as fast as he could; all the time being led by the hand by his, as yet, un-named saviour. He didn't dare look back. He heard the sadistic laugh of the SS officer and his cronies blend into the general street noise of Paris. They darted down one road then scampered along another and then finally switched down a small alley and stopped behind a collection of bins.

George and the Reich

Both still breathing hard they peered over the bins to check the coast was clear. On seeing they'd not been followed, without a word, they both sighed with relief and laughed.

'Thank you so much. I have no idea how to repay you,' George spluttered completely forgetting himself.

The street kid looked at him in shocked amazement.

'You are English?'

'Ah! Oops! Err… Yes,' George said reverting back to French, realising he'd blown his cover.' You won't give me away, will you?'

'Of course not!' the boy said looking almost insulted, 'But what are you doing here?'

'It's a long story,' George said, 'but what should I call you?'

'I am François Loiseau,' the boy said standing up and bowing in mock ceremony.

'And I am George, but my French name is Luc!' he said reciprocating the comical bow.

'Then since you have a French name you must also have a Parisian name too. Since I am small and because of my surname I am known on the streets of Paris as Le Moineau (the sparrow). You shall be…' François thought for a moment looking to the sky for inspiration and rubbing his chin '…butterfly!' he finished, the moment of inspiration showing on his face.

'Butterfly?' George exclaimed sounding puzzled.

'Yes! Butterfly,' François replied 'because you just fluttered into Paris from nowhere.'

George reasoned silently that butterfly — Papillon — in French sounded much better than it did in English.

'OK!' George agreed.

After these initial introductions and preamble they both sat on the cobbles leaning against the crumbling wall down this quiet, seemingly forgotten, alley.

'So, how have you ended up in Paris?' François enquired with a look of disbelief.

'Well,' George began, 'my father was shot down.' George's narrative was loudly interrupted by his stomach groaning.

'You are hungry I think.'

'I'm absolutely famished,' George concurred. 'Do you know where we can get some food?'

'Yes, there are many places,' François replied.

'Great, let's go!' George said firmly.

'But in Paris if you want food, you have to pay,' François shrugged.

'That's not a problem' George said with a satisfied smile; he produced the money he had courtesy of the SS.

'Wow! where did you get that? I haven't seen that much money since before the war!' François said in shocked exclamation.

'Well, let's just say there's one slightly poorer German out there,' George replied clasping his hands behind his head and looking up with his tongue pushing into his right cheek.

'Oh, that is excellent, a little payback.'

'Now let's go and dine at Adolf's expense,' George chuckled.

They bought bread, cheese, ham, cakes — lots of cakes — and several bottles of lemonade. Then clutching their pending feast, François said, 'C'mon I'll show you the best kept secret in Paris.' Darting down another small back alley, François ran toward what looked like an apparent dead end, then with his free arm, reached through a mass of overhanging vines and leaves to reveal a discreet stone archway. François bent down and lifted a miner's lamp from the stone floor, which he was able to light with a match produced from his coat pocket. Enjoying the adventure, George quietly followed his trusted new friend. François then led George into a series of underground tunnels which eventually opened at the base of an old spiral staircase.

The staircase seemed to go up and up, seemingly without end; they eventually arrived at a door; François moved a loose stone in the wall by the doorway and took out a huge mediaeval-looking key. Opening the door he stood back and said, 'After you…' George walked in to a dark room; after putting his share of the food down on the floor, François scampered across the room past George and opened a small shutter. The room instantly filled with the late evening light, revealing a bare stone ancient-looking room. The bedding and burned candles in one corner were evidence that François had lived there for quite a while.

'My dad showed me this room just before the war. He told me then that there was going to be another war, much different from the first and if I ever needed to hide I should use this room. He said it was the best-kept secret in Paris and I should show it to no one. You are the first I've shown it to,' François said,` picking up a battered framed photograph from beside his bed and showing it to George. 'These are my parents,' he continued, passing the photograph to George.

George deduced that something terrible had become of them, since François was living here. George was about to ask about their fate when François said 'They were taken shortly after the

Nazi's occupied Paris. My father is the senior curator at the Louvre. No doubt they are trying to find out where certain art treasures have been hidden; my father won't tell them. The Gestapo came and took them one afternoon while I was out. I was nearly home and I saw the car pull up outside the house, I had to watch helplessly as they took them.' He finished with tears in his eyes and a noticeable warble in his voice. François wiped his eyes.

'So what did you do next?' George asked.

'I waited until dark. I watched the house to see if any Germans were waiting for me or coming back for anything. Then when I thought the coast was clear I went quickly in the back door. I only took absolute essentials that I could carry in one trip, so as not to attract any unwanted attention. I took a little food, some blankets, a few clothes and that picture of my parents. I didn't go back after that. So, now you know my story, what's yours?'

'It's very simple, really,' George said, with a shrug. 'My Dad was shot down, he's a bomber pilot, and I'm here to find him. That's it!'

The nonchalant précis prompted a tirade of questions from François: 'Wow! How did you get across the Channel? Where have you slept? How have you got food? How did the Germans catch you? Did they know you're English? Where is your Dad?'

George realised he had to now take François fully into his confidence and give him chapter and verse. Despite their instant camaraderie, since the incident on the beach, George was now suspicious of anyone he didn't fully know. However, he decided he had to take the leap of faith and trust François on this. He took a deep breath and over the next hour, between mouthfuls of food and gulps of lemonade, he recited the whole saga to the entranced François. George's voice was the only sound in the slight echo of the ancient room, punctuated only by the sound of a car horn outside, or gasps of breath and exclamations of '*Oh là là!*' from François.

George finished the monologue with '…and that brought me to Paris and here.' As he looked around the ceiling of the room, then focussing back on François 'Where exactly is *here*?'

'Look out of the window,' François replied.

George walked to the small window and peered through the weather-beaten glass. The glass was old, very old, the scene was distorted, but George could make out, just, that there was water either side of them. He could also see from the view over rooftops that they were very high up. George turned to impart his findings to François, mimicking the detectives he had heard on radio shows when they were revealing the culprit. 'From the information to hand, I deduce that we are very high up and the river is running either side of us, and judging by our internal surroundings the building we are in is ancient, therefore we must be on the Île de la Cité, not only that — we must be inside Notre Dame!'

François gave George a round of applause. 'That is very good!' he exclaimed.

The light was beginning to fade and the evening chill was beginning to set in. François lit a candle and threw George one of his heavy blankets. 'Here take this; it can get a little chilly in here at night. Make yourself as comfortable as possible then I'll blow out the candle.'

George threw his bag into the corner on the same side of the room as François, who was already wrapped up. He wrapped himself up tight in the blanket using his bag as a pillow.

'Right I'm all set,' he signalled to François, and then the light was extinguished. They talked a little longer but soon fell asleep, George from exhaustion and François from the sheer volume of food, it was the most he'd had in weeks.

George's enigma

Group Captain Victor Hawkshaw had not even sat down before the phone on his desk began to ring.

'Hawkshaw,' he answered.

The gruff voice at the other end simply barked, 'This may be delicate, better scramble.'

Victor pressed the scramble button on his phone. This was a system to prevent anyone who might be listening in to the call from understanding any of the content.

'Hello,' Victor said. 'Ah, good morning Air Commodore, what can I do for you?'

'As you may know a raid was sent across the Channel two nights ago to pick up Scotty's boy who's gone AWOL. And you may also be aware that they were rumbled by Jerry….' bellowed the Air Commodore.

'Yes, an awful shambles by all accounts, sir,' Victor replied.

'Well, SOE want to liaise with you directly since you know the family, I said that you'd naturally co-operate fully.'

'Naturally, sir. But I presume on that basis SOE have more than a casual involvement in this, can you brief me any further, sir?'

'Don't know much more mi-self!' replied the Air Commodore. 'But I do know that before he was separated from the landing party he passed on a great deal of intelligence and SOE have received a strange message which they want you to look into. Quite odd really, just three words: Urchin — Eagle — Pawn!' The Air Commodore then repeated the three words. He then asked, 'Any ideas?'

'Urchin — Eagle — Pawn,' Victor pondered. 'Absolutely no idea…' then he stopped in his tracks and whispered, 'George's table! Yes I have an idea sir. Leave it with me, I'll liaise back with SOE later today.'

The call ended and Victor got to his feet and called through the door to the next office, 'Smithy! Fetch the car, we're off to Scotty's again!'

'Right away sir,' Smithy replied.

The sound of Victor's car arriving prompted the usual welcoming committee of Rachel and the Brigadier to expectantly rush to the front gate.

'Any news?' Rachel asked before Victor had even had a chance to get out of the car.

'Nothing about Scotty as yet,' he replied, 'but I have news and some questions about George. Can we go inside?'

'Of course, Victor,' Rachel replied.

Once inside Victor began bringing Rachel and the Brigadier up to speed. He told them about the raiding party and the, until now, uncertainty of the outcome. Then he said, 'Can we have a look a George's table again? We've had what I believe was a coded message from George: Urchin — Eagle — Pawn. Well I know that Urchin means George but haven't a clue on the other items.'

'Right. Let's go and have a look,' said Rachel leading off at a trot.

For a short while they stood perusing the items arranged on the table.

'Well!' said Rachel, 'That's odd, the eagle is in amongst several things. Look there's an eagle, a train, a car, a boat and a bus. I

George and the Reich

don't know what to make of that — any ideas?' she looked at Victor and the Brigadier.

'It's all double Dutch to me!' grumbled the Brigadier.

'Looking at this from another angle…' Victor said, 'The odd one out is the eagle… so what do the others have in common?' he pondered.

'Transport!' barked the Brigadier in a moment of clarity, 'they're all methods of transport.'

'Transport… so he must be on the move,' said Victor.

'Right! What was the last one again?' the Brigadier commanded.

'Pawn, sir,' he replied.

'Pawn,' Rachel and the Brigadier repeated in unison as they perused the table.

There in the middle of the table was a chess pawn on top of a piece of paper with a swastika drawn on it.

'George — Transport or travel — swastika' Rachel repeated what they'd deciphered. 'So what's the real meaning here?' she questioned looking at Victor.

'Oh God!' Victor exclaimed with a dark look of realisation on his face.

'What? What is it Victor?' Rachel responded anxiously.

'Well I hope I'm wrong, but I think it means that he, George, is travelling either to Germany or with the Germans; unfortunately, I rather believe it to be both, since we have nothing else to go on, other than, strangely, that he has had the opportunity to get a message out. Which I think means he has not been apprehended as such and they're not aware of his true identity. My word, I think he's fooled Jerry!'

Then turning to Rachel, Victor said, 'We can do nothing more at present, this is an incomplete message; we need to wait for the next message which will hopefully reveal his new location. You need to understand that your boy is far wiser than his years and more resourceful than the majority of the men under my command; he's OK.'

Rachel by now was sobbing again with despair.

'I think a cup of tea is in order,' mumbled the Brigadier as he left the room.

By the time Victor and Rachel had followed, Ives was in the kitchen and the kettle was on.

'Tea, Victor?' Rachel enquired.

George and the Reich

'Thank you, no. I'd better get back and report our findings and I have no idea what mess has hit my desk while I've been out.'

With that he showed himself out and shortly after, the staff car started and the sound soon disappeared into the distance.

A rude awakening

George was suddenly woken by the loudest crashing noise
he'd ever heard. The room was shaking. It was light so he knew it
was morning; but that's all he knew. He looked round panicking, it
felt like bombing but it didn't sound like it. Then his eyes fell on
François, who was sitting up against the wall evidently in raptures
of laughter at George's expense. George could see he was laughing
but the only sound he could hear was the crashing. When the noise
stopped George's ears continued ringing. François said, 'Yes, maybe should have warned you about the neighbours!'

'Neighbours, what neighbours do you have this far up?' he
questioned loudly his ears having not fully settled down yet.

'The bells! The bells!' François said pulling a contorted face
and shuffling around the room hunched over, which made them
both laugh.

'George, I know how you got to Paris. So what are you going
to do now?' François puzzled.

'Well, I know what raid Dad was on and when he was shot down; so I know roughly where he would have come down. I'm now on my way there to see if I can find anything out. Someone will know where they were taken. I'm hoping they're not in Germany!'

'Excuse me asking but how do you know he's still alive?'

George ignored the question, not willing to admit that was a possibility.

'François, I need to get in touch with the resistance, quickly!' George said suddenly.

'Of course, not a problem; but why? Won't the British try to get you back before you've found your father?'

'They may, but one attempt has already failed and now I'm deeper into France. I must get in touch so I can get a message back to Mum,' George replied.

'What makes you think they'll relay a message for you?'

'Well, they've already sent a commando raiding party to get me and I've passed on a great deal of intelligence to them, so I think there's a good chance.'

'OK, come on then let's go,' François beckoned, 'No time like the present!'

George followed without question as François skipped down the ancient stone steps like a mountain goat. Very soon they were in the catacombs which criss-crossed beneath the bustling Parisian streets. François had had plenty of time to accustom himself with these ancient caves. 'This is the quickest way across Paris with the added bonus of no Germans,' he called back to George without breaking his stride. 'Here, this is it,' he said arriving at the foot of a rusting vertical ladder.

'This is where?' George enquired with a frustrated tone.

'You wanted to contact the resistance, well one of my resistance contacts may be found in this area of Paris, follow me.'

At the top of the ladder they arrived in another tunnel, evidently closer to the surface from the flickering natural light spilling from one end. François lead George towards the light which on closer inspection was an overgrown tunnel entrance, which George imagined looked a little like being behind a green waterfall; the movement of the leaves in the breeze causing the sunlight, which was permitted to penetrate, to dance on the cave walls.

By placing his index finger over his lips and then pushing the palm of his hand towards George, François silently signalled to George to be quiet and stay put. François then turned towards the cave entrance. He gingerly peered through the foliage, and then edged a little further forward pushing through the branches; he paused momentarily then pushed further again. Save for a leafy silhouette, as far as George could see, François had been absorbed completely by the bushes. A single hand then appeared back through the leaves and beckoned George. George moved forward and pushed his way through the bush. As soon as he emerged François grabbed him and pulled him into a crouched position with him, against the walled cave entrance. 'Shh!' François whispered, 'We have to be careful. This place is frequented by vagabonds and there are often German patrols.'

As his eyes adjusted to the daylight he could see that they had emerged into a rough courtyard which nature was in the process of reclaiming; there were as many weeds as there were cobbles. The courtyard was surrounded on all sides by tall derelict-looking buildings. The windows were smashed, many of the roof slates had long since come loose of their fixings and fallen the five stories to smash on the cobbles below. The perforated roof provided ideal accommodation for what seemed, from the endless activity, like the city's entire population of pigeons. Much of the rendering which once covered the walls of the buildings also now lay with the slate debris on the floor of the square.

François tapped George on the shoulder snapping him out of his semi-daydream, watching the coming and going of the pigeons.

'We go. Now. Quickly,' François whispered. With that he took off at a sprint, George following close on his heels. Other than the tunnel there was only one route out of the courtyard, an alleyway leading to the main road. As they ran through the alley François pointed with his left arm indicating that they would turn left once they were through the alley. George continually looked though the broken windows as he ran between the buildings, which were as dilapidated inside as out. As they rounded the corner George glanced back into the alley to see two dishevelled rough-looking men had emerged from the buildings. They were just seconds too late to accost the two boys for any pickings they might be carrying.

As François had indicated, they turned left, then dashed across that small road and turned right then immediately left. This led them on to a main road with all the day to day bustle of a busy high street. François had instantly stopped running and straightened his left arm in front of George's path to ensure he did so too. The street was lined on each side with colourful shops of every kind punctuated by the occasional café. George was mesmerized by the sights, sound and smells, he was completely knocked off balance when he was firmly yanked from the right and pulled into a narrow passage. 'What the...!' He didn't get to finish his outburst; François had placed his hand over George's mouth. 'You must pay attention!' he said. 'Anyway, we are here.'

'Where?' George asked

'Where you wanted to be, remember?' François replied. 'Come, follow me!' he commanded. The passage led out to the narrow lane which ran along behind the shops. The lane was straight with high walls either side. Every so often there was a door or gate in the wall, with several dustbins standing sentry at each. They stopped outside a solid red back door with four large bins next to it. François took off two of the bin lids and threw one over the wall. It landed on the other side with a loud metallic crash. George froze, his mouth gaping. 'Now we're for it!' he said as he tried to run off.

François grabbed him by the scruff of his neck before he got away. 'Don't be scared, that's my signal,' he explained as he threw another lid over the wall.

Very soon they heard a door slam and footsteps accompanied by loud Gallic grumbling, on the other side of the wall.

'You lousy kids, I'll have your guts for garters,' the voice said as the gate opened and a weathered face of thunder appeared. The man's initial scowl turned to a smile when he greeted François, as he replaced the lids on the bins.

'Hello Pepe,' replied François. Pepe beckoned the boys into the yard and quickly surveyed the alley before bolting the door shut. The man was unshaven, wearing a faded dirty blue jacket, beret and a long since extinguished cigar stump in the corner of his mouth, which enhanced his overall unkempt appearance. He walked round the boys, opened the back door to the house and invited the boys inside.

Once inside the house George saw there were two other equally dishevelled looking men sitting around the table in the kitchen. The conversation fell silent when the boys entered. The two men at the table viewed George with suspicion, but said nothing. George was equally on edge. He knew that the resistance could be brutal with anyone they distrusted and he had no means of escape. Pepe walked around the boys and sat back at the table. The chair squealed in protest as Pepe manoeuvred the chair into position.

'Well Moineau, who is your friend? We have not seen him before. Is he safe?' Pepe got bluntly to the point.

'Of course he is safe! Would I have brought him here if there was any doubt?'

'What proof do you have?' Pepe quizzed bluntly.

'Well, none. But I saved him from a thrashing by a Standartenführer, he is English, his father was shot down; he's a bomber pilot, and he's come across the Channel to rescue him!' François reeled off frantically.

Pepe stood up rapidly sending the chair crashing against the wall, the other two men also stood up. The two boys visibly jumped, almost out of their skin!

'Have you learnt nothing boy?' Pepe bellowed at François. 'Is this the best the mighty German Reich can come up with?' Pepe yelled at George. 'Does Adolf think we French are so stupid as to believe this charade? François my friend you have fallen victim to a poorly-staged, far-fetched Nazi trick!'

George by now was visibly shaking and in fear of his life. Then drawing a knife one of the men leant on the table and said in German, 'I am going to kill you. Slowly!'

George tried desperately not to show that he understood German; he was convinced that if they found out he understood German he would meet his end.

The man turned to his comrades, pointing at George and said, 'He understood!'

For the first time George spoke up, and in the King's English said, 'Well, what do you expect? You were pointing a knife at me; that's an international language.' George knew he had nothing to lose now as he tried to regain his composure. He searched the tatty-looking room for an escape route. There were two doors and a window: The door they'd come in was now blocked by Pepe. The route to the other door, which George presumed led to the front of the house and other rooms, was blocked via the kitchen table and two formidable-looking scowling men. The window, just over his left shoulder, may be his only hope; though he'd have to clamber onto the draining board and either open it or kick his way through. Pepe was closest to him; whilst he was older than the other two, he was probably quick enough to grab him before he'd made it out of the window and restrain him for the second or two it would take the others to cross the room.

George was beginning to realise there was no escape route. He was shaking uncontrollably and tears had started to roll down his cheeks. Just then there was a deliberate, measured knock at the door. The room fell silent. Pepe nodded to the two men; they both produced pistols, one moved through the far door and peered in from there, the other went toward the back door and used the open inner door to shield him from view. Pepe moved toward the back door and put his hand on the knob. Before opening the door, he turned, looking into the kitchen at the boys and put his index finger across his lips, and then pointed to the man behind the door and then pointed at George gesticulating with his hand like a gun. George knew clearly this meant, 'Make a sound and you're dead.'

Pepe turned once again to the door. Cautiously he opened it, just a crack. On seeing the caller, he flung the door open and welcomed the visitor in. Before George had a chance to view the stranger Pepe leaned into the kitchen and pulled the bare wooden inner door shut. Then the back door was closed with a clunk. Behind the door there followed a rapid conversation conducted in a loud whisper. Although he overheard parts of it, he didn't need to hear to know he was the subject of the conversation that might very well seal his fate, unless he could talk his way out. He looked back to the two men holding pistols, who had resumed their seats at the table. This indicated that the caller was familiar to them also.

Just then the door opened and Pepe re-entered the kitchen, followed by the caller. George could see the man was much better dressed than Pepe and his friends: polished black shoes, pressed trousers and a dark trench coat.

'Here he is, the little Nazi vermin!' Pepe pointed to George as the man walked round from behind Pepe to face George.

George looked up at the man. He instantly took a sharp intake of breath which he attempted to mask along with a look of amazement which tried to hijack his face; he didn't want to blow the man's cover in case Pepe and his friends were not fully in the picture.

'*Sacré bleu!*' the man exclaimed. 'This is no Nazi, but I have no idea what he's doing here!' he said to Pepe in flawless French. Then switching to equally perfect English he said, 'George! What on earth are you doing here?'

'You know this boy?' Pepe quizzed and exclaimed in equal proportion.

'Yes. He's from my village in England; he goes to the same school as my boy!'

On hearing this exchange the other two men had relaxed their guard and re-secreted their pistols. A bottle of wine had appeared of which they were both enjoying a glass.

'But, what is he doing here? It couldn't be more dangerous for him. We need to get him home,' replied Pepe.

Having judged his position to be far less precarious than it had been two minutes ago George butted in, 'They've already tried that, a navy launch and a team of commandos… didn't work!' he said with a nonchalant delivery.

'That was you?' the man asked. 'I'd heard of the skirmish and that the raid to recover a boy had failed, but knew no more. I might have known if anyone was up to this kind of mischief it would be you,' the man finished with a wide smile.

'Mr Dulac! I thought you were... err... but you're here... I don't understand!'

'Indeed, here I am! Well let me tell you my story, but first why don't you tell me yours?' Mr Dulac conceded.

'Well, I would sit down if I were you, this may take a while,' François said to Mr Dulac with a giggle.

Pepe offered them all a seat and George, once again, upon request recited the whole story, including the bullying of Mr Dulac's son Peter, and his part in his defence. '...and that's how I'm sitting in this kitchen... in Paris!' he finished.

'My word George, what an adventure! I'm sorry to hear about your father; we'll see if we can find anything out,' said Mr Dulac in complete amazement, 'and thank you so much for sticking up for Peter. Unfortunately, and for many reasons which I can't go into, conscientious objector was the best cover for my apparent disappearance; not even my wife knows the truth.' His words tailed off, in a regretful, slow metre as he looked wistfully through the dirty kitchen window. A single tear rolled down his cheek before he recomposed himself, and stood up. 'Right, I'd better be off. George be careful, no discussing this, especially in a public place, the Gestapo are everywhere. I'll find out what I can and I'll meet you two tomorrow morning at eleven, but not here.'

How about the park near the Place de la Concorde?' François interjected.

'Yes! Excellent,' Mr Dulac responded, 'near the *Bassin Octagonal*.'

'No problem' said François 'I'll have him there.'

'Do you have money for food?' Mr Dulac enquired.

'Yes, plenty,' George replied, 'I lifted it from the SS guard that I gave the slip!'

This made Mr Dulac roar with laughter. He translated it into French for Pepe and his compatriots who were looking puzzled at Mr Dulac's amusement, then they broke out into raucous laughter too. They poured everyone a drink and toasted George.

'Mr Dulac, before you go I have one request, if I may?' asked George.

'I'll try, what is it?' he enquired.

'Can you get a message back to London, please?'

'Not really George, it's too dangerous. I dare not risk it.'

'Please Mr Dulac; it's only three words, which are complete nonsense but if they get to Mum, they may be able to make sense of it.'

'Alright, give them to me, but no promises, OK?

'Yes,' George responded. 'They are: Urchin — Scallop — Tree.'

'Got it. I'll see you two tomorrow.' Then after a quick chat with Pepe and his friends Mr Dulac left.

Soon after, George and François also left the house, as the afternoon was giving way to evening. They returned to the little room high in Notre Dame clutching more food and lemonade.

Mr Parker

'Morning Victor,' said the Brigadier, who was in the garden as Victor's car pulled up.

'Morning sir!' replied Victor, 'Do you mind if I have a word with you and Rachel again and another look at that table of George's, please?'

'I don't see why not!' he said gesticulating for Victor to lead the way.

Once inside, Victor said, 'SOE has another message, this time transmitted from one of their people, they wouldn't tell me any more than that, other than: Urchin — Scallop — Tree.'

Having now become quite in tune with George's codes based on the arrangement of apparently random items, they deciphered this latest message in no time.

'Well, we know that Urchin means George.' Victor began with the obvious whilst looking over the items, 'so… Scallop… there's a mini-Eiffel Tower sitting in the scallop shell, so I imagine that means he's made it to Paris; and by all accounts he's made contact with SOE in Paris!' Victor exclaimed shaking his head with the incredulity of this already surreal situation.

'OK, but what does the tree mean?' The Brigadier pondered, rubbing his chin.

'Look, there's a tree at the back!' Rachel pointed, as she leaned over lifting it. 'It's placed on a piece of paper; there's a swastika crossed out.'

'Well, that's it!' said Victor 'He's in Paris and he's somehow got away from the Nazi's and he's made contact with SOE.' He took a moment, 'I can't believe I've just said that. I need to get back and report this to SOE right now. I don't know how they're going to take this news. Needless to say this stays within these walls,' Victor dictated.

'Oh absolutely Victor! But what are we going tell his school? He's already had so many days off; he can't have a cold for much longer. The last thing I want is Vlad snooping round here,' Rachel responded. 'That man gives me the creeps.'

'Vlad? Who's Vlad?' the Brigadier barked.

'Oh! It's one of the names the boys call Mr Batt,' Rachel shrugged.

This made the Brigadier roar with laughter. All the time Victor was seriously pondering Rachel's question of George's cover story.

'I'll speak to SOE on this as well Rachel. But I think he'll have to go down with something that requires isolation. I'll come back to you on that.'

'OK Victor. Thank you.'

Victor left in quite a hurry. 'Step on it Smithy!' he ordered, 'back to base and don't spare the horses!'

When Victor arrived at the airfield, he leapt out of the car, without waiting for Smithy to open the door; ran into his office, without returning any of the salutes he received from the staff, slammed the door shut, picked up the phone and sat down. Almost all in one fluid movement.

He took a deep breath, and then dialled SOE in Whitehall.

'Ah, yes, good morning; has Mr Parker arrived from Victoria?' he enquired. This was code for clearance at the highest level of secrecy.

'Parker, 3 — 2 — 1,' was the response, which was his cue to press the scramble button on his phone.

'Morning Colonel,' he began, 'we've worked out from the latest set of items that the boy has made it to Paris, but the best bit is that he seems to have shaken off his German escort.'

'The more I hear of this young man, the more I realise he's a resourceful, determined little blighter with nerves of steel; we could do with more of his kind in the fold.'

'Yes, he's always been a bit of a handful,' replied Victor, 'but, question is, what happens next?'

'Well! He's too far inland to send a raiding party; can't send a Lysander into Paris and he's not going to want to return until he's achieved what he went there to do,' the Colonel continued. 'What *do* you think he went out there to achieve Hawkshaw, hmm?'

'Well Colonel,' Victor began, 'There is only one logical reason: his Dad was shot down over France, so I imagine that he's gone out there to rescue him. The other thing is, he's going to need a cover story; at the moment his school think he's off with a cold, but we'll need something which will make an elongated absence seem plausible.'

The Colonel shook his head in disbelief. 'What marvellous courage, or foolhardiness; hard to determine which. One has to hand it to the boy, he's made it this far. But one thing is certain, this is very serious; we will have to inform Number 10. I'll come back to you with a cover once I've done so.'

'Is that really necessary Colonel, I mean informing the Prime Minister?' Victor asked.

'Absolutely, Hawkshaw. We've thrown valuable resources at this already; Winston will have to know. It's likely that he'll hit the roof when he finds out, so I'll have to work on the delivery. The fact that the boy has provided valuable intel on the Nazi defences will go in his favour; anyway, leave that with me, good work so far. Good bye!' with characteristic abruptness the conversation was over.

Our man in Paris

The next morning George and François left their little room high in Notre Dame for the rendezvous with Mr Dulac. They walked over the bridge from the Île de la Cité and then along the river; as they approached the park François produced a dog lead from his pocket.

'What's that for?' George asked.

'If we've lost our dog, we have a reason to speak to an apparent stranger without suspicion,' François replied with a smug grin.

As they entered the leafy park, which was showing the first signs of autumn, François began calling out, 'Pip! Pip! Come on boy.' After calling out to the imaginary dog several times he walked up to a German soldier who was walking around the park.

'Excuse me,' he began 'have you seen a small scruffy-looking grey dog, please?'

'No, I'm sorry I haven't,' the soldier replied politely.

'OK, thank you sir,' François responded.

'That will help our cover,' François whispered to George as they walked toward the *Bassin Octagonal.*

'How?' questioned George, now believing the whole dog story to be a waste of time.

'Don't look back, but we have been watched by two Gestapo officers since we set foot in the park and that German soldier is walking towards them; they will stop and ask him what we wanted.'

'Ah! But how can you tell they're Gestapo? They don't wear a uniform!'

'They have a smell,' François replied curtly.

'A smell?' George said almost too loudly.

'Yes,' replied François. 'When you see Gestapo they have a gap around them like there is zone of bad smell around them, people avoid them at all costs. You look around you with *your eyes open,* you'll get to know what they look like.'

'Look, there's Mr Dulac,' George spotted quietly.

Mr Dulac was sitting on a bench near the *Bassin Octagonal* with his back to the Place de la Concorde, approximately a hundred yards behind him, looking engrossed in a story in the paper. They approached Mr Dulac.

'Excuse me Monsieur,' François said 'have you seen a small scruffy grey dog, please?' He continued holding the lead out to complete the pretence for the potential audience.

Mr Dulac, obviously well-versed at this kind of deceptive conversation, looked over his paper at the boys and began speaking to them. He scratched his head and looked around, he rubbed his chin and then thoughtfully put his finger to his lips and finally moved his paper to his left hand and then pointed with his right hand in the direction the boys had come in. The words he used bore no resemblance to his gesticulations. 'Right,' he began, 'there's no time for questions here. First I've had the acknowledgement code from London; they understood your message, we have no further instructions on that front at present. Secondly, your Dad is in a small holding camp further south which is part of a larger labour camp near the Vichy border, the resistance have details. Thirdly, we must be extra careful; we believe somewhere in the village back home is a German spy. What we really need is someone inside Gestapo HQ. Anyway, it will be safer not to use public transport to travel out of Paris. There will be a barge; it will dock at the Île de la Cité for the evening. The bargee is expecting you at midnight, the barge is called '*Maxime*'. It will take you down river, near to Dijon where you will rendezvous with the resistance; the bargee will have further instructions for you, they will take you the rest of the way. Now you best go and get ready.' Mr Dulac finished and went back to his paper.

'Thank you, sir,' they said as they left.

'Good luck!' Mr Dulac called after them.

'Don't worry, I know a tunnel which leads directly out to the quayside where the barge will dock,' François whispered, 'it will be much safer at that time of night.'

Back at the room, high in Notre Dame, the boys sat and waited for midnight, eating the rest of their food and drinking the last of the lemonade.

'Will you come with me?' George asked.

'No,' said François, 'Thank you, but I know Paris and I am as safe as anyone can be in this war. In any case when you find your Dad and go back to England I can't come with you. How would you explain where you found a French boy?'

'Yes, I suppose that would give the game away,' George conceded. 'So then, we shall make a pact, to meet after war?'

'Agreed!' said François holding his lemonade in the air.

George reciprocated and they toasted their plan to meet at the end of the war.

They both woke with a start at the clock striking the hour. It was midnight; they lit candles and George gathered his few things together in his bag. He reached in his pocket — he still had twenty francs of the SS money in his pocket.

'Here,' he said offering half the money to François.

'I can't take that!' said François.

'Yes, you can and you will; I stole it anyway,' George chuckled.

'Well since you put it like that!' François conceded, taking the money. 'Right. I have to guide you to the quayside.'

François lead the way — the candle light flickered and cast ghostly figures around the cavernous ceiling of the steep, stone staircase as they descended. Once at the bottom of the steps, François led them along a particularly damp and smelly tunnel. Their soggy footsteps echoed around them. In the semi-light of the candles George saw François signal to stop, in the brief silence the dripping from the ceiling played random notes of differing pitch as they hit the tunnel floor.

'We are near the tunnel entrance,' François whispered. 'We must continue without candles and quietly.'

Gingerly they made their way towards the moonlit entrance, groping their way along the damp walls of the tunnel. The sounds of the river began to fill the mouth of the tunnel. They both listened intently, trying to gain a picture of what was immediately outside. The river lapped and slapped the quayside and a boat slowly chugged past. Just as they were about to sneak forward to take a look, they heard voices; they sounded close but not right outside. They both took a breath and then crept forward to the barred tunnel entrance.

'Crikey it's barred,' whispered George.

In the dim light George saw François put his finger to his lip: 'Shht!' quietly indicating for George to maintain silence and then to remain where he was. François very slowly edged the last few inches towards the entrance. In the moonlight he could see the anthracite figures of two German soldiers on the quayside, rifles slung over their shoulders. There was a third figure talking to them from the barge moored to the quay opposite the barred tunnel. The third person was not a soldier, leaning over the railing outside the wheelhouse of the barge about six feet above where the soldiers were standing. François could see the small red glow of a cigarette. The conversation finished, the soldiers bid the bargee goodbye as they slowly sauntered off. Once the slow, damp gravel footsteps had faded into the distance François beckoned George forward.

François took hold of one of the bars with both hands and twisted it. There was a rusty loose metallic grinding screech. Even in this light George could see that with relatively minimum effort François managed to lift one of the bars, sliding it out of the bottom cross member and up through the rusted hole where it was once welded to the top one. George realised that this was another one of François' usual routes. The bar now temporarily removed, the gap was big enough for the boys to squeeze through. François slowly poked his head through the gap, checking left and right carefully several times.

'The coast is clear. Time to go! good luck!' said François holding out his hand.

'Thanks François!' George replied shaking his hand, 'thanks for everything. You can still come with me you know.'

'I know, but I belong in Paris.'

'Well, OK! But if I can ever begin to return the favour, just let me know, OK?' George stated. 'But, would you do one last thing for me? Ask Mr Dulac to pass this message to SOE in London,' then George slowly said, 'Urchin — Eagle — Mussel — Tree.'

'*Bien sûre, Bonne chance!*'

After they said their goodbyes George tentatively peered through the bars left then right and then quickly again. The coast was clear. He stepped out on to the cobbles. It was a damp, slightly misty, cool night. As he stepped away from the tunnel entrance, George looked up behind him. Some twenty feet up he could see the lights and hear the sounds of the Parisian evening: accordion music, laughter, corks popping and glasses chinking. He turned back round. The man was still out on the deck of the barge, his dark silhouette visible against the lighter shade backdrop of the barge. The tiny red glow of his cigarette occasionally moved up to his face and then back down to the railing he was leaning on. George approached cautiously; his senses on red-alert. The image of the man and the barge became clearer as he closed in. He could see the man was now looking directly at him. As he came within speaking distance, he scanned all around him, up and down the quayside; it was deserted. He checked out what he could see of the barge. Just below the skipper's feet he could see the name plate, '*Maxime*'. George looked up and, as he'd been instructed, said 'Do you know a good place to fish?'

'I do!' he replied, 'Where?'

'Down river,' George answered.

'Pike?'

'No, trout.'

'OK!' said the bargee, 'Come aboard, quickly!' He snapped the final word.

Once on board, the skipper ushered George below deck immediately.

'You are younger than I expected,' he stated. 'Listen! before we get started, I have a few rules: 1. I don't know anything about you or what's going on and I don't want or need to. 2. I know your name is Luc; mine is Gérard. 3. When we arrive at your destination you get off. 4. While you are on my barge you do as I say. 5. If we are boarded by the Nazis you hide well; if you are discovered I don't know you, you are a stowaway. Is that all understood?'

'Absolutely Gérard,' George replied obediently.

'Good. Well, make yourself comfortable,' the captain said, handing George some blankets. 'We'll get underway shortly, and then we can be out of Paris before daybreak.'

'Thank you, sir.'

'No! Just Gérard, please,' the Captain said with a little smile and then left the room.

George surveyed his surroundings. He was in a cabin which had not seen an occupant, well not a human one, for a long time.

Instead it seemed that the cabin was store room cum attic; it was filled with crates of wine, rope, tarpaulin, several stacked boxes, some suitcases and a rocking horse among other things, all of which were sporting a rather liberal covering of dust. 'Why does every attic seem to contain a rocking horse?' George thought rhetorically.

He cleared the old bunk of the debris which covered it; mainly broken pieces of wood, a mop and some old rags, all of which looked like it was where they landed when they were thrown in the room. George threw his bag to the head end of the bunk as a pillow, he clambered on to the bed pulling the blankets over himself and lay his head on the makeshift pillow. After a bit of jigging around, fidgeting and a little puffing of his pillow, he was comfortable. He lay awake until the engines began to chug and the barge was underway. It wasn't long before George was rocked to sleep, by the gentle rocking of the boat and the rhythmic rumble of the engines as the barge slipped slowly out of the city and followed the aqueous road into the country.

A bit early

George woke with a start. The engines were silent. He looked towards the porthole of his cabin. Although the tiny flimsy curtain was drawn, he could see that it was not yet fully light. They were not scheduled to make a stop until much later. He was instantly suspicious. Outside, he could hear an ongoing conversation. It was Gérard and the unmistakeable guttural tones of Germans. George listened intently; they were going to board and search the boat. It was evident that Gérard had had no warning of this or he would have alerted George. George quietly, but quickly, got out of the bed, on which he threw some debris to make it look unused. He grabbed his bag and crept out of the cabin. He knew he had to be off the boat before the Germans boarded. All the voices and noise he could hear was aft, so he made his way forward hoping to find an escape route there. He clambered through and over the various boxes, chests and sacks which filled the dark, dusty cargo hold.

At the other end of the hold he found a hatch in the ceiling. Gently, he forced it open just a crack and peered through. He could see nothing but the main hatch to the cargo hold. He'd been hoping for this, it would provide excellent cover. He found a length of rope, about four yards long, in which he tied an overhand loop at one end and a bowline in the other. He opened the hatch wider; as he did the hinge gave off a rusty metallic creak. He froze. Had he been heard? He listened carefully; it seemed the discussion further down the bank was still in full swing. He clambered out, taking with him the rope and his bag. Leaving them by the hatch, he crawled to the main cargo hatch. It was a damp, misty morning and George shivered as the morning chill penetrated his skin with no warning.

Cautiously, he peered over the hatch. In the dim misty light of the morning he could make out the figures of several people one of which he knew was Gérard. He could see they were now moving quickly on to the barge. George lost no time. He fixed the smaller loop of the rope on to rowlock on the starb'd bow of the barge and fed it though the corresponding hole in the gunwale. George then slung on his back pack and climbed over the side; reaching down for the rope, he slipped the large bowline loop up his legs to his bottom and then lowered himself down until the rope took his weight and he was, hopefully, out of sight of the German search party. His head was a good foot below the bow gunwale. He sat there quietly out of sight; the rumbling and crashing could be heard from below deck as the Germans ruthlessly

George and the Reich

searched the barge. He was not certain what they were looking for; it could be contraband, supplies for the resistance, or the resistance being quietly transported under their noses.

After what seemed like an aeon of dangling from the rope, while remaining completely still and trying to not even breathe loudly, the German search party left the barge. George heard an authoritative German voice, whom he presumed was the commanding officer, issue a warning to Gérard that he should ensure he kept he barge clean from the resistance and black-market vermin or he would be shot and his barge blown from the water. 'Crikey!' George thought to himself, 'that sounds permanent.' Shortly after that George heard the barge's engines rumble into life. A cloud of acrid, oily-smelling exhaust momentarily engulfed him and then moved on leaving its sooty fingerprints in his nostrils. George stayed put until the barge was underway and had chugged its way around the next reach.

Once the coast was clear, George hoisted himself back on to the deck. The misty twilight of the early morning had given way to full daylight. He kept low to reduce the chance of attracting attention from anyone on either bank. As quickly as he could, he disappeared back down the small hatch into the hold. The sound of the rusty hinges was now stifled by the noise of the engines. George dropped back down into the hold and clambered over all the cargo once again. He threw his bag back into the cabin that was his home for the next twenty-four hours and climbed the steep steps to the bridge.

'Cor, that was close!' he exclaimed.

'*Merde!*' was all the Gérard could say as he pirouetted better than any ballet dancer and landed in a wide-eyed stare looking straight at George while still retaining his grip on the wheel.

'Please don't do that!' Gérard shouted, 'My nerves are quite shot as it is. I was certain they'd find you; quite what would have happened after that is anyone's guess. Anyway where were you hiding? They turned the boat upside down and didn't find anything.'

'I was dangling from a rope off the bow,' George said nonchalantly. From the bridge he surveyed the passing panorama. They were sailing through rustic France; trees lined each bank, punctuated occasionally by dishevelled-looking buildings: houses, shops, farmsteads and cafés all with cracked rendering and the odd roof tile missing. Some had faded adverts painted on the side.

It was turning out to be a mild, bright day. Along the bank more people were emerging from unhurried rural France and going about their business: gossiping, cycling, walking and fishing; almost oblivious to the war, of which the only reminder was the occasional building flying a swastika; evidently having been commandeered by the occupying forces. As they progressed slowly with the river's meanders, occasional greetings were shouted to Gérard from the bank, to which he retorted, without fail, accompanied with an exaggerated wave of his arm.

George spent the rest of the morning in the wheelhouse with Gérard; sitting back from the windows, as a precaution against being sighted. In the early afternoon Gérard interrupted the hypnotic chugging of the engine. 'You had best go to your cabin and get some rest, you may have a busy night ahead. In any case I have to dock at the next wharf for an hour or so to refuel, load more cargo and get some food.'

George reluctantly conceded that he was probably right, and so went off to bed.

Sometime later, the engines silent, George was woken by Gérard. 'Wake up! Wake up!'

'What's up?' George said rubbing his eyes in the late afternoon light.

'Firstly, I have a message from the resistance: you will be unloaded at the next wharf as planned.'

'Unloaded!' George exclaimed, looking up to make sharp eye contact. 'What do you mean unloaded?'

'Well, you will not walk off the barge in front of the German guards,' Gérard gestured with an exaggerated shrug of his shoulders, 'you will be unloaded on to the quayside in a crate. The resistance, in disguise, will collect you in the crate which they'll load on to a lorry. They'll let you out of the crate when they are at the safe house. If anything goes wrong you will be on your own,' he warned.

'Nothing new there then,' George muttered.

'Pardon?' replied Gérard, having not caught what George had uttered or its sarcastic overtone.

'Nothing,' George dismissed with a shake of his head.

'OK!' Gérard continued. 'Secondly, the crate is through in the hold marked "China, fragile!", come, I'll show you.' Gérard led the way and George followed quietly behind. 'Here! We figured that was innocuous enough to prevent any unwanted attention from either the Germans or the light-fingered stevedores: which may not have been the case if we had marked it coffee or tobacco for instance. You see,' Gérard continued pointing to the latches on each side of the crate, 'these four latches are on the inside so you can lock yourself into the crate from the inside, so in emergencies you can get out quick, but that is only in emergencies. Understood?'

'That's all understood Gérard, thank you,' replied George.

'There are also these straps,' Gérard continued, pulling at one of the thick canvas straps, 'these are to help you hold on when being moved and you will see there is a small box nailed to the bottom to make it a little more comfy. Lastly, you must be hungry, I'll bring you some food down and then we'll get underway again.'

Gérard returned to George's cabin with the food. 'Make sure you get some rest tonight, it will be very suspicious if a crate on the wharf side is snoring,' he chuckled. This amused George, as he pictured the consternation this might cause the goons. 'You should also wrap up warm before you get in the crate; it is going to be cold tonight and I have no idea how long you'll be on the quayside before you're collected.'

'OK,' George replied.

'We should be there at around 1 AM but you will not be unloaded until about 4 AM when the first of the wharf staff arrive.'

'OK, I understand Gérard. Thank you.'

Table again

'Good Morning Smithy; no Victor?' Rachel puzzled as Smithy handed her an envelope.

'No, Ma'am, Sorry Ma'am. The Group Captain sends his compliments and asked me to hand you this.'

'OK Smithy, thank you. Would you like a cup of tea?'

'No thank you Ma'am, I'm under strict orders to RTB immediately.'

As Smithy turned on his heels and trotted back to the car Rachel opened the envelope; the letter inside began:

Good morning Rachel. I didn't call to the house again, so as not to attract any attention from those whom we may wish to avoid. It is plausible to call round once or twice after I lose an airman but to keep calling, may put loved ones in jeopardy. Anyway, we have another message which is: Urchin — Eagle — Mussel — Tree. I'd be grateful if you would you look into it with the utmost urgency please.'

However, best not contact me at the airfield or on the phone. Please, pass your findings on a note to Doctor Pickle. I'll arrange collection from him.

Also, after speaking with SOE, to explain George's continued absence from school etc., it would be best that we use the cover story that George has an as yet undiagnosed fever, and until such time that we know there's no danger he will be quarantined. A military ambulance will turn up this afternoon and stage a mock removal.

Please ensure you burn this letter and discuss its content with no one; this may seem alarmist but we have a suspicion of there being a Nazi spy in the area.

Sincerely,

[Group Captain] Victor Hawkshaw.

Rachel went straight up to George's bedroom. From previous messages she knew that Urchin was George; Eagle meant travel and Tree meant that he'd escaped the Nazis, or was still out of their grasp. After looking over the table she quickly found the mussel shell which stood on a piece of paper with an arrow pointing to an S.

'An arrow, pointing to an S,' she pondered as she paced up and down George's bedroom, whilst tapping her chin. She looked again at the piece of paper, as she did so there was a crunch under foot. 'How many times do I have to tell him to tidy…' her rage tailed off as she looked at the broken object. 'A compass!' She looked from the compass to the paper and then back again. Instantly she flew down the stairs and scribbled on a piece of paper which she placed in an envelope and thrust into her pocket. She ran out of the door and jumped on her bicycle and pedaled towards the village, as fast as she could.

On nearing the village Rachel reduced her speed to a less urgent composure. As she passed along the main road many of the people called greetings, which she returned. She passed by The Block and the Scaff and past the Brigadier's house. As she rounded the bend past the school, the playground deserted and silent, at one end Mr Batt sat in his office; his eyes, she thought, focussed on his desk. In one sharp movement he looked out of the window; his cold black eyes looking straight at hers — she instantly felt them piercing through to the back of her skull. She looked away and shuddered with the icy chill which he instilled.

She propped her bike against the fence outside the doctor's large red brick Georgian house, its frontage covered in ivy. A large weeping willow dominated the front lawn between the white picket fence and gravel drive, which ran along the front of the house. The doctor's surgery was a small building in the front garden.

She entered the surgery and found the small waiting room unusually empty. Closing the door behind her, she stood for a moment looking round the clinical white-painted walls listening for

George and the Reich

a sign of life. From the far door she heard the mumble of a man's voice. Rachel move toward the small coffee table and selected one of the old magazines to pass the time while she waited, before sitting on one of the half dozen eclectic chairs spaced round this side of the room. Distractedly, she leafed through the magazine, whilst exhaling impatiently and constantly checking the door to the consulting room for sign of movement. She looked back at the magazine. 'Oh my! The Titanic sunk! I must have missed that!' She permitted herself a brief chuckle at her joke. After which, she threw the magazine back onto the small table, crossed her legs and folded her arms; her foot automatically began tapping rapidly on the floor. Still the door didn't open. After what seemed like hours, but in fact was no more than a couple of minutes, there was a loud click from behind the door and then a louder scraping sound which Rachel presumed was the doctor pushing back his chair to stand up.

As she moved towards the door, it opened and out walked the doctor. 'Rachel!' he said looking up from the paper he was carrying with a start. He gazed at her over the top of his half-moon reading glasses. 'Is everything OK? Well, as much as can be expected?' he asked qualifying his enquiry.

'Good Morning, doctor. Yes, as you say, as much as can be expected,' she replied.

'I understand that all correspondence from you is now to pass through me to Victor; Smithy dropped me a note earlier.'

'Yes absolutely,' she replied, 'I have the first note here, if you would pass it on, please?' she said handing the note over.

'Of course. Incidentally I'll be arriving with the ambulance this afternoon to *take* George away,' he said tapping the side of his nose 'So if there are any onlookers it will explain why you don't get in the ambulance. The story is, if asked, that he is going to the small medical facility at the air base because that's been identified as the safest place to quarantine him for now.'

'OK doctor, I understand.' With that Rachel thanked the doctor and left the surgery.

She adopted a more leisurely pace as she pedaled the bike home, stopping at the baker for fresh bread. When she arrived home Rachel went to the kitchen and made a pot of tea and some bread and jam with the intention of sitting outside for an hour and enjoying the afternoon sun, which was quite warm for early autumn. As she carried the laden tray towards the French windows, the phone rang. Thinking nothing of it, she put the tray down and casually answered it. 'Hello!' Instantly she winced and shuddered, as if someone had slowly and deliberately walked over her grave.

'Oh! Good afternoon Mr Batt,' she replied, 'what can I do for you?'

'Since George has been absent from school for some days now, will he be returning to school tomorrow?' he enquired in his usual cryptic, cold, slimy tone.

'I believe that Doctor Pickle will be providing you with an official update shortly. But all I can tell you is that George has a fever which is, as yet, undiagnosed; he is due to be collected this afternoon by military ambulance to go into quarantine until they are certain of what he has.' Rachel cringed, hoping she was being plausible.

'I see!' replied Mr Batt. 'Military you say! Why not a civilian ambulance?' His probing question of ice-cold steel, sliced through Rachel, making the hairs on the back of her neck prickle.

'Not that it is any business of yours,' she chastised impatiently. 'But, the doctor asked Victor if part of their medical facility at the airbase might be used as an isolation unit.'

'My apologies Mrs Scott; I wasn't meaning to pry,' he sycophantically hissed with a forked tongue. 'I would, of course, be extremely grateful if you would update me when a diagnosis is reached, please.'

'Of course, Mr Batt. Goodbye!' replacing the receiver as soon as she'd finished, so as not to give him the chance to slither through any more comments. She immediately shook her head and ruffled her hair scratching her scalp to get rid of the imaginary nits which had gathered during the conversation. She took a deep breath, gathered her thoughts, picked up the tray and continued to the garden.

Later the khaki-green ambulance arrived accompanied by Doctor Pickle. The doctor entered the house followed by the two RAF personnel carrying a stretcher. 'Right!' he said to Rachel once inside, 'Victor wants us to make a show of this in case there are any observers; casual or sinister. Do you have a couple of pillows we can put under the stretcher blanket and something to simulate George's head and brown hair; any ideas?'

Rachel looked blankly at the doctor for a moment and then in different directions around the room, shaking her head as if dismissing that location and moving to the next. Then her faced relaxed and simultaneously she made eye contact with the doctor, clicking her fingers in the air next to her face and then pointed her index finger upwards as if to say 'got it'. She ran off up the stairs and soon came back down with a football and a brown fur hat. 'Will that do?' she asked.

'Perfect, Rachel,' the doctor replied, 'But, do you have an old stocking to cover the ball to give it a more skin like appearance?'

'They're rare commodities now doctor you know. I'll have a quick look, I'm sure I have,' as she ran off again, returning rapidly with the required item. 'Excellent! Right chaps let's put this together,' he said, handing one of the airmen the stocking-covered ball and the hat; whilst the other had already placed a blanket over the pillows on the stretcher. With the effigy complete, they all stood back and admired their handiwork. 'Well, up close it doesn't really stand up to inspection, but from a distance I think it might just work,' the doctor assessed.

'I think you may be right there, sir,' agreed the airman tucking the blanket around the ball.

'Right, let's give it a go. Rachel you come out with us. You need to act like you're crying and keep hold of the side of the stretcher until it's in the ambulance. Remember that's your son on there and he's gravely ill.'

'I can manage that easily doctor, I've had plenty of practice over the last week or so,' Rachel commented with a wry smile.

'OK, oh before I forget I have this from Victor.' Doctor Pickle handed her a folded piece of paper. It read: 'Have confirmation from SOE. George heading south by barge and will rendezvous with resistance near Dijon. No further info. Will update when further communication received. Please destroy this note. Victor'.

She screwed the piece of paper up and threw it in the fire; breaking into floods of tears she grabbed her handkerchief in a vain attempt to stem the flow. 'Quick!' she grizzled between the sobs, 'These are real tears; let's put them to good use.' With that the airmen picked up the stretcher and led by the doctor proceeded outside toward the door; alongside Rachel sobbed, her eyes fixed on the ball at the head of the stretcher.

When they were halfway along the garden path the doctor heard, 'Pssst doctor!' in a whisper from the airman immediately behind him. 'Pssst doctor, don't look round but there's a glint and a little movement in the bushes over the road in that field about 11 o'clock.'

'Where?' the doctor whispered, surveying the scene in front as subtly as he could.

'Clump of bushes, hundred yards at 11 o'clock,' the airman replied without breaking his stride.

The doctor studied the area in question and then saw a glint. 'Got it!' he said in triumph. 'Good job we staged this masquerade, we're definitely being observed. Question is by whom? And why?'

he thought to himself 'One thing is certain there is a spy in our midst; better let Victor know,' his thoughts concluded.

All the time Rachel maintained the pretence, whilst feeling the refreshed pain of knowing her son was travelling deeper into occupied France. When they reached the ambulance, Doctor Pickle turned to Rachel as if to offer some comfort, but whilst he was looking at Rachel he spoke to the airmen. 'Once we've got this stretcher inside, do you have a set of binoculars and somewhere concealed to use them, please?'

'Of course, sir. We'll get you inside and make some kind of pantomime of the engine not starting; give you chance to check out our friend in the field.'

Once they were in, Rachel stood at the back as if still talking to George. The airmen tried to start the ambulance; the engine turned over but it wouldn't fire. They lifted the bonnet and began making a show of rummaging around. The doctor carefully observed the field with the binoculars from his clandestine position in the ambulance. He could see that something or someone was in the bushes, every now and then there was a flash, which the doctor believed to be the lenses of binoculars or a telescope, but there was no more he could make out. He banged on the ceiling of the ambulance three times. With that one of the airmen jumped into the driver's seat, turned the key and the engine growled into life.

'Have you spotted anything sir?' the airman enquired.

'Yes, there's definitely someone there. But we're going to have to let him go. If we chase after him now, he'll get away and he'll know something's up because we wouldn't leave a casualty unattended whilst in our care.'

After fastening the bonnet and the rear doors the second airman climbed into the passenger seat. 'Right! We'd best go straight to the airfield,' the doctor ordered.

The driver ground it into first gear and, slowly, the old green ambulance gathered speed.

Some forty-five minutes later when the ambulance had lurched, bumped, rocked and ground its way through the Kent countryside, they arrived at the gatehouse to the airfield. The guards gave a cursory nod to the driver and lifted the barrier. The airfield was just that, a field which had been hastily converted to its present purpose at the beginning of the war. Some old farm buildings had been converted to various uses: barracks and officer's quarters, canteen, a small medical facility and offices; one of the buildings had a second story built on to provide a small control tower. Added to these were some relatively newly-built aircraft hangars and maintenance workshops.

The ambulance pulled up to the medical building where Group Captain Hawkshaw was waiting. The airmen ran to the back to retrieve the stretcher and release the doctor from his torment in the rear of the ambulance.

'Did it all go to plan?' Victor asked as the airmen took the stretcher in to the medical facility.

'Pardon?' responded Doctor Pickle, wiggling his index finger in his ear. 'Damn thing's left me with a bad case of tinnitus and I'm black and blue. Did they forget to fit springs to it?'

This made Victor roar with laughter. They entered the facility behind the airmen carrying the stretcher.

The medical facility was no more than a glorified sickbay with drab décor; it could only be described as functional at best. To the left of the entrance was a small desk, presumably for the duty nurse or medical attendant, the doctor thought. Behind the old desk, a single forlorn-looking sick-note of a grey-green filing cabinet stood sentry. To the right, on the other, longer side of this thin room, stood two unoccupied skeletal metal-framed beds, punctuated only by two small cabinets, all of which stood on the same insipid faded beige linoleum and the walls painted all round in the same dull blue-grey. The only joy given leave to enter was the daylight spilling in through the four large windows. The airmen followed Victor, who disappeared through a door to a much smaller room in the rear which, once the light had been switched on, the doctor could see had suffered a similar decorative travesty to the first, the curtains in this room had been firmly drawn. 'Can't be too careful!' Victor exclaimed gesturing toward the curtains.

'Indeed,' agreed the doctor, 'I'm damn, sure we were being observed earlier. Too far to get a look at, even with binoculars, but there was someone there for sure.'

'Did he get wind you were aware of his presence?' Victor quizzed.

'No, I'm pretty sure he didn't have a clue.'

'OK. Good. Let's hope they've swallowed the charade then, whoever it was.'

Gallic Morning Mist

George awoke to the sound of his cabin door opening. He looked up trying to focus, although still bleary-eyed he could see the outline of a figure in the early twilight. He blinked a few times and focussed on Gérard holding out a cup of coffee. 'Here you go. This should help keep you awake,' he said.

George took a large sip of the coffee, remembering as he swallowed that he severely disliked the stuff; however he persevered in the interests of both politeness and staying awake until the evening. He looked around and realised it was dark. 'What time is it?' George asked.

'It's 3 AM. I thought you should be awake in plenty of time,' Gérard replied.

'Are we at the wharf?' George asked.

'Yes, we docked two hours ago,' Gérard replied 'When the wharf workers arrive we'll load you into your crate. You'll be unloaded with several other crates; the lorry will collect you and three other crates marked: 'China'' He emphasised the word and one corner of his mouth stretched into a lop-sided mischievous smile. George looked curiously at this for a while and then dismissed it as he forced down the last of his coffee and then handed the cup back to Gérard. 'You should get ready,' Gérard said over his shoulder as he was leaving the cabin, 'you'll need to get into that crate at a moment's notice.'

'OK,' George replied, getting sluggishly to his feet with a wide hippopotamus yawn and a stretch.

George washed his face and the sleep from his eyes and got dressed in some warm clothes. Still he shivered a little with the cold, or it could be nerves. He was not looking forward to several hours in a crate, blind to the world. He gathered what few things he had and placed them back in his bag and tried not to think of the forthcoming ordeal. He sat down to breakfast with Gérard at the table in the back of the wheelhouse. It was a simple affair; more tar-like coffee, bread, cheese and ham. Although ordinarily George would have devoured such offerings, today was different — his apprehension was getting the better of him.

Just then the sound of a vehicle came into earshot and got steadily louder. 'You best get below,' Gérard said, 'that'll be the wharf workers coming to start work and they'll want the covers off the hold soon.'

'How can you tell it's them and not a German patrol or any-one else for that matter?'

'That's easy,' Gérard said wiping his mouth with his hand. 'Listen! It's not as fine-tuned and new-sounding as anything the Germans have. In fact it's quite the opposite; it sounds old, tired and it rattles. Come, we'd better get you out of sight. They know nothing of this and believe me, the fewer who know the better; even if they are on the same side.'

George silently conceded by getting to his feet and taking a final swig of the thick coffee, followed by a contorted grimace.

George grabbed his bag from the cabin and walked through to the hold. Climbing into the crate, he sat down with his bag tucked behind his legs, to restrict its movement as much as possible. George looked up at Gérard just as the car seemed to hiccup, belch and fart its way in to the wharf and reach a crescendo of screeching brakes and grinding as it finally stopped and instantly doors were crashed shut. With the car now silenced the only sound was the sound of work boots on the damp gravel. As they seemed to stand still there was a loud shrill whistle. 'Hey! Gérard! Wakey, wakey! This hatch won't open itself, you know!' yelled the evident purveyor of the whistle and owner of one pair of boots. Gérard winked at George, '*Bonne chance!*' he said placing the lid on the crate.

'Thank you,' came a muffled reply from the box. George fastened the inside latches and then tested the lid was fast with a couple of firm upward shoves; it didn't move at all. He signalled his readiness by two firm knocks on the lid. Gérard responded likewise then turned and walked back toward the steps up to the wheelhouse.

Inside the box it was pitch black, George couldn't see his hand in front of his face, although he tried. It was also snug to the point of being cramped. His back was against one wall and his knees the opposite one, with his bag taking up the spare floor space. Shoulder to shoulder it was a little wider than he was and in this seated position it felt like his head had less than two inches clearance from the lid.

Above there was a loud deep grinding sound of the hatches being dragged open. He could hear voices conversing above him, the content of which was stifled by his temporary containment. Slowly, the cold early morning chill was making its introduction to George; he gave a little shiver as he drew in a chilly damp breath. Through the small vents in the box George could hear a slow metallic grinding that was gathering pace. As the grinding seem to reach a crescendo the there was a loud cough and a bang which repeated several times, then the bangs became more frequent as whatever the stevedores outside were playing with seemed to leap into life and began to breathe on its own. The fresh chilled grassy smell of the morning dew was joined and overtaken by the sooty stench of crudely-burned diesel.

Very soon he heard the glassy sound of chains hitting the deck of the hold near his crate. Evidently, by the metallic scraping sound the chains were being man-handled and attached to something. It wasn't George's crate although from his limited sight he couldn't make out what. Then the speed of the engine outside increased and he heard the chain being gathered up. 'Ah! It's a crane,' he thought. Very soon the chains hit the floor again, this time he could feel it was his turn, as the chains were being attached. The engine speed once again increased and the chains took the strain. As the crate left the deck it listed slightly to one side lightly bumping the floor and then swung gently. George grappled for the canvas straps to hold himself steady, pushing forward with his feet and his back against the wall to brace himself and feeling more than a little nervous as the crate swung gently in the air. Hoping, as he was lowered to the dockside, that the noisy crane had a little more work to do; at present silence would surely give him away due to his heavy breathing. He needed just a few minutes to compose himself.

The chains were removed and the crane's old engine revved again. George could hear the loose chains drag briefly along the wharf side before being lifted once again. The process was repeated half a dozen or so more times before the crane fell silent. At this time George relied heavily on his ears to help him see what was going on, as the noise of the crane had rendered him, temporarily, blind. Now the luxury of relative silence had been restored to him, George began to build a picture of his surroundings and the goings-on. He was aware of the first glimmers of early light and that the wharf side sounded deserted: no footsteps or chatter. Now his adrenaline levels were dropping he could feel the chilly bite of the early morning air nibbling at his nose, ears and finger tips. George folded his arms with his hands firmly placed in his arm-pits for warmth. The frosty air seeped under his jumper and he began to shiver. Keeping his jaw clenched tight George successfully prevented his teeth from chattering, at least for the time being.

All of George's senses, especially his hearing, were in a heightened state of alert. The early morning was eerily quiet. The silence was broken, suddenly, by the bark of a German voice. There shortly after followed the sound of what George deduced were two pairs of feet: one was loud sharp and deliberate, a sound he had come to recognise as jack boots; the other was a stooped-sounding subservient trudge. He knew from this that a German soldier and one of the dockers were coming to inspect the newly

George and the Reich

unloaded cargo. As they approached, he heard the rustling of paper and a French voice explaining the content of the crates. They seemed to walk round the crates and after a short while walked away. George realised as he breathed out, heavily, that he had been holding his breath.

Slivers of light broke through the darkness of the crate as daylight reclaimed its realm; the mist of his breath in the cold air traced the beams of light. Although there was no longer any human noise, the birds and wildlife were making a racket as they woke. After what seemed to George like hours, but was in reality only about twenty minutes, a truck pulled on to the wharf side and stopped with a squeal of brakes some distance from George's location; a door slammed. George could hear a voice in the distance directing the truck driver towards the crates. The truck pulled up closer to the crates; George heard voices, including one German, closer to him, with another rustling of paper; after which a sheet was ripped and then a pair of boots turned and walked away rapidly. This was evidently German boots, because once out of earshot a French voice grimaced 'Les boches!' and then spat. This was followed by chuckles. Although George couldn't see for certain he ascertained that there were three or four Frenchmen outside. George's crate was then loaded on to the truck with the three others. George was thrown around in his crate as the truck bounced out of the wharf and on to the road, which felt like it was long overdue for resurfacing.

After around half an hour, the truck stopped. There was a metallic screech, a wooden crash and then dark and quiet again. George heard the men get out of the truck and talk to each other quietly. His heart was in his mouth; where was he? From inside his crate he managed to overhear parts of the whispered conversation. From what he pieced together, one man was going to stay with the truck while the other two did a sweep outside to ensure they weren't followed and they have no unwelcome guests lurking.

Five minutes later the two-man patrol returned and declared that the coast was clear. One of the men banged the side of the truck twice, and then said, in a loud voice, 'Luc! You can come out now it's safe.'

With all his wits assembled George slowly unfastened the catches and gradually lifted the lid. He paused when the lid was opened a crack and surveyed what he could see, the majority of which was other crates, the cab of the truck and not much more in the darkness. He stood up and put the lid to the side of the crate. Clambering out he turned and delved inside the crate to grab his bag; slinging it over one shoulder, he made his way to the back of the truck and jumped down. As his eyes once again adjusted to the darkness he could see that he was inside a fairly dishevelled barn.

George and the Reich

'*Sacré bleu!*' one of the men exclaimed, as they clapped eyes on George for the first time.

'There has been some mistake, I think,' said another, 'You are but a boy. We were told this was a strange mission, but not exactly how strange,' he chuckled.

In his best French George replied, 'It is true, I am a boy, but trapped inside this boy's body I have the heart of a man and an Englishman at that,' as he finished paraphrasing Queen Elizabeth I.

'Your heart is of no concern!' said the third man, 'It is your stomach that is paramount. Do you have the stomach for what comes next, and the nerve to hold your own?'

George paused at the back of the truck. Slowly he looked from one man to the next, calmly hiding the fact that he was quite unnerved by the situation. 'Well, I've made it all the way here from England, through occupied France right under the noses of the Germans; I even gave one the slip that was trying to take me to Germany; whilst pinching his money. So I think I can hold my nerve. So what's the plan?'

The men appeared to accept the explanation and one of them replied, 'We were told to collect the crates, one of which was containing you, and bring you here; we are to await further instructions from SOE.'

Several hours passed while they waited; the three men took it in turns to keep watch. The afternoon was fast slipping towards evening; George could see, through the crack in the old barn's wooden walls, that the light was fading.

Then, after what seemed to George like an eternity, the man keeping watch said, 'Someone's coming!' The other two jumped up and produced hand-guns as if by magic, and blew out the three candles which had been lit only moments earlier and provided a mere famine of light. George moved to a position along the side of the truck to provide cover between him and the barn doors. Systematically he scanned for an alternative means of escape, should those approaching be foe. Almost immediately a small motorbike was audible becoming rapidly louder. George instantly relaxed and sat down again. He knew the sound of the motorbikes the Germans used; this one had a much smaller engine and higher tone. As the motor bike came into the sight of the man on watch, he slung his rifle over his shoulder and signalled to the others to stand down. 'It's OK! It's them,' he said, opening the barn door enough to let the bike in. It was a very slight-looking motorbike with a side-car that didn't look powerful enough to carry one man let alone the pillion passenger and the man in the side car.

The barn door was closed, after the guard had looked up and down the road and across the fields and then up and down the road again. The newcomers got off the bike and removed their goggles; the candles were relit.

'Good to see you made it OK George, or is it Luc?' said the man who had ridden in the side car.

'Monsieur Dulac!' George exclaimed, 'I didn't expect to see you.'

'No, I wasn't going to come, but there is something I need you to report back in England; I couldn't risk transmitting it in case the codes were broken.'

'What is it?'

'Well, I suppose you're in this up to your neck now anyway,' Dulac said with the hint of a chuckle and ruffling George's hair. 'We have information to indicate that there is a German spy operating in coastal Kent. So when you get back, you'll need to pass this intel on to Victor, he'll know where to send it and keep your eyes and ears open and your mouth closed; there are too many lives at stake. Understood? What we are trying to achieve is getting someone into Gestapo HQ to verify and identify this person; as you can appreciate, that's easier said than done and is not a job for the faint-hearted.'

'Absolutely, Monsieur!' George replied.

'OK, right to the matter at hand,' Dulac began again, this time in French. 'The plan is that George, or Luc as we should call him, will be smuggled into the prison camp tomorrow late afternoon in Monsieur Forgeron's truck during his regular grocery delivery; we'll give you the details on that a little later Luc, OK?'

George said nothing, he just nodded, his face fixed in concentration and disbelief: he'd almost made it to his Dad!

Monsieur Dulac continued, 'OK, the rest of you have your instructions and will meet at the rendezvous tomorrow at 20:00hrs.' Then, turning back to face George he continued, 'You will stay here for the night, there is a small hideout below the floor of the barn — it used to be used by smugglers and poachers; you'll be comfortable enough.' One of the men reached down and lifted a trap door which, until then had been covered in a thick layer of dusty dirt and straw.

'Monsieur Forgeron will collect you from here at around six.'

Most of the men then dispersed in different directions out of the barn door, leaving only Messieurs Dulac and Forgeron. 'There is a compartment in one of the fuel tanks big enough to fit you in. When Monsieur Forgeron gives you the signal, which is two firm kicks to the tank you'll be in, you carefully climb out and crawl to the back of the truck and under the building which the lorry will have reversed up against; this is the kitchen. You will hide under there until it is fully dark, which will be a matter of ten minutes. The kitchen is surrounded by various huts and buildings. Your father and other British airmen are housed in the row of six huts running along the south side of the kitchen; the truck will be on the north side.' Dulac drew a diagram in the dust on the barn floor; pointing he said, 'Neither your father or any of the airmen inside are aware of your imminent arrival; we've kept it quiet to avoid any potential "leakage" so you will need to manage their surprise. Your father is in the second one, here. OK?'

'Yep, got it,' George replied.

'Right the next bit is trickier,' Dulac began again. 'We, obviously, can't leave you in there and you won't be able to get out without a careful escape plan. So, once you are in there, it is your job to prepare all the airmen for escape at 1 AM. You need to instruct the men that once they're out, they must split up in different directions; if they stick together they'll be easily captured or worse. At 12.30 AM you will make your way to the watch tower on the perimeter, here,' he said pointing to the edge of the dirt diagram. 'Now, this is the dicey bit. By the time you are at the watch tower one of our chaps will be at the perimeter fence; take what he hands you and then climb as high as you dare up the tower and attach it.

Once you are down and back in the hut, go to the window nearest the perimeter and using your torch signal the letter A; got it? Dot dash.'

'OK, got it! One question though: what will be the signal to start the breakout?'

'Oh!' Monsieur du Lac chuckled, 'you'll know when, believe me! After you are out and across to the road here,' Dulac continued indicating again on the dirt map, 'you'll need to head off towards a small wooded hill in this direction which, if you have a compass, is north east. This hill should assist to conceal your silhouettes across these fields; it is about three kilometres with several hedges for cover. At the foot of the hill there is a gate to the road in which will be parked a farmer's truck taking produce to market. This farmer, like Monsieur Forgeron, is used to carrying items that he doesn't wish to be discovered.' They all chuckled whilst Monsieur Forgeron made an exaggerated face of innocence. 'He is one of the few who have a permit to be on the road at that time of night and is well known to the Germans. Once you have met the farmer you must ask him if he has any limes, to which he will answer no; then you must say, 'Would you like two more,' after which he will show you where to conceal yourself. You must be there at 2 AM at the latest or he will leave without you. At around 7 AM he will stop and let you out. You must then make your way up the track where you've stopped. This will lead you to a farm, which is one of our safe "houses". On the right there are three barns, you need to enter the middle one which is full of hay and climb the ladder to the enclosed loft. The farmer's wife will leave you a food basket. You will lie low there for the day; you won't be staying longer. We have to anticipate that the Germans will, by then, be extending the search, but should have their hands full with the mayhem caused by the escape. Within twenty-four hours of arriving there the RAF will pick you up, you will receive instructions at the time; OK any questions?

'No questions thank you Monsieur, but I do have one favour to ask please,' George replied.

'If I can I will.'

'After Dad and I are clear, would you transmit the following message to SOE please? Oak leaf — eagle — cork.

'These are strange George but, we are taught to ask no questions, no problem I'll see to it.'

Handing George a small case Dulac said, 'Right, as soon as we've got this trap door covered we'll be off. We'll cover it with some of the bales of straw to better conceal it, so don't worry that you can't open it from below. In the case is enough food, water and candles to last until tomorrow evening,' Dulac said pointing to the trap door '…you'll find a raised bed and blankets. Right we'll see you tomorrow; *Bonne chance*, Luc!'

'You too!' George replied, descending down the ladder into the dugout.

Before the trapdoor crashed back into place, George had lit one of the candles, so he wasn't left fumbling in the dark. There was a great deal of scraping and thudding above his head as all traces of the trapdoor were hidden. Holding the candle up, as the dust falling between the cracks above began to settle, he examined the surroundings that would constitute his lodgings for the next twenty-four hours or so. The ceiling was fairly low, so much so that he had to stoop slightly; a grown adult would have to positively crouch, he thought. Whilst there was a dirt floor, the walls and ceiling were roughly boarded. George presumed the floor had been left bare to reduce sound. In the corner was a bucket with an old newspaper next to it, '*En-suite* as well, ' George chuckled to himself. The only other features were the bed and a small upturned crate to act as a table, on which George placed the case and candle, before testing the bed which to his surprise had a thin mattress on top of the boarding so providing a little in the way of creature comfort.

Since there was little else to do, George carefully set the candle on the crate and lay on the bed. For the first time in what seemed like weeks he was lying down in relative safety and comfort; pulling the blankets around him he was soon sound asleep. He woke several hours later to find the candle burned to a stump; he lit a new candle from the last of the first one and set it firmly in the warm wax on the crate. The crackle of the new candle broke the eerie silence. Nothing moved. George could hear no sounds and although he listened carefully, there was no movement outside; not even a rat stirred in the barn above or the pit below. George pulled the covers back over his shoulder and turned on his side watching the flickering shadows created by the candle light and very soon he was asleep again.

The objective

George was down to his last candle, as evening approached; when he heard the muffled sound of a vehicle stop outside the barn with abrupt metallic crunch as the handbrake was roughly applied. The barn doors groaned open briefly and then closed with a crash. George was, by now, sitting up and listening intently to the noises that had broken the eternal silence. As a precaution he blew out the candle. From the activity above him, he could tell that whoever this was, was not just randomly searching the barn, they knew what to do. 'It must be Monsieur Forgeron,' he thought, and relaxed again while the movement and scraping continued above him. He reclined back on the improvised bed while dust descended all around him. Finally, the trap door opened, George looked up. As the dust cleared he saw the beaming smile of Monsieur Forgeron. George grabbed his things and, covered in dust, climbed out of the pit.

'I hope your stay wasn't too uncomfortable,' Monsieur Forgeron greeted him.

'No, Monsieur Forgeron, your hospitality was exemplary,' George replied holding out his hand in gratitude, which Monsieur Forgeron naturally grasped.

'Ooh, by the way,' George continued, 'you might want to provide your next guest with some paper by the bucket.'

Monsieur Forgeron instantly examined the hand with which he had only moments ago shaken George's, and then looked sharply at George who was already in raptures of laughter. Monsieur Forgeron instantly got the joke and slapping George on the back likewise guffawed at the humour with a laugh generated deep within his ample stomach.

'*Allez!*' Monsieur Forgeron ordered once he had re-composed himself. 'We must go; the Germans are strict about delivery times.'

At the barn door Monsieur Forgeron signalled silently for George to remain just inside. He scanned the surrounding fields and the road for movement. Having satisfied himself that the coast was clear he beckoned George out towards the truck. 'For safety's sake we'll put you straight in the fuel tank compartment,' he cautioned. 'If you crawl under the truck, look above and behind you there's a catch which opens the hatch.'

George, who was already under the rather rusty chassis of the truck, said, 'Yep, I can see it,' as he released the catch and the hatch swung open.

'But mind your head,' Monsieur Forgeron completed his sentence, realising it was too late as the resonating sound of corroded steel struck cranium. And George yelped, '*Ouch!*' He half crawled out from under the truck and stared crossly up at Monsieur Forgeron clutching his now tender head and displaying a rust-encrusted lump which had already started to form.

'Are you OK?'

'I'll be fine,' George replied with gritted teeth as he crawled back under the truck and into the fuel tank.

The journey to the camp took about half an hour, during which George was thrown around in the small filthy compartment as the truck rattled and crunched its way over every lump and into every pothole in the road. It felt like he'd managed to collect bruises over 90% of his body. Although he had no way of ascertaining his location from his concealed position, he knew they were close; the road was smoother and the truck was slowing. It ground to a halt with a screech followed by the loud clatter of the handbrake ratchet as it was brutally applied. George froze in his rusty sarcophagus and tempered his breathing to ensure silence. He listened intently to the muffled conversation between the guard and Monsieur Forgeron. Monsieur Forgeron was evidently applying copious amounts of sycophancy and jovial humour to hide his intense dislike for the Germans and the fact that he was carrying live contraband. He likened his resonant expressive French lilt to that of a tuba in an orchestra whilst the voice of the German guard grated on his nerves like the excessive use of a football rattle. The pleasantries evidently having been completed, the truck lunged back in to action. He felt a corner and then it stopped again. Next to his head he heard, and felt, the gearbox vehemently protest as it was forced with a cog-crunching grind into reverse. The truck kangarooed backward towards, George assumed, the loading bay; it stopped and this time the engine was turned off. It was finally quiet but George's ears were still ringing and his body was aching from the bumpy ordeal.

Now on high alert he waited for the signal to disembark. More conversation ensued, some of which was above him along with heavy footsteps and scraping as Monsieur Forgeron unloaded his produce. Monsieur Forgeron said his farewells and closed the truck doors. George then heard heavy footsteps on the gravel and he knew this was Monsieur Forgeron; there was nothing light about him at all. Suddenly the signal came, 'Thunk! Thunk!' George rolled out of the tank with the mastery of a commando.

He blinked a little in the light and looked around. He saw the face of Monsieur Forgeron who had feigned tying his shoe laces. He winked at him and then stood up. George lost no time — as quietly as he could, he crawled to the end of the truck and under the kitchen hut. He saw the truck pull away in a cloud of dust and thick exhaust. He was on his own, again. 'This is going to have to stop,' he chuckled quietly. Now he had to wait until dark. 'This shouldn't be long,' he thought. It was now six o'clock and the late summer daylight was beginning to fade.

Lying on his front in the dusty soil under the centre of the kitchen hut, behind one of its many large concrete supports which, coupled with the service pipes on his other side, concealed his presence well. George surveyed his surroundings. From what he could see from his rat's eye vantage point, Monsieur Dulac's description of the layout was quite accurate. As the light faded, the guards settled in to a routine patrol which George studied as he began to plan his next move. Under cover of twilight he moved to a position behind one of the supports at the edge of the hut. He spat in his hand and mixed in a fist full of dust, he wiped the muddy paste over his face to assist with his camouflage. George checked his bag was properly buckled up. He held it tight as he prepared to make his move. He could hear the murmur and laughter of many light conversations and the jangling sound of eating coming from a hut behind him. The main garrison must have been at supper now. He surveyed again. Night was falling rapidly. He knew from observation that the guards were now approaching their furthest distance from him before they commenced their return. They had their backs to him. He looked again with his head now fully exposed. There were no torches or search lights on, the dusty alley between the kitchen hut and the hut where his Dad was held was no more than five yards and dimly lit with a row of six or seven dark huts stretching along either side of the alley to his right. To his left there were no buildings for a good twenty yards, although there were a further four huts on the far side next to what he believed was his Dad's hut. He took a deep breath and crawled out from his cover. He remained crouched; looked left and right then straight ahead. Quietly in a crouched run he made it to the other side and crouched down on his knees again. He took another look all around and then disappeared under the new hut. The guards were now making their way back towards him intermittently shining torches in what seemed to be random places. He waited for them to converge and pass then crawled right under the hut to the left side. Again he cautiously peered out. The next hut was only three yards away which provided excellent cover. The shutters on all the holding huts were closed which added further security against his detection. Satisfied it was as safe as it could be, he scrambled out from under the hut, dusted off a little and then up the step and tried the door; it wasn't yet locked. So he went in and closed it behind himself immediately. Instantly he lent his back against the door, dropped his shoulders and with his head tilted back breathed a sigh of relief.

The hut was sparsely furnished with several bunks dispersed around the three walls with windows. On the fourth, internal wall, which bisected the room from the left of the main door where George stood, there was a large pot-bellied stove in the middle; there were two small tables in the centre of the room with basic chairs around, most of which were occupied. As he re-composed himself it was then he realised that he was not alone and several pairs of eyes were firmly fixed on him in silent astonishment. One, whom George recognised as Flying Officer John 'Charlie' Chaplin, broke the silence. 'Scotty! You might want to get yourself in here!' he called through to another room, his eyes remaining firmly fixed on George.

'What is it?' came a voice from the next room which George hadn't heard for what seemed like years but was still as familiar as the smell of roast beef.

'You really need to see this!' he reiterated while the room remained motionless.

Scotty entered the room 'What is it Charlie?'

Having now used up all the words he could remember, given the state of shock, Charlie could do no more that point.

Scotty followed the direction indicated. When his eyes fell on the dusty apparition at the door his mouth fell open. For a second he was rooted to the spot. George broke the silence as he ran across the room forgetting the situation shouted '*Daaaaad!*' and then leapt at his father nearly knocking Scotty off his feet. They hugged tightly with tears streaming down their faces.

The moment was interrupted by a banging on the shuttered window bringing reality crashing back. 'What is going on?' came the voice on the other side.

'Nothing Fritz! Just a little high spirits that's all!' replied the nearest airman.

Charlie signalled to Scotty with a wave of his hand to conceal George quickly. George was bundled into the next room a split second before the door crashed open and two of the guards walked in scanning the room for irregularities. They proceeded to do a cursory search of the room and then to the room into which George and Scotty had disappeared moments before. This was a smaller room with two bunks, a table, chair and small cupboard with nothing in the way of decoration. Scotty was on a bunk with a book in his hand.

'Squadron Leader Scott!' barked the guard.

'Yes, sergeant, how may I be of service?' he replied without looking up from his book.

'As the senior British officer you are expected to be responsible for discipline and behaviour of the subordinate ranks; the behaviour we experienced some moments ago is unacceptable, do you understand?'

With a face like thunder he deliberately closed his book and, placing it on the bunk beside him, stood up and approached the guard. 'What I do understand, Sergeant, is that, by the terms of the 1929 Geneva convention, I am entitled to be spoken to on matters of discipline by an equal or senior officer; do you hold such a rank?'

'Of course not Squadron Leader but...' he was already sweating with nerves and unable to finish his sentence when Scotty yelled at him.

'Well then sergeant you will address me as military convention dictates and I expect to be saluted before that address. Any issues you have with my men or I should be reported to your senior officer who will then discuss those issues with me. I also expect to be addressed by a soldier who is presented correctly; that means top tunic button fastened, cap straight and polished boots, do I make myself clear, sergeant?

'*Jawohl!*' he yelled, getting his finger caught in his top button hole and dropping his weapon, as he tried to fasten his button, salute, stand to attention and straighten his cap simultaneously, by now in a complete panic and sweating profusely. With that, red-faced and puffing like a steam train, he picked up his weapon, turned and ran for the door. As the door closed with an indignant clatter the occupants of the hut broke out in uncontrollable laughter and applause.

Once the coast was clear a small section of the wood panels in Scotty's room, no larger than two and half foot square were lifted and removed to reveal a storage area for anything the Germans may consider contraband; this would include George who emerged covered in dust and cobwebs.

'Dad, you were awesome!' George exclaimed.

'Phew! It was a bit nerve racking!' Scotty replied, while wiping his brow and smiling.

'I'm used to that after the journey I've had,' shrugged George with a nonchalant air.

'I'll bet! But for God's sake Urchin what possessed you to do such a thing and, really, what did you think you'd achieve?'

'Do you really think I'd come all this way without a plan, hmmm?' George replied in a mock superior tone.

'OK then Mr Big Shot,' Scotty began with a big smile on his face, 'now you've got in here what's the plan?'

George spent the next hour going over the mass escape plan with his Dad and then the rest of the hut occupants. The plan was then relayed to the rest of the huts containing POW's and all watches were synchronised to George's. Once the excitement had died down and all were fully briefed, they all turned in to get what little sleep they could before being woken again at 12.15 AM.

Zero hour

Just after midnight George was woken from his unusually light sleep by the scant activity in the hut. A few, but not all, were already awake, whispering and preparing in dull, shaded candle-light. He'd already started bracing himself for what would be one of his diciest exploits in a recent long list, and who knew what else was to come. He was feeling more nervous than usual, he put this down to the fact that usually the situations were not of his making and he was in them before he had a chance to realise. This time he was to be the sole instigator and if anything went wrong he could be on his own facing the unfriendly end of many German rifles. He tried to override his nerves and focus his thoughts by repeating the plan over and over in his head. He did this in quiet meditation until it was nearly time to go. As he stood up and looked around the hut he realised that the whole hut was awake and quietly milling around, all were evidently trying to keep a lid on their nerves.

'OK Urchin, are you ready?' came the familiar voice of his father over his left shoulder.

'Yes, all ready!' he replied, turning in the direction of the voice with an apprehensive smile.

'Good luck Urchin, I'm very proud of you; it's a good job your mother's not fully aware of all the facts. If it all goes pear-shaped out there just get behind the nearest cover you can find, OK?' he cautioned.

'OK, Dad, will do.'

'George! Standby!' the lookout by the door alerted.

'OK, this is it!' his Dad said with a big hug before releasing him and gently pushing him in the direction of the door.

A section of floorboards had been removed for George to drop through under the hut. 'We did this so we could still move between huts after the goons locked the doors at night. Right we've rigged up a small piece of string so we can signal when the guards are in the ideal position for you to run to the perimeter fence. The signal is two firm tugs, OK?' the lookout instructed.

'OK!' George replied with a thumbs-up, before jumping through the makeshift trapdoor.

Once down, he laid as flat and still as possible firmly grasping the string. The night air was cold almost frosty and he covered his mouth with his gloved hand to prevent the tell-tale sign of steamy breath being emitted from under the hut. Luckily there was little in the way of moonlight, so although cold it was a very dark night. His ears and eyes were on full alert. Looking and listening for the least bit of movement in the dark midnight stillness, all his senses were now concentrated on his right hand clutching the signal string. His heart was beating hard and fast in anticipation of the order to go. There was a little noise coming from the onsite mess rooms, however he imagined that the evening's frivolity was now dying out. The only other discernible noise above the breeze rustling the nearby trees in the wood was that of the guard's boots as they trudged slowly away from the hut. 'Any minute now,' he thought. He looked all around him; it was particularly dark under the hut so much so that to each side and behind him he could make out nothing. In front, although he knew there was another hut, he could make out very little.

Then it came, two hard tugs. 'This is it, here we go again!' he said under his breath. He looked all around again, nothing. He crawled out from under the hut and stood up. Pressing his back against the rough wood cladding, looking left then right, he carefully side stepped to the end of the hut. Gingerly he peered round the corner to the left and then to the right behind the next door hut, then back left. 'The resistance planned this very carefully,' he thought. The watch tower, like the rest of the camp, was in darkness. It stood about six or seven yards diagonally from the opposite corner of the hut from George's current position. He looked up towards the top and could make out very little of the shape let alone any detail. He took comfort that the same should be true of the reciprocal view; this is if the searchlight remained off. Unfortunately, whilst the dead of night provided a great deal of camouflage, there was nothing in the way of sound cover. George knew he had to be careful to make no noise.

He looked towards the watch tower again, this time studying what little he could see of the base. Heeding his father's warning he tried to make out the wire which ran around the inside of the whole perimeter which, stood only one and a half feet tall: 'Just the right height to trip over and make a racket,' he thought. The watch tower was positioned between this 'trip' wire and the high perimeter fence. He knew he had to hold his nerve and step carefully to the watchtower suppressing the overwhelming desire to run for cover. Before he had any further conscious thoughts he found he'd already started to make the crossing. Carefully he made one deliberate step after another maintaining a slightly hunched posture; all the time he was looking left then right then up at the tower. He'd made it! He took a deep but quiet breath, realising he had not dared to breathe on his way across. He stepped over the barely visibly 'trip' wire and cautiously crouched under the watch tower with

George and the Reich

his back to the main perimeter fence, checking again for any movement or sound in either direction. 'OK! Now for the next bit,' he uttered barely audibly under his breath. He silently scrambled on all fours to the perimeter and maintained his crouched position, palms of his hands against the fence. He could see nothing beyond the vague crisscross of the fence wire. All his senses were on high alert but for what he was unsure. Just then something rough touched his hand; this made his nerves jolt. Quite how he managed to stifle the vocal accompaniment that would usually accompany such a start he didn't know; however, since this self-imposed ordeal had begun what seemed like a life time ago, his brain had been reprogrammed to deal silently with stress of this nature.

Moving his fingers, George tentatively touched the rough object. On closer inspection it felt like fairly heavy-duty rope. George grasped the rope and began pulling, so he had enough gathered to climb the tower with little resistance or chance of noise. The rope slid easily through the chain link, it was obviously being quietly fed through by the ghost from the other side. Feeling the coil of rope at his feet he assessed that he had enough to start the climb. Feeling for the end of the rope he tied it around his waist and was preparing to climb when he heard the unmistakably sound of jackboots getting closer. He immediately crouched in against one of the tower's main supports. It was a solitary guard. He stopped next to the watch tower, only a few feet from George. George could see from the silhouette that he was facing away from him and his gun was shouldered. The guard shone his torch under the huts in from of him and then continued to pan around to his right, getting closer to George's position. He continued round shining his torch high into the land beyond the fence 'Nichts, nichts!' he mumbled, passing his beam over George's head and missing him completely, after which he lit a cigarette and gave a heavily despondent sigh before moving on. George rested his head against the tower support momentarily, sighed with relief and then began his careful climb.

When he was as high as he dared go, given the fact that he had to get down again in the pitch black, he tied the rope securely at an intersection between the main support and a cross member to prevent any chance of it slipping. He slowly retraced his steps back down. On reaching the ground he checked all around and then carefully scurried across the gap between the perimeter and huts and back under the hut and in the trap door.

'How did it go Urchin?' his Dad asked. 'We couldn't see a thing; apart from when the guard used his torch but then we had to duck.'

'Piece of cake!' George replied nonchalantly.

'All ready?' Scotty asked of the amassed men. There was a general muffled response to the affirmative.

'Right George, send the signal!'

As George went toward the window, a queue formed by the trapdoor; silently, one by one, the men were descending under the hut ready for the off. There was a large hole in the shutter where a knot in the wood had fallen or been pushed out. George placed his torch against the hole. He glanced at his Dad who said nothing but nodded once. George took a deep breath and sent the signal. Silence!

'What's wrong? Have they not seen it? Shall I send it again?' George questioned his father in a panicked rant.

'Just wait!' was his Dad's only reply. George could tell from his father's expression that he, also, was on tenterhooks.

Then the sound of an engine broke the early morning quiet. 'Come on Urchin, time to go!' said Scotty as he pushed George toward the trap door; George grabbed his bag *en route*.

They scrambled under the hut to where the rest of the men were waiting. Over the sound of the engine, there was a splintering crack; somewhat akin to the sound of a tree being felled. This was followed by an almighty crash. 'What on earth was that?' George exclaimed.

'Your handiwork!' his Dad chuckled, 'Right let's go!'

As they emerged from under the hut, men from other huts on either side were doing the same; all were making for the huge breach in the fence left by the lookout tower which had seconds before crashed straight through it. There was a feeling of shocked silence as George and his father, in the crowd of men, clambered over the wreckage and through the breach in the fence to freedom. As they fanned out in different directions armed resistance men were running towards the camp. Then the camp klaxons began their strained throaty alarm call signalling that the honeymoon period of silence was over. This was quickly followed by gunfire from, in many cases, half asleep Germans in pyjamas and boots. The resistance happily returned fire causing the semi-slumbered Germans to run for cover. George and his dad ran the shortest distance to the trees at the edge of the road. In the darkness this thin line of trees and hedgerow formed a wall-like silhouette providing excellent cover to anything behind it. Climbing the gate, which was the only break in the arboreal wall, they proceed to follow the plan heading northeast across the road into the next field towards the wooded hill.

As they made their escape, the gunfire became less intense and they were on their own in the dull moonlight. The voices of the German soldiers faded into the distance. They kept up a steady trot towards the rendezvous, keeping a regular vigil behind them to ensure they were not being tailed. As they neared the wooded hill the pace slowed to a walk, both on full alert. In the dead of night the long grass which bordered the field made a regular percussive brushing sound against their legs as they progressed through it. They tentatively approached the gate. Across the road exactly as described, was the shadowy outline of the farmer's truck, evidently in fairly poor repair even in the darkness. Scotty climbed over first followed quickly by George. As they approached the truck, George one step behind his dad, the driver's door creaked open. A stout grey figure emerged, displaying no observable signs of urgency in the greyness. He clattered the door shut and approached with a slightly stooped ambling gait. Scotty took the lead, 'Do you have any limes?'

'Pardon?' replies the man sounding puzzled and scratching his head through his beret.

'Do you have any limes?' Scotty repeats.

'Oh! *Oui… Oui… Oui…* ' he says evidently trying to remember his line. 'Ah… *Oui!… Non!*' he finally replies.

'Would, you, like, two, more?' Scotty replied with second part of the code, with slight overarticulation.

'Oh! *Mais oui!*' the farmer replied grabbing Scotty by the shoulders and kissing him on both cheeks like a long-lost friend.

George thanked his lucky stars that he was subjected to no more than a ruffle of his hair by the farmer's shovel-like rough hand.

Then looking all around him in the gloom the farmer gestured the way to the truck's hidey hole '*Maintenant, allons vite!*' George then Scotty followed him into the back. In the back of the truck what little light had been available outside was repelled by the thick tarpaulin canopy. The farmer took out a match and lit a small oil lamp which cast a dim, eerie, orange light around the truck. The cargo was neatly stacked at the front in crates followed by rows of bulging sacks towards the back. The farmer moved four of the sacks and then bent down and lifted a well concealed small trap door in the bed of the truck. He gestured to George and Scotty to get in. The space was large enough for them both to lie down with little else in the way of creature comforts. After their entry, the trap door was unceremoniously clattered back in to place and the sacks dragged back to conceal it. During the five or so hours they were in the confined space they felt every bump and pothole that the truck went over and amassed a collection of bruises to prove it. The farmer had in his mercy permitted one 'comfort' break during the whole journey. As dawn was breaking the truck lumbered and

George and the Reich

clattered to a halt on a rough verge. They heard sounds of effort as the farmer clambered into the back of the truck and moved the sacks. He lifted the trap door and relied on it for support as he offered his hand to assist them up with a '*Vite! Vite!*', not wanting to hang around there any longer than was absolutely necessary. Once they were off the truck, the farmer wished them '*Bonne chance*' with a saluting wave as he restarted the truck and clattered away.

George and Scotty started up the dirt track as instructed. The last remnants of night had now receded. The sun was not yet out of bed and the air was still with a biting chill; a light mist stretching across the rough stony track from the fields either side. Straggly hedges bordered the track; giving the impression that interest in their maintenance had long since diminished. They walked as briskly as they could, given the unkempt rocky nature of the track, their joints still stiff from the uncomfortable journey and complaining with every movement. After two hundred yards or so the track opened out in to an equally dishevelled farm yard, littered with old farm implements. The three barns as George remembered from the description stood to their right and on the left stood a rather large farm house still displaying echoes of its once grand status.

'Dad, we need to head for the middle one,' George gestured toward the barn. They both looked nervously all around, in an attempt to ensure no one was following and then headed for the barn. As per his briefing the barn was stacked floor to ceiling with hay and straw. The large wooden doors to the barn looked like they hadn't moved for the best part of a century and stood wide open, one of which was flat against the outside wall. Just inside, to the right, was a tall ladder leading up to a small doorway. 'Right, up here!' George instructed.

'Yes Sir!' Scotty replied, standing to attention and saluting. As George passed him and started up the ladder, Scotty playfully cuffed the back of George's head.

In the hayloft there was plenty of hay to bed down and a large basket hanging from a rafter. The light was provided by a small window, on the farmyard side of the barn which was open and hanging on by one rusty hinge. George could just about peer out of it if he stood on tiptoe. Scotty took the basket down; on the top was a short note in English which said, 'Welcome, you will receive further instructions this evening.' Under the note was bread, cheese, ham, salami, wine and water. They demolished the contents of the basket, and relaxed in the hay; the excitement of the night behind them they were soon fast asleep.

George and the Reich

Back to the table

'Ahh! Good afternoon Mrs Scott.' Rachel shuddered and a cold chill ran down her spine. She didn't need to look to put a face to that unctuous, slimy voice over her right shoulder. 'Good afternoon, Mr Batt,' she replied in a polite yet cold form. She continued to browse the shelves in the village shop without making eye contact.

'Is there any change in George's condition? Is he likely to return to school soon?' Mr Batt pressed while studying for a reaction.

Rachel calmly turned around and looked him squarely in the eyes 'No! There is no change and the doctors are struggling with a diagnosis and therefore a prognosis is, as yet, unlikely; wouldn't you agree?' all of which was said through slightly gritted teeth while she longed to put the odious man in his place and walk away.

'Well, as headmaster of the school it is my job to provide a first-hand account to the board of education regarding all long-term absences; so I shall need to visit George personally to complete my report,' he smarmed with a smile like a spider approaching a juicy fly.

Rachel felt her jaw tense and her fists clench momentarily, then she once again composed herself. 'Mr Batt, if you won't accept my testimony as George's mother then perhaps the doctor will be able to provide the necessary authentication you require, I will ask him to provide this as a matter of urgency. However!' she continued, raising her voice with venom and pointing her index figure within half an inch of Mr Batt's nose, attracting the attention of others in the shop, 'I will *not* permit you to visit him, potentially upsetting him in his present condition; I hope I have made my position quite clear. Good day Mr Batt!' with that she turned and marched out of the shop, opening the door with such force that the bell rang violently.

On leaving the shop Rachel lost her composure and burst into floods of tears. She kept walking and didn't turn around, not wanting to give Mr Batt the satisfaction of knowing he'd got to her. She resolved to phone the doctor when she got home and recount her conversation with Mr Batt. And request that he fabricate a narrative of George's 'illness' to placate Mr Batt.

'Rachel! Rachel!' instantly Rachel was snapped out of her thoughts by a much friendlier voice from across the road.

George and the Reich

'Oh, Victor, hello!'

'My word, are you OK? What's happened?'

As Rachel told Victor of her encounter with Mr Batt she welled up again.

'The hideous man!' was the only comment Victor could bring himself to make, in the presence of a lady. 'Come on, let's get you home, Smithy's got the car just across the road.' Gently and discreetly, he led Rachel to the car; Smithy had already jumped out and was holding the door open.

'Smithy we'll take Mrs Scott home.'

'Very good, sir.'

In the car Rachel composed herself and took a deep breath. 'Would you have some tea when we get to the house Victor?'

'Well, it's actually quite fortunate that I ran into you without contriving some kind of meeting. We've had another coded message.'

'From George!' Rachel exclaimed with a big smile unable to contain her excitement; this was the boost she needed.

'Yes, it would seem to be; it's certainly in the same format,' Victor responded coolly.

When they arrived at the house the Brigadier, who had all but moved in during this trying time, 'to provide his support', was snoozing on a chair on the patio, snoring with porcine resonance. As they entered the house Ives greeted them clad in an apron with a feather duster in hand.

'Ives, you don't have to do any of that!' pleaded Rachel.

'Sorry Ma'am, I'm under strict orders that while the situation continues we must muck in to lighten your load.'

'By "we", you mean you do the work and Dad supervises, when he's awake enough,' she said with a wry smile.

'Good arf'noon sir!' Ives said, coming to attention and saluting Victor.

'As you were Ives,' Victor returned the salute.

'Yes sir, thank you sir. Should I prepare some tea Ma'am?'

'Yes please Ives that would be very kind of you,' Rachel replied.

'Not at all Ma'am; coming right up.'

As Ives disappeared to the kitchen Rachel turned to Victor, 'Right, what's the message this time?'

'It is Oak, Leaf, Eagle, Cork' replied Victor.

'We need to look at the table again; follow me.' Rachel lead the way to George's room once again.

'Right we know eagle means travelling, so he's on the move again.' Victor began in a matter of fact analytical tone whilst perusing the other items.

'What was the first one again?'

'Oak leaf,' replied Victor 'There's an oak leaf on the picture of him and Scotty.'

'My God, do you think it means he's found John?' Rachel almost screamed.

'I think it does but, I also think it means he's actually with Scotty,' Victor added.

'OK so we know he's with John and travelling,' said Rachel.

'Well, that either means he's been captured or he's managed to spring Scotty out from under the German's noses. Since we have an absence of a swastika or German reference I think it's the latter!' Victor paused and looked at Rachel, 'Good Lord! A young boy has got the better of the German war machine!'

'Right, what about the next bit then Victor; cork wasn't it?'

'Yes.'

'There's a cork next to that baseball bat, well that's puzzling!'

'OK, what do we know about baseball?' Victor began brain-storming.

'The bowler is the pitcher, the pitch is called the park…' he continued.

'Bat, ball, stand, run!' Rachel added.

Then they tried adding these words into what they already knew.

'George and John, travelling, bowler…?'

'No' they said in unison, and it went on

'George and John, travelling… pitcher… park… bat… ball… run!'

'They're running… they're on foot?' Rachel became more excited.

'But why a baseball bat?' Victor pondered rubbing his chin, he began pacing looking up at the ceiling, out the window, at the bat and then back to the ceiling.

'Babe Ruth is the only baseball player I know, if that's any help?' Rachel said.

Victor spun round and looked directly at her, 'Yes, and his name is George as well.'

'Do you think that's the link?' she queried.

'It must be something linked with Babe Ruth, but quite what eludes me.' He went back to pacing again.

'What's he famous for? I mean in cricket you hear of those that good at bowling and batting, rugby has forwards and backs with preferred positions and I believe it's the same in football.'

'I believe he's the most successful batsman of all time,' Victor replied.

'Has he scored more... goals... than anyone else?' Rachel grimaced at her lack of sport knowledge.

'No, they don't score goals like football, it's more like cricket except they go round bases rather than back and forth between wickets but they're also called...' he paused and looked at the bat.

'Called what?' Rachel pressed.

'*Runs!*' Victor became excited 'he's famous for hitting *home runs!* Scotty and George are on the home run! I'd better relay this to SOE in case their chaps haven't got the message through.'

Victor ran down the stairs, leaving Rachel sobbing with joy. As he burst out of the front door, Ives was emerging from the kitchen with the tea tray.

'You've forgotten your tea sir!' Ives called after him.

'Sorry Ives, no time; got an emergency!' Then Victor shouted, 'Smithy start the car, back to base; quick as you can!'

'Right you are sir!' Smithy replied pulling away before Victor had both feet in the car.

When he arrived back at his office he immediately dialled SOE in Whitehall.

'Good afternoon; has Mr Parker arrived from Victoria, please?'

The phone was answered, 'Parker, 3 — 2 — 1,' as usual the cue to scramble.

'Morning Colonel, Hawkshaw here. We've deciphered the latest code from George.'

'Well, has the boy won the war for us yet?' The colonel guffawed at his own joke, while Victor waited patiently for him to finish.

'Colonel, the last set of words sent through mean that George is with his father and they're heading back; does that concur with your intelligence sir?'

'Absolutely, in fact we know they are now a few hours north at a safe house. There's some good fields round there, we've used some of them in the past for night drops and pickups. One of the

George and the Reich

clandestine ops boys is going for them tonight, all being well. They're further than we usually like to send a Lysander but doable in fair conditions; no point sending a Hudson for two, Hawkshaw, what?'

'Indeed, sir. Who's flying it sir?'

'Verity, a chap from 161; keep it under your hat though.'

'Of course sir, I hear he's one of the best at these ops.'

'Absolutely, no point sending a novice when there's no spare fuel for mistakes. In any case the PM's quite taken by this boy's grit and ability. Right Hawkshaw that's all for now, toodle-pip.'

Then the receiver went dead in Victor's hand before he'd had a chance to say good bye.

That night

After sleeping restfully throughout the day Scotty awoke with a start at about 5 PM. He could hear voices outside, which broke the silence of the ramshackle farmyard. Scotty peered carefully through the broken window. Carefully, he crept over to where George was still asleep. He put his hand over George's mouth then gave him a nudge. George made a noise then tried to speak all of which was muffled by Scotty's hand. Scotty gestured with his finger to his lips and then took his hand off George's mouth.

'We've got company Urchin; it looks like they're going to search the farm.'

George rubbed his eyes and stood up. He tiptoed to the window; he didn't attempt to look out but he listened to the conversation.

'You're right Dad,' George confirmed. 'The Germans that are there are telling the farmer that the SS are ten minutes behind them, so if they've got anything or anyone they are hiding then they need to confess now and the authorities will look upon them leniently.'

George and the Reich

'Yes, we know all about German leniency!' Scotty scoffed. 'It could all be a ruse and there are no SS coming but I'm not willing to take that chance; come on let's pack up and get out of here. Make sure you take any evidence of us being here with you; we'll have to go it alone from now on.'

'Well that's nothing new,' George replied.

'Hark at the big shot,' Scotty mocked, 'anyhow when did you learn how to speak German?'

'I've had to learn what I could while I've been over here; anyway they were also trying to speak French to the farmer, but failing miserably.'

'OK, are you fit?' Scotty said.

'Fitter than you,' George smirked.

'Right we'll have to see if there's a back entrance to the barn then we'll head directly away from it, so we keep the barn between us and the Germans.

'Right, let's go!' Scotty ordered. Gingerly he went down the ladder first, once he was at the bottom George followed. It was a particularly warm afternoon; the smell of hot dust was blowing into the barn entrance and mingling with the aroma of warm hay.

Once George had descended Scotty edged slowly towards the barn doors, pressing himself hard against the wall next the open doorway he slowly peered round for a split second. Holding up two fingers, Scotty indicated to George that there were two Germans. He then indicated that they should now move to the back of the barn. Looking round again, he gesticulated to George with a sweeping motion of his right hand that he should go. Once George had moved, Scotty followed. They darted to the back of the barn between the two huge stacks of hay. At the back of the barn were two huge doors, similar to those at the front, but these were firmly shut. Scotty tried pushing each of them but they were stuck fast. 'It looks like this is not an option,' Scotty whispered. George tapped his Dad on the shoulder and pointed to the right-hand door. In the dim light of the barn it was hard to see but there was a domestic-size door in the bigger barn door. Its secret was only given away by the thin lines of light entering at points where the door had warped away from its original frame. Scotty tried the door. It was stiff but opened with a grinding creak. Scotty grimaced with the noise. They waited in silence to see if they had been heard; there was silence. 'OK, clever clogs, let's go!'

They clambered through the door and ran to a wood which was two hundred yards away from the barn across a meadow. They ran into the wood and stopped behind a large beech tree. They both peered around the tree simultaneously. The two German soldiers were casually, it seemed, looking around the area outside the barn. 'They obviously didn't treat the sound as too suspicious or they'd have followed it more urgently, then we'd have been in the *merde'*, George whispered, waiting for his dad's reaction to his French expletive.

'If your mother heard that, she'd wash your mouth out with soap,' Scotty chuckled.

After watching the soldiers lose interest and re-shoulder their weapons, George and Scotty slumped down in relief with their backs against the tree.

'Right, any idea where we are?' Scotty enquired looking around.

George, having produced a map from his bag, replied 'Well, looking at the map…'

'Map, what map!' Scotty exclaimed whipping his head around. 'Where did you get that?'

'I brought it from home,' George casually replied.

'Don't suppose you have a…'

'Compass!' George interrupted holding it out to his Dad.

'10 out of 10 Urchin; what else have you got in that bag?'

'Oh, just essentials,' George answered nonchalantly.

'OK professor where are we then?'

'Well as far as I can work out,' George replied setting the map out in front of them, 'given the length of time we were in the truck, its speed and the direction we set off in, we should be anywhere on this radius,' he pointed an arc on the map with his finger, 'and given the terrain I would guess we are here, near Barbizon.' George sat back feeling quite smug and impressed with himself.

'I think you're right Urchin, well done.

'Hey, look at this,' Scotty pointed to the map.

'What is it?' George asked, not recognising the symbol on the map.

'It's an airfield; we may be able to speed up our return home, if we can get in.'

'It's in the right direction so it's worth a look. But, doubtful we'll get in, the goons will have it heavily guarded,' George cautioned.

'Well, we've got about two and a half hours of daylight left; we'll start heading north at dusk. From the map it looks fairly rural so we should have cover.'

'That won't matter, it'll be dark,' George remarked.

'Yes, but even at night you need cover to disguise your silhouette; that's why we're trained to stick away from high ground when evading capture because that will potentially give a clear silhouette against the night sky.'

They rested for a couple of hours while the sun went down, taking it in turns to keep an eye out for anyone approaching. The wood they were in was quite lush and fairly dense. It was made up, predominantly, of deciduous trees with, in places, thick bracken undergrowth.

'We're best to stick to the more trodden paths within the wood,' George determined, 'so we leave a minimal trail and don't get ourselves cut to shreds in the process.'

'I wish we'd brought the rest of that food with us,' Scotty declared, 'I'm starving.'

George rummaged in his rucksack again, 'We've got some bread, a little salami, a lump of cheese, an apple and a little water.'

'Urchin, you're a genius.'

They tucked in to the remaining food, then, fully refreshed and the sun in its last throes, set off in a northerly direction.

They kept as straight a line as they could but, in the interests of safety, stuck away from roads and darted from wood to hedge to bushes. The going was relatively easy; after approximately five hours of continuous vigilant trudging they came to a small airfield. Cautiously they approached, maintaining their cover and good observation. Quite by chance they had approached from the darkest part of the airfield perimeter, which was free from the usual eye-watering floodlighting. The airfield seemed to be surrounded by a very high, fifteen-foot by George's estimation, chain-link fence topped with barbed wire. Just the other side of the fence was a line of six large aircraft hangars and to the left of these was the main gate which was guarded and well lit. George couldn't see how many guards there were in total because some were out of sight in the guard house. He could, however, see two guards both of whom were struggling to keep hold of two snarling Alsatian dogs. To the right of the hangars just in front of them was a small collection of outbuildings which were in complete darkness. George continued to review the situation looking for the best route to circumnavigate this obstacle. However, Scotty seemed preoccupied and unwilling to make a move.

'I wonder where we are,' whispered Scotty.

'Melun Villaroche,' George whispered in reply.

'How did you work that out?' Scotty enquired incredulously.

'It says so above the gate over there,' George giggled.

'Remind me to clip you round the ear when we get home!'

'Talking of which, Dad, we need to be well past here by dawn,' George warned. 'We'd best get moving.'

'Yes, just a minute; I'm watching something,' Scotty replied, without glancing back at George, completely transfixed.

'What is it?'

Scotty ignored the question and just kept watching avidly with feline attention.

'Dad!' George persisted. This was greeted with a dismissive '*Shhh!*'

Petulantly George sat back unable to review the map in the dark and obviously unable to use a torch.

After ten minutes Scotty broke his silence. 'George!' he whispered as loudly as he could. George crept up to his side. 'I don't suppose you have anything like wire cutters or pliers in that bag of yours do you?'

George rummaged in his bag and produced a fairly substantial looking pair of side cutters.

'You're a genius, Urchin.'

'What have you got in mind?' George asked, knowing he wasn't going to like the answer.

'I've been watching the German movements in that airbase. Firstly: They all seem preoccupied in bombing up the Heinkels they have out on the field; see the lights between these hangars. Secondly: there are no perimeter guards at the fence near us and this part of the perimeter is a blind spot to any watchtowers given these two hangars. Thirdly: there's a little two-seater parked just next to this hangar on the right; if we can get in through the fence we can pinch it and *fly* back to England, so we're back in time for breakfast.'

'Won't the gun emplacements shoot us to pieces before we've taken off?'

'We won't use the runway, that's a very short take off plane. We'll head off to the right across that far perimeter fence away from the guns, using the building and their planes for cover. Once we're airborne, we'll head north again giving Paris a wide berth and then change our heading to north north west which should take us across the Channel around Boulogne; we may even fly over the Beauchamp's place.'

'OK, but we'll run a gauntlet of anti-aircraft guns especially at the coast; if you keep as close as you can to the Beauchamp's hotel it should be minimal, they haven't installed the big guns along there yet,' George instructed.

'Yes sir wing-commander!' Scotty mocked 'Well, anywhere it's liable to get a bit hot we'll need to keep low. But we've got to get it first. When we're up I'll need you to help navigate; do you think you're up to that?'

'Absolutely! Let's get home!' George replied with a big smile.

'OK, we're clear!' said Scotty looking left and right, 'Let's go!'

They ran the short distance between their vantage point and the fence. Crouching at the fence they looked all around again, Scotty was right; they were in a blind spot.

Scotty cut the chain link fence vertically for just over a foot and then to the left at ground level for a foot. He held it back for George to crawl through. George reciprocated and they were in. Looking around again they were in reasonable darkness and sheltered from the attention of the guards by the hangar to their left. The small single engine plane was only a few yards away.

'This may be here because it's a lame duck,' Scotty warned. 'If it is, our goose may be cooked.'

They both trotted to the plane in a low crouched position. Scotty climbed on to the wing and opened the door. 'Right. Get in!' he ordered. George unquestioningly obliged. Scotty removed the chocks from the wheels then clambered in and frantically commenced a shortened version of the RAF pre-flight checks.

Once he was happy that everything was, as far as he could ascertain, working he lent across to George and said, 'Put these headphones on and brace yourself; once I start this engine we will be fair game. The tanks are just about full; we should have enough to make it home.'

George took a deep breath and said, 'I'm ready, England here we come!'

With that Scotty started the ignition process. The engine coughed and choked into life. Scotty wasted no time and commenced taxiing. George looked across the instruments and turned on the radio. After few crackles and belches they could hear the odd matter-of-fact German aeronautical transmission.

'Why have you turned that racket on?' Scotty barked.

'It may forewarn us if they've noticed us and if anyone is coming after us,' George responded via his headset.

'OK, point taken,' Scotty conceded as he recalled that his son now had a good working knowledge of German.

'As soon as these transmissions get frantic you won't need me to translate that they know one of their planes has been stolen.'

With the limited light Scotty taxied the plane as far as he dared, turning toward the far-right perimeter fence as they'd planned and using the hangar and parked Heinkels as cover.

'This is it!' Scotty shouted, opening the throttle up fully. They were heading directly for the perimeter fence. The plane bounced over the uneven ground as they gained speed. The first knowledge they had that they were being shot at was the tracer fire passing by on either side. As George had predicted it wasn't necessary to have a working knowledge of German to understand, from their radio communications, that they were a 'little' upset.

'Dad, they've been ordered to cease fire until we take off in case they hit one of their own planes.'

'Well the heat won't be off for long,' Scotty exclaimed pulling back on the controls. As he did, the nose lifted and he allowed the small plane to climb just enough to clear the perimeter fence. He flew directly away from the airfield maintaining a low altitude which kept them just above treetop height. Tracer fire had re-commenced but was way short of the mark as the Germans lost track of the plane's exact location. Searchlights were now scanning the skies high and low in an attempt to pinpoint the plane.

'They've lost us!' Scotty laughed as he began a slow left bank to bring the plane to their intended northerly homeward heading.

'I'll keep her fairly low until we get past the airfield, then it will be sensible to climb to three thousand feet or so.'

'OK, Dad.'

At the point where Scotty was completing the bank and levelling the plane into the northerly heading, a searchlight skimmed the tail. The vigilant operator quickly focussed the whole beam on the small plane, directing the machine guns and light anti-aircraft fire directly on them. Scotty manoeuvred the little plane to avoid the blinding light, dropping down even lower then rapidly climbing and banking away. Each time the searchlight regained its target re-focussing the fire at them. Reaching into his bag George said, 'I've got an idea; but don't tell Mum I had these,' withdrawing five strings of Chinese fire-crackers and a zippo lighter.

'George this is no time to play with fireworks!' Scotty shouted. 'What are you doing?'

'Just watch!' he grinned, opening the small window hatch to his left. As he did so the sound of the wind became intensified.

In quick succession he lit each string of fire crackers and dropped them out of the window. He looked round to see the flashes as the crackers exploded as they dropped. Almost instantly the searchlights and indeed any lighting on the airfield were extinguished and the machine gun fire redirected towards the fire crackers. George turned the radio up. 'What are they saying?' Scotty asked as he took full advantage of the halt in hostilities and banked away to the right ensuring there was enough distance between them and the airfield once the Germans realised they'd been hoaxed.

George listened carefully to the transmissions, 'They think they're under attack,' he laughed.

Once out of range Scotty climbed to three thousand feet and set their heading due north once again. Leaving the Germans to deal with the mêlée they had created, George and Scotty both looked at each other and let out a huge sigh of relief and then screamed with joy, '*We're going home!*' After they had calmed down and settled in for the long haul George asked, 'What's our equivalent ground speed?'

'About 120 mph; Why?'

'Well, I only have a ground map to go by so it makes the calculation a little easier. OK by my calculations, if things go to plan, we should be over the Kent coast in just over two hours.'

'OK!' Scotty replied, 'that should be fun; we'll have to convince them not to shoot us down given the fact that we're in a German plane. That's if we get there — once Melun Villaroche have got the word around, every German in France will be on the lookout for us.'

George took a deep breath and shook his head; now was not the time for considering failure.

'By my reckoning, you'll need to maintain this course for about one hour fifteen and then head north west around Arras,' he told his father.

'OK navigator, all understood.'

After about thirty minutes of peaceful flying two search lights were switched on, evidently at the sound of the solitary plane. 'Brace yourself!' Scotty warned, 'If they get a lock on us I'll have to dive and turn and there will be fireworks!'

After what felt like ages, with their hearts in their mouths, the worst happened. A searchlight landed on them. Scotty held his nerve in the anticipation of ak-ak. Silence. Neither of them dared to breathe. Then suddenly, the lights were switched off.

'The news obviously hasn't reached them yet,' but as quickly as George said that, the searchlights were switched back on.

'You spoke too soon Urchin! They've heard.'

The searchlights were frantically scanning the skies in what looked like random patterns to regain a lock on the stolen plane.

'Hold on tight Urchin, this time if they spot us, they will be firing. If they get a lock on us I will make a sudden manoeuvre and you need to be ready.'

'I'm ready.'

Scotty was concentrating on flying the plane and looking out for night fighters while George was looking in the direction of the searchlights; his face pressed against the cockpit window. The searchlight position was now behind them; but one beam glanced off the nose of the plane and instantly began a close search to gain a full lock. Immediately, tracer fire rose from the ground, seemingly surrounding the plane like an escort of fireflies. Scotty reacted instinctively; rolling the plane to the left and into a short dive then banking away to the right and climbing. He banked slowly to the left again and then rolled over to the right sharply. With the searchlights now too far behind to identify them, the anti-aircraft fire ceased while the lights searched in vain for the little plane. They had evaded this attempt to bring them down. Scotty reset the course and adjusted the altitude.

'Are you ok? Nothing damaged?' Scotty enquired as he checked the instruments and controls for evidence of damage.

'I'm fine,' George confirmed, looking round the cabin with his torch and then to the parts of the plane's outer structure that were in his view, he further confirmed, 'No damage.'

'That was lucky,' Scotty smiled 'I thought they had us.'

For the next forty-five minutes or so things were peaceful during which George and his dad only spoke a few words. This was due in the most part to the fatigue brought on by the last forty-eight hours of stress, excitement and lack of sleep and the anticipation of the potential fire storms they still had to run through.

'We should be around Arras now. Yes, there are a few lights below,' George stated looking at the town below which was under black-out conditions, 'Change course to north north west, that's 337.5 degrees.'

'Check, 337.5 north north west,' Scotty confirmed.

'We should be at the coast in about forty minutes.'

Steering this course kept them clear of Paris and other major built-up areas that may have had anti-aircraft firepower.

The next half an hour passed without incident, apart from the odd course and altitude adjustments. Then the engine spluttered and cut out for a split second. George and Scotty both sat straight up at full alert, from their relaxed repose; George looking plaintively at his father; Scotty studying the instruments.

'That can't be right!' Scotty shouted with panic in his voice, 'The fuel tanks are showing almost empty, when they should be at least half full. George, use your torch to check the wings; see if you can see any sign of a fuel leak.'

The engine briefly cut out again.

With a heightened sense of urgency, George shone his torch along the rear edge of the wing on his side. 'No sign my side; lean forward Dad, so I can look at your side.'

He leant across behind Scotty's neck and scanned the back of that wing slowly 'No… no… nothing… Hang on,' he cried out, 'it looks like some liquid is coming off the wing at this end. Crikey, we must have taken a bullet when we were under fire.'

The engine cut out again, but didn't recover; the prop ground to a halt.

'Well this is *déjà vu!*' Scotty replied 'It looks like we'll need to make an emergency landing shortly, hold tight!'

'We're near the coast,' George said, 'By my reckoning and from what I can see in the dark, we're near the Beauchamp's hotel; Dad you need to steer to the right!'

'*Why*, for God's sake? We'll be lucky to get out alive,' Scotty yelled.

'There's no time to tell you, just do it and then land as close as you can to the small wood, which will be in front of you once we're flying parallel with the coast. If you don't, we'll ditch in the sea, then we'll have to swim; that's if we make it.'

'OK, Urchin, I'll trust you on this, let's do it,' Scotty declared as he banked hard right while gliding the plane and keeping the nose up as best he could, then straightening out to follow the coast, all the time losing height.

'*There it is! There's the wood!*' George shouted.

'OK, I hope you have a plan Urchin; we're going in.'

'When we land just follow me,' George instructed.

They were losing height rapidly; and were little higher than tree level.

'Alright Urchin, but we've got to land first and that's going to be rough.'

They were less than three hundred yards from the wood and thirty feet up and losing height rapidly.

'*Hold tight!*' Scotty yelled, as the plane dropped lower and the fixed under-carriage hit the scrub land for the first time. The plane bounced and came down again hard, bouncing roughly on the uneven ground and lurching from side to side violently. Scotty struggled to keep it under control. They finally hit a large rock which sent the plane onto its side, snapping the starboard wing and grinding it to a halt in a circular motion pivoting on the wing stump.

When the plane had stopped spinning. Scotty was first to break the silence 'You OK?'

'Yes, I think so,' replied the dazed George. 'You?'

'I'm alright; I think.'

After a few moments, where the shock of the situation left them unable to move, the guttural sound of the German alarms and the barking of approaching dogs snapped them out of their daze.

'Time to get moving Urchin.'

'I'm with you; let's go.'

George flung open the door on his side of the plane; which was now facing upward to the sky. The door fell back on the hinges with an almighty crash. The port wing was still intact, pointing toward the sky as if to suggest this is from where the problem had fallen.

George climbed out and jumped to the ground, looking all around for the Germans that were closing in. He knew that being caught could prove fatal for the Beauchamps and numerous others, so he had to get out without being detected. Scotty followed him out and landed next to him. 'OK Urchin, what's the plan?' Scotty enquired with an air of doom.

'*Dylan!*' George replied.

'*Dylan?*' Scotty repeated with an incredulous tone.

'Yes,' George reasoned, smiling. 'This is the wood where I used to play. Below here is a cave where I hid *Dylan* on my arrival, he's going to get us out of here.'

'Good Lord! You must be feline, bloody clever or both!' Scotty declared.

The Germans were close enough now that they could hear orders being barked at almost the same metre as the dogs were barking. Trucks could be heard approaching. George assumed these would contain more troops and searchlights; the sounds were accompanied by the flashing of distant torchlight. At that point George took note that there was a good breeze blowing towards the sea, meaning for once that fate seemed to be on their side providing the best conditions for a quick getaway once they were seaborne from the cave. But they had to get to *Dylan* first.

George and the Reich

'I think we've got a weather shore. Quick, follow me,' George ordered as he ran along the fence using his knowledge of the terrain to help him in the darkness, now he was in familiar territory. They were now roughly in the same position as George had been when he was escaping back to the hotel after the beach rescue had gone so horribly wrong.

'Stop! Get down!' George ordered in a strained whisper. Scotty complied without question.

'Right,' George said lifting the bottom of the fence, 'Get under there and wait for me by the bracken just over there.'

'It's a bit tight,' Scotty strained, as he wiggled his way under the fence. 'Yes. You've got a bit podgy; Jerry must have fed you too well,' George giggled as he followed him under the fence. When George caught up with Scotty he kept going in crouched run, 'Follow me!'

'Follow you where? There's nowhere to go,' Scotty declared, fearing the worst as the Germans were now swarming around the now smouldering crashed aeroplane and spreading out in all directions looking for the elusive fugitives.

'Quick! This way!' was the only reply George gave. Scotty followed George deeper in to the wood through the thick scrub and all the time getting caught on the brambles. George stopped and said, 'Here we are.'

'What do you mean, "Here we are"? Where are we? We have got to get out of here George; the German army are less than two hundred yards away. How are we going to get out of here?' Scotty was by now two steps away from blind panic.

'Down there,' George replied calmly pointing to the secluded hole. 'Just follow me.' Once in the hole, George turned on his torch, followed closely by Scotty. 'They're at the fence,' Scotty whispered to George as they crawled down the short tunnel to the cave. 'So this is where you used to disappear to is it?' Scotty said as he stood up, grabbing the torch from George to have good look round.

'We best get moving Dad, it won't be long before the dogs have our scent,' as he began removing *Dylan*'s tarpaulin. George stowed the tarpaulin in the locker and began making the sails ready for a quick getaway. 'Dad, can you check how far in the sea is please.'

Scotty took four paces towards the cave entrance, 'I'm standing in water here.'

The water in the cave was gently lapping the walls. 'OK, that's great! That means the cave is pretty much flooded and it sounds fairly calm; we'll be fully afloat long before we reach the cave mouth! C'mon help me get *Dylan* in the water.' Just as George said that a shrill dog barking was a sharp reminder of their precarious situation. 'They must be at the tunnel entrance!' Scotty exclaimed as he pulled *Dylan* towards the water; George pushing from the back. As soon as *Dylan* was afloat he unclipped the wheels, threw them in the boat and jumped in. Scotty jumped on the bow and tumbled in unceremoniously. 'Dad, get the jib up now so we can catch the wind as soon as we're out of the cave.'

'Aye, aye skipper!'

They moved *Dylan* slowly through the shallow water using the paddles in the darkness to feel along and fend off the cave walls, heading ever closer towards the dark blue cave mouth. Suddenly their attention was torn from the task of navigating the boat to a flash of light and the aggressive bark of a dog in full hunting mode. With that they automatically began pushing harder to get *Dylan* moving faster. They knew it would be seconds before the dogs were unleashed into the hole after them followed closely by soldiers, angry at the effort of scrambling into a filthy hole.

Then it came: the sound of two, three or maybe more dogs scrambling quickly down the passage at the back of the cave. In the darkness George couldn't see and he wasn't going turn to his torch on to provide an accurate target. The dogs continued at full gallop, splashing into the water, barking as if manically possessed by the prey only seconds from their jaws. George being at the rear of the boat froze with fear. The splashing stopped but the barking continued. 'It's too deep for them, they have to swim!' George shouted almost hysterically, his heart racing with the combination of fear and relief. He was ready with a paddle to repel any canine that may attempt boarding. *Dylan's* nose cleared the cave entrance. They heard the heart-warming sound of flapping as the jib filled with wind. The boat jerked forward as the full sail propelled *Dylan* into motion. George grabbed the tiller. He knew, as with entering the cave, that he had to steer a fine line to avoid ripping *Dylan's* hull even at high tide. Scotty trimmed the jib and made it fast in the jamming cleat. 'Dad, get the mainsail up, I can't let go of the rudder here.'

'OK, George,' he replied scrambling to the mast and hoisting the mainsail. George unlashed the boom, it swung as the mainsail caught the running wind, nearly knocking Scotty for six. They were at full speed. The dogs had given up the chase and retraced their paw prints back to their masters. George and Scotty scanned the top of the cliffs, beach and cave entrance for any sign of that their escape had been spotted. There was nothing. 'Chances are they're still searching inland since the dogs came back with nothing,' George hypothesized.

'Yes but, if one of those goons has half a brain he'll realise that the dogs are wet because they chased the scent into the water, and didn't just go for a nice swim; then they'll be looking out here,' Scotty cautioned.

'The voice of doom!' George grinned. 'Let's just hope it's not before we've put some distance between us and them.'

'Oh crikey! It looks like they heard you Dad!' George cried out, the panic in his voice was palpable as several searchlights began scanning the beach and shoreline.

'We need to get as far out to sea as we can before they start expanding the search; at this moment, they will not yet have realised we have a boat,' Scotty said, trimming the jib to goose wing the sails to maximise the running wind. They sailed into the night on a direct course to England. After some time the only evidence of the coastline they had just left were the search lights. Suddenly one of the searchlights swept out to sea, momentarily illuminating them and then carrying on. Then a split second later they froze with renewed fear as the searchlight halted its scan and rapidly backtracked; they'd been seen! Unable to move with the dark anticipation that had overcome them, they looked back in the direction of the beach, waiting. The searchlight landed back on *Dylan's* stern. Instantaneously what sounded like several machine guns opened fire. Many of the bullets were falling short or wide; a few hit *Dylan*'s stern but with barely enough velocity to puncture the wood as they sailed out of range. George and Scotty both slouched back relaxing for the first time in days. 'Ha-ha! England here we come!' George shouted, thrusting his clenched fist in the air. After an hour of uneventful sailing Scotty had taken over the helm and George had dozed off, exhausted. An hour or so later, Scotty woke him, roughly shaking his leg. 'What is it?' George said, rubbing his eyes.

'We've got company,' Scotty said quietly pointing dead ahead. George scrambled to the bow and peered into the night. Silhouetted by the moonlight was a familiar sight. He sighed with relief and shuffled back down to the stern to his father. 'It's not what you think; it's a moored rescue pod for German airmen shot down over the Channel.'

'Well, if that's the case George; why have hatches just opened on the deck and why are there now people standing of the top of the conning tower?' Scotty asked rhetorically.

'Oh crikey! I hadn't seen the deck rise out of the water.'

Suddenly, a search light fell instantly upon them, followed by a burst of machine gun fire that entered the sea less than two yards in front of them.

'That was a warning shot; George put your arms up, the game is over!' Scotty warned. Slowly they both put their hands up. From a loudhailer came a voice in what was, by now, familiar harsh German.

'He's ordering us to heave to!' George translated.

'Well, just do as he says!' Scotty ordered.

Before George had a chance to fully comply with the order, the message was repeated, and then again in English with the usual thick German accent. 'You will heave to or I will blow you and your tiny boat from the water!'

George had dropped the sails and was now standing with his father, their arms stretched above their heads. They could hear many excited German voices as they stood motionless, save for the jostling caused by the slight swell, and *Dylan* slowly drifted towards the submarine.

Abruptly, the excitement quadrupled to near hysterics as orders were barked and rasping alarms sounded. The reason soon became apparent when George picked up on the word 'torpedo' being yelled. The submarine crew disappeared except those blindly firing the deck guns in the direction of the torpedo. George and Scotty lost no time in exploiting this mêlée to their advantage. With the sails once again hoisted they disappeared into the darkness; once clear the course was again set for England. As they left, the submarine was taking action to avoid the path of the torpedo; turning violently to port and commencing a crash dive. There was a large explosion; the sub had been hit. George and Scotty waited with baited breath for subsequent explosions as the submarine's fuel and magazine were ignited. There were no further explosions and the submarine continued to dive evidently still in an operational condition, although damaged. At the same time a launch moving at high speed passed them, throwing *Dylan* and its passengers around fiercely. 'That's a British MTB!' Scotty declared at the top of his voice pointing at the launch. 'We need to make contact with them once they've finished their current task.'

'It's too dangerous Dad.'

'It won't be once all the firing's stopped; quick hoist the Union Jack so they know we're friendly,' Scotty ordered and George immediately complied.

'Let's get clear for the time being, they'll be laying depth charges to finish her off, we don't want to get in the way of those,' Scotty further cautioned.

Sure enough, as if Poseidon's full fury had been unleashed, there shortly came a succession of sinister rumbling explosions deep down in Davey Jones locker followed by a drenching shower of sea water as the shockwaves broke the surface one after another. After the last explosion the quiet of the maritime night regained its composure, save for the quiet chugging and searchlights of the naval launch scanning the area for evidence of a hit. As the search area of the navy expanded the inevitable happened, and the search light fell upon *Dylan* with George and Scotty looking directly into the beam.

Wide eyed and with baited breath they held their hands up in the air. 'We're English!' they both yelled at the top of their voices. Various orders were shouted and the launch turned and cautiously coasted towards them. As little *Dylan* came alongside the comparatively large launch, two sailors reached for the little boat with boat hooks while two others kept a distrusting vigil on George and Scotty with submachine guns continually trained on them. They were assisted on to the launch and silently escorted into the vessel.

'Please look after my boat until we get back,' George requested nervously.

'Just keep moving, son,' said one of the armed sailors.

The silence was maintained until they were brought in front of the vessel's commander.

'These are the two in the small sailing boat sir,' one of the escorting sailors said saluting the commander, 'It seems they can speak English, sir.'

'We are English!' Scotty said.

'Speak only when you are spoken to!' yelled the sailor.

'That's quite alright Soames. I'll handle it from here.'

'Very good sir,' Soames backed down.

'Well… erm,' the commander stuttered in a manner leading Scotty to speak.

'Squadron Leader John Scott, sir!'

'Well Squadron Leader I'm sure you appreciate this is pretty queer. A man and a boy alone at night in a sailing dinghy in the middle of the Channel, in the middle of the war. It may be more plausible if you were alone; escaping back to Blighty after being shot down, would it not?'

'Indeed sir it does seem more than odd. However, I'm not sure how much of the complete story I can give you until we've made contact with my CO.'

'Of course, Scott; that may speed up the verification in any case; now how about a cup of tea,' the commander enquired.

'Tea would be great; I haven't had a decent cup of tea in weeks.'

'Me too!' George, who had thus far remained silent, interjected.

'Of course,' replied the commander 'and we may even manage to rustle up a biscuit too.'

Shortly after the tea arrived and they had been chatting for no more than five minutes, a junior officer approached and spoke quietly with the commander.

'Well that was quick; it seems they are keen to get you both back sharpish and that this is rather "hush-hush". But, and I quote — "We need some items to table this motion" — any idea what that means?'

Scotty was completely bemused 'None at all!'

'This is where I come in,' George said smugly leaning forward from his reclined position. 'The items are: oak leaf, pistol, eagle and Tower Bridge.'

'That's all?' exclaimed the commander.

'That's it!' George replied

'OK!' he passed details of the three items to the sublieutenant to transmit.

'This may take twenty minutes or so,' George informed the commander, 'you see the Group Captain will take a while to decipher the code.'

'Well you are a self-assured little blighter aren't you!' the commander smirked and winked at Scotty.

Scramble

'Right colonel, got it; on my way. I'll call back in twenty minutes!' Victor immediately picked up the phone again and dialled. 'Smithy, need the car right away, Yes now!' he barked, jumping out of bed and grabbing his uniform. Smithy was waiting by the car with the door open, as Victor ran to the car whilst still fastening his tie.

'Where to sir?' Smithy asked as Victor got in.

'Scotty's place as fast as you can; but don't make it look like you're going fast.'

'Pardon sir?' Smithy puzzled.

'Drive as fast as you can without drawing any attention, if you know what I mean.'

'Very good sir,' Smithy replied, still puzzled as he drove away.

'Well done Smithy,' Victor said as they drew up to the Scott house a few minutes later. 'Turn round ready to go back the same way.'

'Yes sir.'

Victor suppressed his instinct, given the urgency of the situation, to run to the door, choosing to walk in as casual a manner as he could manage. With his left hand in his trouser pocket, he knocked on the front door and scuffed the sole of his right shoe until the door opened.

'Victor! This is a surprise; is there news?' Rachel enquired, standing back and gesticulating for him to enter, still blinking and squinting from being woken only seconds before.

'Sorry I didn't call, could not trust that the phones were secure. Yes actually, we need check the table again.'

Once in George's room and poring over the table Rachel said, 'Right, what is the code this time?'

'Oak leaf, pistol, eagle, Tower Bridge,' Victor recited.

'OK, well we know that oak leaf means George and John together, we also know that eagle means travelling,' Rachel began while they surveyed the collection for the other items.

'Look the model of Tower Bridge is placed on a little White Ensign,' Victor said lifting the bridge and holding up the small flag.

'A what?'

'A White Ensign; it's the flag that all Royal Navy ships fly.'

'OK and the pistol is with a little picture of George's boat, *Dylan*. So what does this all mean?' Rachel sighed.

'Well!' Victor began scratching his head 'George and Scotty, *Dylan*, Royal Navy. OK, well that all rings true.'

'What does? What's happening Victor?' Rachel began to lose her composure knowing there was something Victor was withholding.

'Alright, you do have a right to know, but…'

'I know, don't breath a word etc., etc.!' Rachel impatiently completed Victor's sentence undertaking the unofficial vow of secrecy.

'OK, sit down,' Victor instructed. Rachel sat on George's bed while Victor perched on George's desk chair. 'There's been a message from one of the Channel patrols — they have two people in their charge, match the description of George and Scotty. Due to the coding procedure we could not be certain until verified by George's particular code. I now know it is them and they should be back in a matter of hours.'

At this news Rachel could hold on no longer and wailed with tears of joy and relief that the ordeal was nearly over.

'I have to get back and call this in so we can get them back ASAP.' said Victor.

'What is all this racket?' barked a gruff voice from down the hall. Then a bleary-eyed Brigadier entered the room having been attracted, moth-like, by the light on in George's room. He stood in the doorway swaddled in his dressing gown blinking and scratching, looking from Victor to Rachel and back again. 'What is so important as to wake everyone at this hour of the night?' the Brigadier demanded.

'George and John have been picked up in the Channel, they should be back in Blighty in a couple of hours,' Victor reported.

'Oh! Right! Well under the circumstance I suppose the commotion is justified. Shall we have some tea?'

'Not for me thank you sir; I have to get back post haste. I'll keep you posted on developments; I'll show myself out,' Victor declined standing up and taking his leave.

'Don't wake Ives up just for tea, Dad,' Rachel pleaded, still tearful.

'Why ever not? I can't see any of us getting any more sleep tonight so it won't be long before we shall need breakfast and possibly transport,' the Brigadier barked in his usual manner.

Home-coming

'We've received the all-clear that your "strange" code checks out and we are to deliver you both back with the utmost urgency,' said the commander over the remains of the cup of tea provided earlier by the steward.

'What about *Dylan*?' George piped up spitting tea and biscuit over everything and everyone in a five-foot radius.

'*Dylan*! Who is *Dylan*?' the commander asked, wiping his face and sleeve.

'*Dylan*…' George replied having now finished his mouthful '…is my sailing boat outside.'

'I'm sorry but we have to leave her,' the commander replied insincerely.

'In that case I will not need your assistance in getting home, I'll sail there myself!' George said firmly and precociously.

'You can't sail across the Channel single-handed, in wartime and at night,' the commander condescended.

'Well for your information I already have. And I made it across occupied France, twice,' George informed the bridge loudly and arrogantly, imparting more information than he perhaps should. Then looking directly into the commander's eyes and stepping in closer, he continued, 'Anyway how will you explain returning empty-handed when the order was to return with "the utmost urgency"?'

'Very well' the commander conceded, and gave orders for the small boat to be hauled aboard and fastened.

George turned with a smirk and winked at his Dad. Scotty, sitting back with his arms folded and the tea cup resting on the inside of his elbow, chuckled, 'Nicely done Urchin; you've become quite a force to be reckoned with.'

'*Torpedo!* Starb'd bow!' yelled one of the lookouts.

'Full ahead!' ordered the sub-lieutenant.

'Full ahead, sir!' confirmed the sailor at the helm.

'20 degrees to starb'd.'

'20 degrees to starb'd, sir.'

Those not directly involved with the evasion process observed in nervous silence.

'We'd better move before we attract more attention; Number 1, set course for home at full speed!' ordered the commander.

'Aye Aye, sir!'

The course was set and the launch, already at full speed, was making a sweeping turn heading directly for Dover.

'You chaps can settle down for a while, we should be in port in about an hour and a half,' the first officer informed them as the steward handed them more tea.

'Squadron Leader, we're just entering the harbour,' the sub-lieutenant said gently as Scotty blinked and tried to rehydrate his tongue. He nudged George who was fast asleep on his shoulder.

'What? Where are we?' George said slightly startled.

'We're just coming in to Dover; we must have dozed off,' Scotty informed him.

'Looks like there's a welcoming committee there for you Squadron Leader,' commented the first officer pointing to the quay wall.

'So there is, but I wonder what the ambulance is for? Did you report us as injured Lieutenant?' Scotty enquired.

'No sir!'

As the launch tied up alongside, Scotty spied a familiar face. 'Look George, there's Victor, come to meet us.'

'Crikey!' George said with a gulp, 'bet I'm for the high jump!'

'Permission to come aboard Commander?' Victor requested.

'Of course Group Captain, please do.'

Victor made his way in to the small bridge area of the launch; as he did he took his cap off and placed his hands on his hips with an incredulous shake of his head. 'My God, you made it! And against all odds George *you* did it! That is both the daftest and bravest act I have ever seen; well done!' Victor turned to George's father, shaking his hand, 'How are you Scotty?'

'I'm fine, thanks to George and no thanks to Nazi hospitality; but tell me, what is the ambulance for: are there some casualties coming?'

'No it's for George,' Victor replied. 'That's why I've come aboard before you disembark. We believe there is a Nazi spy operating in the area so we've had to concoct a cock and bull story about George being too ill to go to school. So if we stretcher George off and into an ambulance no one, apart from us, will know it is him and hopefully no unnecessary attention will be aroused.'

'Ah, I see! So what about me?' Scotty asked.

'You can just walk off; after all you're just escaped aircrew. Besides it will give my presence credibility if I'm seen with rescued aircrew.'

'Well Victor you have a way of making a chap feel important,' Scotty chuckled. 'Shall we disembark?' Victor gestured towards the door and a stretcher was brought aboard for George. George was soon secured to the stretcher and carried to the ambulance. The ambulance set away followed by Victor's staff car with Victor and Scotty in the back.

Once back behind the strict security of the airfield and away from prying eyes George stepped out of the ambulance and joined his father in the administration building. Once inside, Rachel who had been waiting patiently for over an hour screamed and embraced both of them together kissing them alternately on the cheek.

'Oh Mum!' George moaned, as if having never been away.

'Don't you ever do that to me again either of you,' Rachel scolded in floods of tears.

Then Victor approached tentatively and gently cleared his throat. The three of them looked up.

'Sorry to break up the reunion but we need to complete a quick debrief then you can go home.'

'Oh really, Victor, now?' Scotty protested.

' 'fraid so. Can't be avoided old chap.'

'Right, well let's get it over with,' Scotty conceded standing up.

'We need George as well.'

'OK come on George; let's get this done then home.'

George tagged along behind his father towards Victor's office. When Victor opened the door there was a strong smell of cigar smoke. As they stepped into the office George took a sharp intake of breath, 'Mr Churchill!'

THE END

Printed in Great Britain
by Amazon